Table of Contents

Perseus Corbett
and the
Forbidden Valley

By David Breitenbeck

Noble Cobra Publishing, August 2022

www.noblecobra.com

In my beginning is my end.
-T.S. Eliot, *The Four Quartets: East Corker*

Chapter One
The Kiss

Pause you who read this, and think for the moment of the long chain of
iron or gold, of thorns or flowers, that would never have bound you,
but for the formation of the first link on one memorable day.
-Charles Dickens, *Great Expectations*

It all started with a kiss.

That is to say, though there were many other things that laid the foundations for what ultimately happened, still the great events that occurred and all that proceeded from them were initiated in that one simple kiss. A kiss which, in the ordinary course of events, itself ought never to have taken place at all.

The events that led up to that all-important kiss began on a hot afternoon in the spring of 1912 at Sangral House in Kent. Sangral, as may be found in any competent guidebook, is a magnificent old manor house nestled back among the hills and attended by columns of oak trees. Its earliest stones had been laid in the fifteenth century, and since that time it had been added to and pulled about many, many times, giving it the rambling, unplanned appearance of something that had rather grown than been made. Its east wing drives out before the front entrance like a defensive arm, ending in a conical tower, while the west wing retreats back, as though seeking the quiet shelter of the trees.

It is a house with character, the kind of house that might have been (and indeed has been) the inspiration for many a romance, many a history, many a ghost story.

Sangral, of course, was the ancestral seat of Baron Darrow. But at present our interest is not in the illustrious family of the house, but rather with a twelve-year-old boy weeding the flowerbeds along the side of the east wing. This boy's name, somewhat improbably, was Perseus Corbett.

On that morning, young Perseus was repeatedly pausing in his work to gaze up at the magnificent house, for he was a new arrival upon the estate. He was born in London, the only child of a father who had once had aspirations of being an inventor and a mother who had been the daughter of a classics professor and who had not long outlived his birth. The boy had suffered from asthma, a condition aggravated by the smogs and fumes of the city, and which had required him to remain at home most of the time. Yet his condition had grown steadily worse despite all precautions. His father, upon consulting a doctor, decided that the fresh air of Kent, coupled with a moderate amount of exercise in performing simple gardening duties, were his best hope of survival, and had accordingly packed the boy off to his brother, a gardener on the Sangral estate.

Thus far, weeding had been Perseus's main occupation, and he had been at the job for several hours that morning, working his way slowly along the perimeter of the house. His back ached and the sun beat down upon him, but he was still so overawed by the novelty of the country, the fresh air, the beautiful, fragrant flowers, and most of all the sight of the great house itself that he found it difficult to care much about his discomfort.

For Perseus, from having been thus far obliged to find most of his amusement in reading, was an imaginative, sensitive boy. To his young eyes, Sangral House had looked from the start like something straight out of a fairy tale. Under its shadow, he felt almost as though he were back in the middle ages, or the time of the cavaliers; some dutiful servant laboring on behalf of a noble lord, or some great lady.

Sangral House was just shy of a castle, after all, he thought. All it needed was a princess.

It was about the time this thought occurred to him, while he was teasing out a particularly troublesome weed from between two bushes, when something flashed by within a foot of his head and landed with a soft thud in the dirt beside him, making him jump. He looked and saw a gleaming silver circle lying in the dirt, flashing in the afternoon sun. Picking it up and dusting off the dirt, he discovered it to be an intricately cast medal with the image of a man's head on one side and an oak tree on the other.

"You there! Boy!"

Perseus looked up to see a girl's head with a lot of tangled red hair sticking out of an upstairs window. "Bring that back up to me!"

"What'd you want to drop it for?" he called back.

"I didn't do it on purpose!" she answered. "Could you just bring it to me, please?"

Perseus felt a sudden thrill of exultation, as boys do feel when they're asked to do something important. His imagination, already travelling along such lines, conjured images of himself as a knight errant, retrieving the princess's lost treasure.

"All right, then!" he called back, which was not a very knightly thing to say, but it was his first attempt after all. Forgetting all about his work, he got up, dusted himself off a bit, and ran for the kitchen door, which was nearest. It seemed very dim after the bright sunlight outside, and he had a fleeting impression of a large, smoky kind of room full of delightful smells and a lot of activity. He darted through before anyone had time to realize he wasn't supposed to be there and hurtled up the servants' stairs.

"Here now!" said a commanding voice that caused him to stop. A tall, stern-looking butler stood before him on the first floor landing, glaring down on him like an imperious judge from behind a flashing pince-nez. "What do you think you're doing in here?" he said.

"The girl upstairs dropped this out the window," said Perseus, holding up the medal. "She asked me to bring it up to her."

The butler grunted, as though to say that he was not surprised. "Very well," he said. "I shall take it from here."

He held out a hand for it. He was such a commanding presence that Perseus, who had always been used to obeying his elders, nearly handed it over without thinking. But the fantasy that had taken root in his mind was strong, and he hesitated. "No," he said, clutching it close to him. "She asked *me* to do it."

"That is no part of your duties," the butler answered. "Now hand it over."

Perseus hesitated a moment longer. Then, bourne by a sudden reckless courage that came from he knew not where, he darted past the butler, ducking under his arm, and raced up the stairs two at a time while the old man shouted after him.

He reached the third-floor landing and burst out into the corridor, finding himself suddenly in a glorious blaze of rich, patterned carpet, dark oak panelling, and fine paintings. He would have had no idea where to go from there, but the girl was visible at the end of the passage, leaning over the bannister that overlooked the main staircase. Perseus ran to her, and she jumped a little as he suddenly appeared from behind.

"Here...it is..." he gasped, holding the medal out to her. His bad lungs were rebelling against the sudden and unprecedented burst of energy he had demanded of them.

"Oh! Thank you," she said, looking bemused. Then she frowned at him, seeing his distress. "Are you all right?"

He nodded, hoping devoutly that he wasn't about to be sick. Meanwhile, the butler arrived behind him.

"My apologies, Miss Elizabeth," he said. "A recently arrived apprentice undergardener. He has no business being here...."

"That's all right, Tredwell," she said. "I told him to bring my medal back up. I dropped again, you see, and he was right there."

"Yes, ma'am," he answered stiffly. "Nevertheless, it is highly improper that he should force his way in..."

"Oh, never mind that!" she said carelessly, turning back to Perseus, who was leaning against the banister trying to breathe. "Look, boy, are you all right? Here, come and sit down. Tredwell, fetch a glass of water, there's a good fellow."

She led Perseus to a comfortable seat beneath one of the windows. Tredwell gave a stiff bow that spoke volumes and disappeared.

As Perseus slowly got his breath back, he was able to get a better idea of the Hon. Miss Elizabeth. She was about his own age (though being a girl she of course conveyed the impression of being older), tall and bony, with a good-natured, freckled face that had clearly seen a lot of sun and bright hazel-green eyes. There was something of the air of a young colt about her, in her long, bony limbs and the restless, rather awkward energy of her movements. She sat now on the edge of the seat with her hands crossed on her knees, looking at him with the eager interest she might have shown to a new dog.

"I say, you're not very strong for a gardener," she commented.

"I'm strong enough," he answered defensively, though his choked voice rather undermined the assertion. "It's only that my lungs aren't quite right. That's why I'm here with Uncle Roger. They say the country air will make me better."

"How long have you been here?"

"Two days."

"Oh, I see. Well, that's not very long, so I suppose it still might work."

Tredwell returned with the glass of water, which Perseus eagerly gulped down as Elizabeth sent the butler back about his duties. The man frowned at the *tet-a-tet*, but did as he was bid.

"What's your name, boy?" she asked when he'd gone.

"Perseus Corbett."

"I say, what a funny name!" she said, laughing.

"It is not! It's the name of a great hero who chopped a gorgon's head off and used it to kill a sea monster and save a princess."

"I know all that, but I've never met a 'Perseus' before," she said. "Have you slain any sea monsters lately?"

"No," he admitted grudgingly. "Has anyone fed you to one lately?"

"I'd like to see them try!" she answered, throwing her head back and laughing with the careless ease of one who was used to having her own way.

"What's so important about that medal, anyway?" he asked, feeling he ought to take the offensive.

"What's important about it?" she exclaimed. "It's only from King Charles the First is all. He made a collection of these during the Civil War and handed them out as gifts to people who'd done him particular service, like my great-great-great...oh, I forget how many greats grandfather, Lord John."

"You're joking!" said Perseus, suddenly interested. He knew a bit of history, and the idea that he had been carrying something that once belonged to the unhappy king filled him with awe. "Shouldn't that be in a museum, then?"

"No, because it's *mine*," she said. "My grandfather gave it to *me* personally."

"So why did you drop it out the window?"

"I told you, that was an accident! I was just leaning out the window, looking at it and thinking about those days – it just slipped."

"I've never met anyone related to a real-life cavalier," he said.

"Oh, yes; we're a very old family, didn't you know? Fourteenth century I think we got started, and Lords and ladies all the way down. If you like that, we've got plenty more like it. I'll show you them, if you want...."

"Well, now," said booming voice. "What's all this?"

A look of pure, unrestrained joy suddenly covered Elizabeth's face as she sprang up and ran to greet the man who had just ascended the stairs.

Perseus had met Lord Peter Alban, Baron Darrow briefly when he'd first come to Sangral, and his impression had been that, without actually being of great size, he conveyed the sense of being larger than life. He was a tall, soldierly man whose sharp eyes shone with a kind of benevolent mastery.

Elizabeth gave him a quick and rather disjointed account of what had happened, while Perseus stood awkwardly trying to remember the right things to say and do.

"But I thought you had to go up to London today?" she concluded.

"I met a wire at the station putting it off," he answered. "So, I suppose you and I ought to go down over the farms, oughtn't we?"

"Yes, we certainly ought," she answered with a mock solemnity that didn't remotely disguise her intense pleasure at the idea.

The three of them – Elizabeth beckoned Perseus to follow – descended down the main staircase and back out into the grounds. As they walked, Lord Darrow spoke with Perseus, asking how he liked Sangral so far and questioning him on his opinion of the gardens. Finding the boy knew very little of the subject, he began leading him and Elizabeth around the flower beds, instructing them in the names and proper care of the various plants.

It was while he was thus engaged that Uncle Roger found them. Quick explanations and assurances that it was all quite all right followed. Lord Darrow and Elizabeth departed for the stables and Perseus was left to resume his duties with only the mildest of scoldings. But even a more severe punishment would have hardly mattered compared with the great fact that he had now become friends with the young lady of the house.

From then on, whenever Perseus wasn't working and Elizabeth wasn't busy with lessons (and sometimes when one or both ought to have been), the two would be off exploring the grounds in fine weather and the house in bad. She showed him all the treasures of her ancestral home, telling him what she knew of their history. He saw the portraits of her ancestors and heard what each one had done. He saw the landscapes and miniatures painted by famous artists, the furniture that had been in use for longer than the oldest servant had been alive. He saw the suits of armour, the secret passages, and the marks on the wall showing where some long-dead relative had thrown a silver tureen of soup in a fit of madness. He saw the woods and ponds that had been cultivated by generations of gardeners. He saw the stables with their fine horses, the kennels with their barking dogs, the pseudo-Greek folly down by the pond that Elizabeth's grandfather had built....

Most importantly, the very day after their chance meeting, he saw the library, with its hundreds upon hundreds of books gathered across many generations. They were books of the kind that creaked when you opened them and breathed forth a wonderfully musty smell, so that even if you didn't read them, you wanted to pull them down and page through them anyway. Having practically been raised on books, the sight of this infinitude of words filled Perseus with the same feeling as if he had found Aladdin's cave.

Elizabeth, he found, was not a great reader. Or rather, she was not at all fond of being *made* to read. She had shown him the library mostly on account of some suits of armour that stood by the library fireplace and the portrait of an ancestor who had been a famous poet in his day. Perseus's accounts of *The Jungle Book*, *Treasure Island*, and *The Count of Monte Cristo*, however, could not fail to pique her interest, and after they had explored the house from top to bottom and back again, their favourite pastime became finding a book to share. They would then race about the park, imagining themselves as part of the stories, or making plans for going on their own adventures; of voyaging in the West Indies like Robinson Crusoe, or trekking in darkest Africa like Allan Quatermain, or traveling in India like Mr. Kipling.

***

And so two years passed rapidly away at Sangral House. Perseus's lungs recovered and his body grew strong under the stern direction of his uncle. He learned to ride, to fish, to shoot, and to climb trees. He learned more about history, about art, about music. He and Elizabeth got into the most frightful trouble over a series of ingenious pranks (all at her instigation). Two years of almost unmitigated happiness and wonder, broken only by occasional visits home, where the dust and grime and squalor of the London neighbourhood – so different from the romantic images of the city that he found in his books – seemed almost like a bad dream. Or, what is worse, like the coming from a good dream into a sad awakening.

The only other check to his happiness was Elizabeth's mother. At first she paid little heed to the friendship between her daughter and the gardener's nephew. They were children, and children would have their escapades. She didn't much care for her daughter's climbing trees or catching snakes, but Elizabeth had been doing those sorts of things long before Perseus showed up, and at least now she was reading.

But as time went on, Lady Darrow began to disrupt their escapades more and more. They would be having a great game in the conservatory and she would look in to say, "It is time for your music lessons, Elizabeth," or they would be sitting reading together on the hillside and she would send to say he was wanted on the grounds. More and more it seemed their time together was being curtailed.

On the other hand, they had a staunch ally in Lord Darrow, who regarded their friendship with an indulgent eye and often joined in their escapades whenever he was home. The trouble was that Army business frequently took him to London or even to the continent for long periods, which meant that most of the time there was nothing they could do but make the best of what they had.

Then came the end of it, the final awakening. A letter arrived from home to inform him that, as his health had so clearly improved, his father wanted him to come home to stay. He had, it said, found him a job in London, which would bring in twice what he was making as an apprentice undergardener, money that would be sorely needed.

Perseus was prepared to argue the matter out, that though the money was not very good, he was on his way to having a perfectly suitable job right here. He would be a full undergardener before long, and had a chance of being head gardener in the end. But when he mentioned this to Uncle Roger, he put the final stop to the boy's wishes.

"Fact is," he told him. "I think Lady Darrow had a hand in asking your father to take you home. She's not too keen on the way you and Miss Elizabeth are so familiar, as I've warned you time and time again."

So it was settled. He would be going home to London for good. Home, where there would be no armour, no paintings, no old books, no secret passages, no ponies, no lake, and no woods.

Worst of all, there would be no Elizabeth.

Shortly after the summons home had arrived, Elizabeth learned that her parents were making plans to go on holiday to America, an extended stay of some months' duration at least. That meant that on top of everything else, they would now be separated by a whole ocean.

The decision was made, the bags were packed, and the tickets purchased. All that now remained were the last few precious hours at Sangral. The Baroness, though she did not approve of their friendship, was at least softhearted enough to allow them to spend those last hours in uninterrupted company.

Perseus and Elizabeth sat side by side on the hill, overlooking the house and grounds. They had spent many a happy hour there over the years, reading or dreaming or playing. But now there didn't seem anything to be done except to be together while they could.

Elizabeth sat with her knees drawn up, resting her chin upon them, idly watching a rabbit grazing by its burrow some way off.

"It's not fair," she grumbled. "Why couldn't you have come with us to America?"

"Just be sure to watch out for sea monsters," he said, making an effort to be cheerful. "I'd hate for you to be gobbled up while I'm not around."

"That's sweet of you," she answered, smiling at what had become a long-running joke between them. "But I keep telling you I'm not going to need it. No one's chaining *me* to a rock!"

They laughed, but not as wholeheartedly as they were used to. It was but the faint flicker of something that was dying.

"You're not going to forget about me, are you?" she asked after a pause.

"Of course not!" he said. "I'm going to be working in a bloody shop; thinking about this place is probably going to be the only thing that'll make it tolerable. You're the one who's going to be having parties and meeting interesting people and having adventures and all that."

"Well, just to make sure you don't, I decided to give you a present," she said, reaching into the pocket of her frock and handing him a small box.

He opened it, and to his astonishment found the Charles the First medal that he had retrieved for her when they first met.

"You can't give me this!" he said. "It was your grandfather's! It's a historical treasure."

"Yes, and now it's mine and I can do what I like with it," she said. "Since I know you like it so much, I thought I should give it to you. Besides, you earned it; heroically risking the wrath of Tredwell to bring it to me, when any sensible boy would have just given it to him. I thought if I gave it to you, then you'd stay gallant and delightfully silly even working in some dreary old shop."

Hesitantly, he put the medal about his neck.

"Thanks so much," he said, fingering the ancient silver with affection and awe. "I'll never, never take it off."

"Don't *never* take it off; you'll spoil the silver. Just see you take good care of it. When my time comes, I don't want to have to explain to either grandfather or Lord John that I gave their medal to someone who went and lost it."

Perseus laughed, but again it soon faded, like a small fire in a cold stove. Their time was almost up.

"I didn't even think to get you anything," he said. "And you're by far the more likely to forget about me."

He didn't add that he wouldn't have known what to get her, even if he had.

"Oh, I don't think that's likely," she said.

"Still, I'd like to give you *something*. Something important. But I don't have anything like that."

Elizabeth thought a moment.

"Well," she said slowly, looking away as though embarrassed. "There is one thing you could give me."

"What?" he asked eagerly.

"It's not really much, of course," she said. "Though I think it is important. And I don't know if I really ought to ask, but since you're so eager..."

"Well? What is it?"

She swallowed and fixed her eyes on a bit of grass by his feet. Her face was as red as her hair.

"A kiss."

Perseus felt as though the bottom had dropped out of his stomach. "A what?"

"My first kiss," she said, playing with the grass. "It's a special thing. Ought to be, at least, I think. Something I can always take with me. That way I'd be sure never to forget you."

Perseus felt himself going red as well. He had never yet seriously thought of kissing anyone. It was the sort of thing one read about in books and imagined doing, but which existed totally apart from the real world. It was as if she had told him that there was a dragon that needed slaying or pirate treasure to be dug up.

Yet, he certainly didn't *dislike* the idea.

"I suppose so," he said.

Judging by the way they focused on it, one would have thought that there was something infinitely fascinating about the grass about their feet.

"So...will you?" she asked after a moment.

He forced himself to look at her, and she forced herself to look at him, and he swallowed and nodded. "I'm game if you are."

He had no real idea what he was doing. It seemed far more complicated in real life that it had sounded in books. But there wasn't anything for it but to simply try their best. Elizabeth shut her eyes tight and learned forward a little. Perseus thrust his face forward and their lips met.

It was wetter than he had expected. But really quite nice.

They broke apart, both breathing rather fast. Then they began to giggle uncontrollably.

A moment later, Uncle Roger came stumping up the hill to tell them it was time, and they walked back down together. At the gate, the moment of parting came. They shook hands and said their goodbyes.

"Have a good time in America," he said.

"Have a good time in London," she answered. "Or at least, not too frightful of one."

He smiled. And just like that, they parted, him walking away beside his uncle to the train station for the last time.

"I'll send for you if that sea monster shows up!" she called after him as a parting shot.

"See that you do!" he called back.

As the train rode away back to London, Perseus found his mind kept going back to that kiss. That first and only kiss. He felt different for it; stronger, bolder, more sure of himself. And all at once, he seemed to see his path clear before him.

In that moment, Perseus Corbett made a vow. He had no idea how he would do it, but he swore he would or die trying. He swore to himself that, some day, he would become a gentleman. He would have a house like that: beautiful grounds, horses, servants, fine old objects, all of it.

Most of all, he vowed that he would marry Elizabeth Alban.

Chapter Two
Dead Man's Gift

"I was first mate, I was, old Flint's first mate, and I'm the on'y one as knows the place."
-Billy Bones, *Treasure Island*

Fourteen years later, Perseus Corbett was still a thousand miles from his heart's desire.

He stood on a pier in Istanbul on a warm, clear night, before the gangplank of the steamer *Aeneas*, bound for New York, and was just wondering whether he had forgotten anything. The visas were all right; perfectly genuine. He'd gotten them blank, but pre-approved from a friend in the American State Department a few years before, following a job in that country which hadn't quite worked out. He was sure they had shaken off all pursuit, and in any case he doubted the Soviets would follow them all the way to Istanbul for the sake of retrieving their property.

Said property took the very pleasing form of a young lady with shiny, jet-black hair and deep grey eyes, accompanied by her young son. Dressed in the rude garb of a working woman and clutching her shawl tight about her head with one white hand, the Countess Nadezhda Vladimirovich looked very little like the great lady she had once been, save for the distinction in her face and carriage, which all her years of fear and suffering had not yet erased. And though Perseus had assured her again and again that the danger was passed, her eyes nevertheless darted fearfully about and she clutched her son's hand tight in her own.

"I believe that is all, your highness," Perseus said at last. "If you have any trouble in New York, ask for Daniel Kirby of the State Department and tell him that I sent you. Can you think of anything else, Martin?"

He turned to the tall, straight-backed man with faded gold hair who stood at his side.

"I think not," Martin answered in a voice flavoured with the air of Vienna. "I have spoken with one of the crew. He is sympathetic to her highness's plight and has promised to attend to her during the voyage."

"Then I think there is nothing more to say," said Perseus. "Have a lovely trip, your highness, and the best of luck to you."

"Good messieurs's!" she said in her rich, husky voice. "I can never, never thank you enough! You have saved our lives! Still I cannot believe that you should run such risks, show such gallantry on our behalf, and to ask nothing in return!"

"Oh, think nothing of it," said Perseus, though inwardly he flinched a little. "No more than what a gentleman ought to do. Particularly these days."

"And to send us on to America," she continued. "I almost fear to accept such kindness!"

"Please," said Perseus. "It is clear enough that Istanbul is no place for you. You had much better go to America, where you can be far away from all of this. You will have a new life ahead of you. A chance to start over."

He smiled down at little Foma as he said this. The boy had still not spoken a word since they met. But now that the moment of parting had arrived, he stole a furtive look at Perseus before turning away once more. Perhaps once in America, far from the horrors he had been forced to witness, he would begin to heal.

"I shall pray for you every day," the countess promised.

"That shall be most appreciated," said Perseus with a bow.

It felt odd to be saying goodbye. They had spent the better part of the past two weeks in company with the countess and her son and had been through some very stiff times together. Smuggling them out of Soviet Russia had been no easy task, and it had cost most of what Perseus and Martin had been able to save. In such circumstances, twelve days are the equivalent of a lifetime, and the two men had almost come to feel that the countess were family. But they would not be going to America. There was, at present, nothing there for them.

The whistle of the steamer blew to signal it was time for all to be aboard. The countess kissed Martin and then went to do the same to Perseus. But when she approached him, he held up a gently declining hand and settled for a simple embrace. They then bid farewell to little Foma, and with a final, grateful smile the countess picked up her small bundle of baggage and ascended the gangplank.

"So ends our attempt to retrieve the jewels of Russia," Perseus sighed.

"I should say we succeeded quite admirably," said Martin.

"Oh, I agree," Perseus replied. "Don't regret it for a moment. Rather have that lovely creature and that sweet little boy in the world than all the jewels the Tsars ever had in my pocket. I'm only noting that it seems a bit of a pattern with us, what?"

He fingered the Charles I medal that lay concealed under his clothing. Perseus had grown considerably in the years since he'd left England. He was tall and broad of shoulder, tanned from long days under tropical suns, and muscular from constant exertion. Long, careful study and practice had given decision and grace to his movements and eloquence to his manners, belying his shabby clothes. His brown hair had faded a little from his time in the sun, and there was a new thoughtfulness and cunning in his dark eyes.

The two men sat down upon a set of crates. Perseus produced a battered cigarette case and they smoked in silence while they watched the *Aeneas* get underway. The countess, a small, dark figure on the stern, waved to them, and they waved back. Little Foma, they were pleased to see, waved shyly alongside his mother.

"It occurs to me," said Perseus after the ship had disappeared on its trip down the Bosporus. "That the problem with becoming a gentleman is that gentlemanlike behavior is not at all conducive to making sufficient wealth for a gentleman's lifestyle."

"Indeed," said Martin. "That is why most try to be born into wealth."

"Bit late in the day for that," Perseus said morosely, fingering his cigarette and glaring at it in some disgust. "How much money have we got left?"

Martin drew out their purse and counted.

"About fifty pounds," he said.

"I suppose that's just enough to start over, if we had an idea of where to start," said Perseus."

"I am quite certain you will think of something," said Martin.

Perseus glanced at him. He wasn't quite sure how to take that, but the Austrian was too well-trained to give anything away by his severely lined face.

Martin Halritter had once been valet to an Austrian count. After having his leg shot off by the Italians and his Empire dissolved by the Americans, the count had retired in disgust to the West Indies, where he soon died and Martin had been left to ply his trade for tourists at a hotel. Perseus had taken him on to help dig up some pirate treasure some years ago, but yet another inconvenient revolution had left them with little to show for it beyond a fast friendship.

Ever since leaving England, Perseus had hunted treasure all around the world. He'd gone to sea as a boy just before the Great War (lying about his age to do so), did his part in the conflict from the deck of the destroyer *Dauntless*, and then scoured the globe for the chance to strike it rich enough to make himself a gentleman. A mere business enterprise wouldn't satisfy him; he recalled the tales of the Barons Darrow that had been, and of the knights and cavaliers he'd read about in books, and the spirit of commerce seemed as far removed from them as could be imagined.

No, a real gentleman, he thought, earned his place by deeds, adventure, and daring. It was not something that could simply be bought by accumulating enough in a bank account. Wealth, of course, he needed, but wealth with a history, wealth earned by acts of courage, not by plodding.

It had seemed straightforward enough when he began, and so it seemed with each new endeavour. He had dug for pirate treasure in the Caribbean, chased lost gold mines in the Rocky Mountains, sought hidden kingdoms in the jungles of Africa and India, dredged for shipwrecks in the East Indies, and dug for tombs in the Egyptian desert. Yet, somehow, each had left him as poor as ever, if not poorer. Many was the time he had stood at the brink of success, had handled ancient gold and hidden treasures, yet each time they had slipped through his fingers like sand.

And something else had slipped away as well; time. Years ago, the thought had formed in his mind that Elizabeth was not likely to remain unmarried for long. In fact, it was likely as not that she had already moved on and forgotten about him. There was no particular reason she *should* remember him, let alone wait for him.

This thought had grown like a cancer with his every delay and failure, and was now like a permanent cramp in his brain. Ever since the end of the war he had carefully avoided returning to England, or even reading English newspapers, lest he find his worst fears confirmed. As long as he didn't know, he could still hope.

Perseus threw his cigarette away in frustration and stood up. The *Aeneas* was almost out of sight down the Bosporus. "Come on," he grunted. "I need a drink."

They left the docks and made for one of the numerous taverns that clustered like barnacles around the port. As they approached it, however, a large man in a black felt hat, with a closely trimmed beard stepped forward out of the shadows.

"Excuse," he said in a husky Slavic accent. "But I am waiting for some friends of mine. Have you seen them, perhaps? Two men, a dark-haired and very pretty woman, and her little child? They were supposed to arrive in Istanbul today, but I have not seen them."

Perseus carefully concealed the alarm that this question had raised. They had arrived at the port of Istanbul that afternoon and had immediately booked the countess passage on the *Aeneas*, not leaving the docks the entire time. He was now immensely thankful they hadn't.

"I can't say I have," he answered. "Didn't notice any particularly pretty women on our ship coming in, and I generally do notice that sort of thing."

The man smiled. "Most unfortunate. Perhaps they have been delayed."

"Perhaps."

"Where have you come from, might I ask?"

"Naples," said Martin. "And you?"

The man looked hard at him, which nearly made Perseus smile. He doubted there was a man alive who could read Martin's face if he didn't want it read.

"Oh, I have been here many years," the man answered. "I have much business in this city. I am most apologetic to have troubled you. Might I buy you a drink?"

"No thank you," said Perseus. "We have business of our own to deal with. Good evening."

The man bowed and they walked on down the winding streets of Constantinople.

"Well," Perseus sighed once he was sure they were out of sight and that the man had not followed them. "It is a damn good thing we sent her off when we did. I never would have thought the Russians would be so keen on getting her back. What made you say Naples, by the way?"

"I happened to recall that the *Karnak* was the most recent arrival, so it seemed to me the most plausible."

"Good lord, what a head for detail you have," said Perseus. "Well, let's find ourselves another tavern; preferably one without any Bolsheviks, if there is such a place."

They turned down a narrow street and saw what they were looking for up ahead; a hole-in-the-wall tavern, the sort no doubt frequented by sailors and local working-class. As they approached it a thin old man came stumbling out and nearly walked right into them.

"'Scuse me, gentlemen," he muttered in English. "Much pardon," he added in broken Turkish.

"After you, father," said Perseus in the former language.

The drunk's eyes lit up. "By God, is that a man of my own country I hear?" he said. "What are you doing in this forsaken place, my fine fellow?"

"Seeking my fortune, as are we all," Perseus answered.

"Not I!" said the man with some dignity, drawing himself up and swaying as he did so. "Not I! I have found mine! Found it long ago. But I will say no more...no. Not another word. It is mine. Mine alone."

"As you say, father," said Perseus kindly.

"Don't you tell a soul," he said, pressing a finger to his withered lip. "Not a soul. Mine alone. I shall go collect it one of these days. But tonight, I think I must go rest."

"Quite," said Perseus. "Do you need any help, father?"

"I need no one!" said the old man, pushing he way past them. "Mine alone. I need only time...yes. Time alone..."

He stumbled on to the end of the street. Perseus and Martin watched him go, Perseus giving his friend a bemused look.

"Poor old fellow," he said. "Wonder what his story is."

"A sad one, I should say," said Martin. "But common enough."

They got no further, for at that moment the night exploded into violence.

Just as the old man reached the end of the street, three figures jumped out and set upon him. The old man cried out, and struck one of them a solid blow, but was knocked down in an instant.

"Here!" Perseus shouted, running to his aid. "You leave him alone!"

The three attackers turned in evident surprise as the two men charged them. The nearest brandished a blood-stained knife at Perseus, who checked himself and raised his hands in defence. The assassin thrust at him, and Perseus dodged the stab and caught him by the wrist, pulling the man between himself and the second attacker while driving his fist into his stomach. He grunted and dropped the knife, and Perseus shoved him into his comrade.

Martin, meanwhile, engaged the third attacker. This man was just bending over the fallen drunk, and Martin kicked him hard in the ribs, knocking him over. The assassin grunted and tried to roll to his feet. Martin caught him on the way up and struck him back to the ground.

The toughs had evidently not been expecting this kind of resistance. They had jumped a defenceless, drunken old man, but now they suddenly found themselves facing two young, fit, and experienced fighters. They stumbled to their feet and scattered as soon as they were able.

"Bastards," Perseus grumbled as he knelt over the fallen drunk. "Here, father, are you all right?"

The old man was clutching his side, right under his heart. A dark stain was spreading over his ragged clothing and onto his withered old hand.

"Thank you, friends," he breathed. "Thank you very much. No one has done so much for me these many, many long years. Oh, but I have deserved no more! May God have mercy on my soul...."

"Here now, it isn't so bad," said Perseus, looking significantly at Martin. "We'll get you a doctor and you'll be right as rain."

Martin nodded and set off at a run.

"No, no," said the old man. "It is over, I feel it. I have wasted my life, lost my chance." His face suddenly became anxious and he felt inside his shirt. Then relief spilled over it. "It is there," he gasped. "It is safe."

He drew out a small, square bundle wrapped in dirty leather rags and pressed it on Perseus.

"I give it to you," he said. "My treasure! My fortune! All I have in the world."

At these words, Perseus's eyes lit up and his heart leapt in spite of himself. "What do you mean?" he asked, keeping his voice steady.

"Read it," the man said. He was fading fast. "Follow it. And when you are rich beyond mortals, remember old Joe."

Perseus took the bundle, the old man's warm blood staining his hands, and mechanically put it into his pocket.

"Treasure house of the gods," the man breathed. "Forbidden...Valley..."

His hand dropped and he breathed no more.

A moment later, Martin appeared, a constable in tow. He paused upon seeing the huddled, shrunken old body and silently made the Sign of the Cross.

Perseus and Martin explained what had happened to the policeman, and the body of Old Joe was given up to the state. The Turkish authorities, who had many such bodies, disposed of it in their own fashion. Probably no one in that city thought of or remembered the old man ever again. He slipped below the surface of history as a tiny, unremarked pebble, even as the ripples he had set into motion began to spread.

Perseus did not mention the bundle to the police, and it remained tucked away in his pocket until he and Martin had found a secluded spot in a still half-ruined part of the city to camp out for the night. There, under the veiled glow of an old lantern and having made sure that no eavesdroppers were present, Perseus told Martin what had happened after he left and showed him the bundle.

"Why did you not mention it to the police?" the Austrian asked.

"I was worried they might take it in evidence," Perseus answered. "Anyway, I don't suppose they care, and the old boy gave it to me expressly."

"Hm," said Martin, a faint crease appearing between his well-trained eyebrows. "What is it?"

"No idea, but he said it was the way to treasure beyond the lot of mortals. Let's have a look, shall we?"

He carefully unwrapped the dirty bundle and found that it was a small notebook. Or rather, part of a notebook; the second half or more of the book had been torn away, leaving only the cover and the first few pages. Perseus opened it and read the following on the front leaf:

"True Narrative of Certain Events in the Brazilian Jungle, by Robert Cooper"

Chapter Three

"A Once-In-A-Lifetime Kind of Chance"

What is that which I should turn to,
Lighting upon days like these?
Every door is barr'd with gold, and opens
but to golden keys
-Alfred Lord Tennyson, *Locksley Hall*

Two steerage tickets to London was the most that their scanty resources could command. Perseus was reluctant to return to England and had argued against the idea, but Martin had quite rightly pointed out that it was the only likely place within their reach where they could put their new plans into motion. They could not afford the passage to New York, and no one in the Parisian scientific community would dream of helping them after that expedition to the Congo.

And so it was that, two days after the death of Old Joe on the streets of Istanbul, Perseus Corbett was en route to his home country for the first time in nearly a decade.

To avoid thinking of the fact, he spent most of the passage pouring over Cooper's notebook, and especially the opening words:

January 1915

I have undertaken to write a faithful account of the events of the ill-fated expedition of the late Professor Applegate in the year 1911. The events described in these pages will differ considerably from the narrative which I and the others of our party presented to the world

25

regarding the deaths of Professor Applegate, John Miller, and the comaradas, Simplicio and Angelo, but I hope the reason for our deception will become clear over the course of my narrative. It was agreed between ourselves (that is to say, between Professor Arnold Prosser and myself) that, in the light of the fantastic things we witnessed, that the truth simply would not be acceptable, all the more so in that we did not and do not understand just what it is we have discovered. I hope that my narrative shall make this clear.

As for why I have determined, with the concurrence of my friend, to write the true account these four years later, that is far simpler. I shall be going to the Front soon. If I do not return, as seems all too likely, then the truth risks being lost forever. Prosser is in poor health; he never quite recovered from the experience. As I feel that some whom we have deceived, particularly Mrs. Applegate and her children, have a right to know the truth, I am now committing these memories to paper while I am still able to. If they ever read this, I can only beg their forgiveness for the deception we have played upon them.

At the same time, I must beg them, if they ever do read these pages, to never allow them to become public. I hope, when they have read my account of what we found, they shall feel the same. The Treasure House of the Gods, the man called it. That was enough to tempt us to that damn valley, and it sure would be enough to tempt others....

What followed was a strange and rather rambling narrative, written in an often difficult hand. Cooper had been a big game hunter and British Army Officer who was commissioned by Professor Applegate, an eminent zoologist, to take him and some companions up a little-explored river deep in the interior of South America. The river was a tributary of a tributary of the Amazon called "Rio Noite," or the River of Night on account of its black colouring.

The first part of the narrative was merely a summary of his own life and how he had become involved in the expedition on recommendation of a friend of his named John Miller, who would become one of the expedition's casualties. Several more were taken up with an account of their journey to and up the Noite.

Then came the interesting part.

One evening, when it came time to make camp, they spotted a large black stone idol beside the river. Against Cooper's advice they decided to make camp there, as they had already been some time looking for a landing place. One of the *comaradas* or native bearers, a man named Angelo, said that he had seen this same idol before. His tale was that he had been part of a surveying expedition with a Brazilian army officer some years before, which had followed the Noite to a little beyond this point until fever and lack of supplies forced them to turn back. It was, he said, on their return journey that they found the idol.

What was far stranger, there was a man sitting beneath it. An ancient man, almost like a mummy. Thinking he might be lost and in need of help, they stopped and approached him. When they spoke to him, the man began to chant in fluent Portuguese:

"Forbidden. Forbidden. Forbidden. Three days to the rising sun is the place forbidden."

However they addressed him, he never said anything else. He died that very hour, and they buried him beside the Amazon. Angelo said that when he had asked his father about it after returning home, he had said that the 'place forbidden' was a place in many of their legends, also known as the Treasure House of the Gods.

Once the man had shared his story, Professors Applegate and Prosser had become immensely curious to know what this 'place forbidden' might be. Cooper himself was intrigued by the name 'Treasure House of the Gods.' After some more consultation, it was decided that part of the expedition should attempt the three-day journey into the jungle, just to see what, if anything, was out there. Cooper, Miller, Applegate, and Prosser, along with two comaradas (including Angelo) went off into the jungle, leaving the rest of the party behind.

On the third day from the river, they indeed found the place; a great valley or pit in the middle of the jungle, with walls so steep that it would be impossible for anything to climb out of it.

"What struck the eye the most, however, was that at the exact centre..."

But here the manuscript broke off in mid-sentence.

It was intensely frustrating to have so tantalizing and yet so incomplete a narrative. If it were not for that introduction, there would be little to interest him.

Yet, throughout there was something; a sense that it was not only fear of the world's skepticism that compelled the two men to hold their tongues. Whatever they had found there, it had astonished them, frightened them even, though wonder as much as horror was likewise stamped on every page.

Perseus bitterly wished that he had the whole thing, particularly the account of what they actually *found* in the valley that had been so fantastic or so terrible as to make it impossible to render a true account to the world. But even these faint hints were enough to awaken the very feelings that Cooper had hoped to avoid. Perseus was now dead set on finding the valley for himself and discovering what it contained.

Other than this curiosity and his anxiety at the thought of returning home, it was a perfectly comfortable voyage. When they weren't studying the book, Perseus and Martin walked about on deck, exchanging greetings with the other passengers and forming plans.

They had already decided that it would require professional support to fund and equip an expedition to the valley. The two of them could not practically travel into the depths of the Amazon and carry out whatever was to be found there, even if they had money for passage and equipment. The account in Cooper's book was unfortunately spare, but Perseus thought there was enough to convince someone of the location's being of archeological or zoological significance – if they could be convinced of the book's veracity.

Martin was more skeptical. He thought the book as likely to put off any potential backers as otherwise. In any case two vagabonds such as themselves showing up with a wild tale of lost worlds in the Amazon was not likely to get much of a hearing.

"Of course," he said as they walked about the deck one afternoon. "We may have better success if we had a contact, someone well-known in society and of good reputation."

"Naturally," said Corbett. "But what good is that? We don't. At least, not in English society. Perhaps if we work our way across to America..."

"Pardon me, but I believe we do," said Martin.

"Do you? Then it must be one of your governor's cronies. Remember, I haven't been in the country since the end of the war."

"Yes, but before that, as I recall..."

Perseus suddenly saw where he was going and felt his stomach clench. He looked around, saw a thin, spectacled man reading a newspaper nearby and pulled Martin away.

"If you mean Miss Alban," he said sharply, lowering his voice. "That is out of the question."

"And why, if I may ask?"

"In the first place, it is odds on against her remembering me at all. In the second, I do not intend to show up after all this time simply to beg her for money. And in the third...well, those two will do."

Martin's well-trained eyebrows rose a little, but he only said, "As you wish," and let the subject drop.

They discussed other plans for a time, but they all shipwrecked on the same problem; that they needed money, and this journey was taking most of what they had.

"If I may," said Martin at last. "Perhaps the simplest solution would be best. This valley is not going anywhere. If we were to once more ply a trade for a time, save our wages, we may be able to arrange something within a few months."

Perseus hated this solution. It was, he knew, very sensible, but it meant delay, and the recent allusion to Elizabeth had made him all the more impatient. He could almost see her now, ensconced at Sangral with her husband, whom he pictured as a fat, elderly man rolling in money and who didn't care tuppence for her. The thought of it was like burning venom in his veins, though it was not nearly so painful as another possibility, which Perseus never allowed himself to fully imagine; that of her married to a good man who loved her dearly, and whom she cared for more than she had ever cared for him...

But though he didn't like the plan, he accepted it, at least for the present. They went to dinner and Martin retired to their cabin, while Perseus, restless and irritable after their conversation of the afternoon, paced the deck for several hours more, fingering the silver medal about his throat.

Though she was constantly in his thoughts, it had been some time since Elizabeth's name had been mentioned between them, and Perseus was surprised by the vehemence of the emotions that had been aroused by it. It made him feel old; old and tired. The years behind him seemed to blend together into a haze of wasted time and opportunity. If only he had done this, or that, or not done the other, then he might have been rich long ago and things might have been different. If only...

"Of all the words of tongue and pen," he quoted aloud to himself. "The saddest are these; it might have been."

He leaned over the rail, watching the dark Atlantic pass by beneath him. Whatever happened, he promised himself, he would not miss this one. There would be no more delay. If he had to lie or cheat or steal, he would do whatever it took. *Whatever* it took.

"Nice night," said a voice behind him.

Perseus, shaken out of his reverie, turned around. The thin, spectacled man was standing behind him, leaning against the wall and gazing up at the clear sky.

"Yes, very," said Perseus, glancing up. His instincts were telling him that there was something not quite right here. He looked closer at the man; thin, young, with a pronounced Adam's apple and slicked, straw-coloured hair. American, to judge by his voice.

"You don't mind my talking to you, do you?" the man asked. "It's a bit of a habit of mine, talking to strangers on ship."

"Not at all. Glad for the company," said Perseus.

"You see, I couldn't help overhearing a little of your conversation this afternoon. You are an archeologist, I think you said?"

"Something of that sort."

"Fascinating subject. Is that what brought you to Istanbul?"

"No, that was a matter of fetching a package for a friend."

"Ah. Well, you see, I represent the Museum of Natural History in New York, and what I heard intrigued me. You say you have found the record of an expedition that discovered an unknown region of the Amazon?"

"My goodness, you overheard quite a lot."

The man laughed a little.

"I'm afraid so. I was so interested I couldn't help it. I also heard you say you were looking for backers. Now I can vouch for it that if the book is verified, my organization would be more than happy to arrange for an expedition."

Perseus's eyes lit up. It was tempting; almost too tempting.

"That is extremely generous," he said.

"I can understand your surprise," said the other. "But see, it isn't a matter of charity. I'm looking for an opportunity to get ahead in my profession. Get away from just running errands for the stuffed shirts who run the show. As soon as I heard what you had, I knew that this was my chance: a once-in-a-lifetime kind of chance!"

"I feel much the same way," Perseus answered.

"You have the book, of course?"

"Oh, yes," he said, patting his jacket pocket.

"If I might take a look at it tonight, I could verify it and then wire from London when we arrive," said the man.

Yes, definitely too tempting.

"What is your name, sir?"

"Dang it if I didn't forget to even mention it!" the man laughed. "It's Byron."

"And what brought *you* to Istanbul?"

"Work. As I say, I work with the Natural History Museum."

"Is there a great deal of natural history in Constantinople?"

Byron's Adam's apple twitched a little.

"Well, see, it was like this; we were arranging with the Istanbul University to have an exhibit on Turkish wildlife. I was trying to convince them to lend us some excellent specimens they have. That fell through, I'm afraid."

"And so you are going to London?"

"Yes, I have family there."

Perseus nodded. "And, excuse me, but if our conversation this afternoon was so fascinating to you, why did you wait until now to mention all of this? Seems an odd approach to a once-in-a-lifetime kind of chance."

There was a pause.

"My offer is perfectly genuine," said Byron. "But if you don't like that, I can make another one. How much do you want for that book?"

Perseus's eyebrows rose.

"That is a bit of a shift in tone," he said. "But I suppose I could consider letting it go for...ten-thousand pounds?"

"Done," said Byron. "I'll wire for the money as soon as we reach London."

"Pardon me, it is *not* done," said Perseus. "I said I could *consider* the possibility. Now that it has been confirmed, I might reconsider at fifty thousand."

"That could be arranged," said Byron.

Perseus smiled and shook his head. The American was not very good at this game.

"Exactly how high are you willing to go, Mr. Byron?" he asked.

The American scowled. One hand had been resting inside his coat pocket the whole conversation. Now it emerged, holding a revolver.

"Not a penny," he said. "Hand it over."

The hand holding the gun was steady. Evidently, though Byron was not a very good negotiator, he knew his way around firearms. As Perseus knew that the man couldn't bluff, he evidently was serious.

Perseus, who had been leaning against the rail this whole time, now shifted his weight and sat atop it. He folded his arms and once more shook his head.

"No, I don't think so," he said. "And I don't think you're going to shoot me either."

"What makes you so sure?"

"In the first place, the shot will certainly be heard, and if you were willing to risk that you might have done so while we were talking and spared yourself a good deal of self-inflicted humiliation. In the second, you have already given away just how important this book is to you, which means you cannot afford to have it go tumbling into the bosom of the wine-dark sea along with my corpse.

As that almost certainly will happen if you shoot me now, I'm reasonably sure you will not try it."

He reached into his coat pocket.

"Don't move!" Byron barked.

Perseus ignored him and produced his cigarette case. He drew one out and offered it to Byron, who shook his head irritably. Perseus lit his cigarette with a perfectly steady hand and tossed the match over the side before returning the case to his pocket.

"Are you willing to get shot just to keep that book out of my hands?" Byron demanded.

"Not at all, but as I say, you are not going to shoot me as long as there is a chance you will lose the book in the process," said Perseus. "Now, if you have any sense at all – which I am willing to assume for the sake of argument – you will see that we are at an impasse. If you shoot me, I take the book to the bottom of the Mediterranean and you yourself will likely be arrested. If you attempt to approach and take the book from me, you risk being thrown into the briny deep along with me. Or even just by yourself."

Byron swallowed. Perseus could almost see him trying to figure out a way around the dilemma.

"So, it seems to me," Perseus went on. "That at present your only options are to clear off and try again some other time, or to simply wait there with that gun in your hands until someone comes along and sees what a bloody great fool you look."

Byron's face twitched and his Adam's apple jerked with anger. But Perseus's sketch of the situation was far too clear to admit of any argument, and besides which he was, as Perseus guessed, an amateur at this game. He was clever and had the stomach to kill, but he lacked experience. He looked up and down the deck, then returned the gun to this pocket.

"Wise move," said Perseus.

"This isn't over," Byron growled.

"It never occurred to me that it was."

Byron slouched off into the night. Perseus let him get a fair distance away before setting off in the opposite direction.

His first move was to report the matter to the crew. He suspected Byron would be clever enough to get off the ship before he was caught, but it would at least keep the fellow busy for a while.

His story was truthful as far as it went. He told them that the man calling himself Mr. Byron had approached him regarding certain private papers he had and first attempted to buy them, then demanded them at gunpoint. Just what made them so important to the fellow, he could not say, but evidently the man was a crook and a gangster. The officer in charge apologized profusely for the incident, commended him for handling of the situation, and offered to make compensation in the name of the Cunard Shipping Line. Perseus accepted, and following a friendly exchange of anecdotes regarding their respective experiences in the Royal Navy was able to return to his cabin, confident that Byron would be kept safe one way or another, at least for the remainder of the voyage.

But in the meantime, this changed things. In the first place, it dispelled any idea of the book being some kind of gigantic hoax or delusion on the part of the old man. It also removed any doubts he may have had whether its secrets included any kind of treasure. Someone evidently thought it both real and valuable enough to kill for.

And that same someone knew he had it.

That once-in-a-lifetime chance of his was looking chancier by the minute. That meant that, even apart from his own fears, time was no longer something they could count on.

The rest of the voyage passed quietly, as expected. Byron was not discovered, making them suspect he had somehow found a way off the ship. This at least, as Perseus said, would give them some breathing space once they arrived.

***

London. Perseus had not been back to his home city for ten years, had not lived there for almost fourteen, and had carefully avoided any news from England all that time. His father had died of pneumonia very early in the war, leaving him with no remaining connection to the place, and afterwards Perseus had only returned long enough to settle his affairs before setting off on his quest.

The old city was still much as it had been. There were more motorcars and omnibuses these days, and the smog was perhaps a trifle thicker. But it was still the same vast sea of people churning over the remains of age piled upon age, like ants swarming on a cathedral floor.

Having now been all over the world and having lived in tropical places, where the colours were stark and the people alive, Perseus was struck by how drab and pale the English were. They went about in browns and greys, muttering familiar platitudes to one another in reluctant voices, as though the greatest ambition of each Englishman was to pass unnoticed in the world.

Men, he reflected, had their wild and tamed breeds. He had lived among wild men; men conscious of their own power and exulting in its use. Here were domesticated men; men who, to the extent they knew of it, were terrified of their own strength. They were like a Mastiff who shies at the advances of a small cat, not because he fears the cat, but because he fears what he might do to the cat.

There was something to be said for either side. At least in London the odds of being murdered in your sleep was rather lower than in, say, Senegal. But then, it was always depressing to see a magnificent animal reduced to pulling carts.

Their first move in London, as they had settled, would be to find a way into the kind of scientific circles that could arrange for an expedition to the Amazon. Perseus left this in Martin's infinitely capable hands. There was another, equally important matter that he alone could see to. For their financial situation was nearly desperate. Money would be necessary to approach those with money; they could hardly show up in the stained, battered clothing they had worn in Istanbul.

More to the point, they needed it fast. Martin's idea of simply working a trade for a time was no longer practical. They needed to get under way as soon as possible if they were to stay ahead of Byron and his people.

This left Perseus with a painful choice to make, for he had only one possession of any value and he had never parted from it before.

But this is the one, he told himself. *The one that will make me. It is not forever.*

So it was that, not without a great effort of will, he entered an upscale pawn shop, slipped the Charles I medal from his neck, and asked for a price.

"Hm," said the pawnbroker, squinting at it through his glass. "Difficult to say..."

"Perhaps I should save us both some time," said Perseus, whose patience was already a little strained under the circumstances. "I know for a fact that it is real silver and that the object is of considerable antiquity and historical interest. If you suggest a price under three hundred pounds, I will take it elsewhere."

The pawnbroker took the glass from his eye and glared at him. "Is that a fact?"

"It is. I could take it to the British Museum and they would give me ten times that amount. The only reason I've brought it here is that I should like to be able to redeem it at some point."

"But look here," said the pawnbroker. "I run a business. The question is not how special this is to you, but how valuable it is to me..."

"And you cannot tell me that rich collectors don't stop by here like clockwork," said Perseus, indicating the forest of expensive curios. "You could name your own price for this with any such man who has the least amount of brains. Look here," he pointed to the back of the medallion. "You see that? Do you know what it is? Seal of Charles the First of unhappy memory. This was given by him to a certain lord who provided service to him during the Civil War. Any collector with even an iota of historical knowledge would recognize that. Why, it's as if I'm handing you a thousand-pound check!"

Perseus didn't like the words coming out of his own mouth. How often had he looked over that medal, tracing the ancient markings and thinking of all they meant; of cavaliers and knights, of horses and guns and swords raised in loyal and religious fervour. Thinking also of the hand that had given it to him. Now he was speaking of it as a mere bit of coin; a thing to be sold and made a profit off of. He hated it, but it was necessary for the moment.

The pawnbroker hemmed and hawed a while longer, evidently trying to find a way to dispute the indisputable, but in the end he gave in and paid out three-hundred and fifty pounds.

"Look here, though," said Perseus after pocketing the money. "I want to make a deal with you. I am soon to leave England, but I mean to redeem that object when I return. How much, honestly, do you intend to sell it for?"

"As you say," said the pawnbroker. "It is a unique and very valuable object. I wouldn't part from it for under nine hundred pounds."

"Well," said Perseus. "If you will be so good as to promise to hold it for one year, then I will pledge to pay two thousand for it within that time."

The pawnbroker's heavy brows lifted.

"You're rather sure of yourself," he said.

"I am," said Perseus. "But think of that; it's practically money in the bank. *Either* you're assured of two-thousand pounds within the next year or you're assured of at least nine hundred afterwards. Rather a good deal that."

The pawnbroker ran a long finger down his chin. Perseus could tell that he was searching for a catch.

"Very well," he said. "I shall put this in the safe until this day next year. Until then, I shall eagerly await your return."

He bowed and Perseus, his conscience somewhat mollified by the arrangement, left the shop.

This is the only way, the last chance, he told himself. *It will be worth it.*

Chapter Four

The Unexpected Outcome of a Museum Gala

"...if you will not think me impertinent I may say that I like you, and I believe that we shall come up well to the yoke together. That is something, let me tell you, when one has a long journey like this before one."
-Allan Quatermain, *King Solomon's Mines*

On the following evening, Perseus found himself at the Natural History Museum, dressed in a rented suit and tails, with a ticket in hand that had cost almost as much, and scanning the crowed of richly dressed guests in much the way a lion scans a herd of zebras.

Martin had outdone himself. The gala was being held in honour of an expedition to Borneo that had returned in triumph with several new species of insects, reptiles, and birds. One of these – dubbed the Silver Eagle for its striking feathers and nocturnal habits – had made a sensation among the public.

The reception was held in the central hall of the museum, with specimens from the expedition on triumphal display at temporary stands between the pillars of the gothic space (the live specimen of the Silver Eagle was perched in a large cage in the centre of the hall, shooting warning looks at anyone who ventured too close). Virtually all the most important and influential zoological men of the Royal Academy and the major universities were there, along with their patrons. All, no doubt, were eager for a 'Silver Eagle' of their own. Here if anywhere, he would find what he sought.

He got some champagne and, putting on his best winning manner – the one that he'd used to flirt with tourists when he had worked on a Nile steamer – he selected the elderly Lord Worthing and his wife (Martin had provided him a list of notable people who would be present) and began making small talk. They were charmed, particularly Lady Worthing, and a few anecdotes and compliments were enough to establish a rapport.

But just as he was laying the foundations for his attack, there was a momentary lull in the chatter around him and a voice reached his ears from across the hall.

"Tell me, your ladyship, will you be making another donation to the museum this year?"

Instinctively, Perseus's eyes drifted in the direction of the voice. And that is when he saw her, standing beside the diplodocus skeleton, not twenty feet away from him.

The same, and yet not the same. The skinny, rambunctious girl, all arms and legs, covered in freckles and insect bites, had become an elegant woman; grace and refinement in every line. The tangled red hair was now smooth and done up in a kind of crown, like a halo of flame. The dirty, torn frocks had been replaced by a green dress trimmed in gold which emphasized her fiery hair, not to mention her firm and blooming figure. Her face was much as it had been, yet somehow more. Beautiful, certainly; it was a face made for the open air, for the adoring, obedient eyes of dogs and horses. An open, kind face that looked as though it ought to be quick to laughter.

But the eyes—the bright, hazel-green eyes, sparkling with life—those hadn't changed.

Martin hadn't said a word...perhaps she was a late addition to the guest list? Or had he deliberately kept quiet to ensure Perseus ran into her? He might have to have words with him later.

And she had been called *your ladyship*. But did that mean....

"I suspect I shall," Elizabeth was saying without interest. "I always find human knowledge a good investment."

"I just wondered," said the other woman, whom Perseus had barely noticed. "As I'd heard you'd recently purchased yourself a new horse."

"Apparently to my shame, I have money for both," said Elizabeth, colouring slightly. "Horses needs homes just like anyone else."

Perseus disengaged himself from his new acquaintances without noticing what he said and crossed the room.

"Of course," said the other, making a note. She was evidently a reporter of some kind.

"Oh, bother, you're going to make that sound horrible, aren't you? That I see people on a level with horses, or something."

"My, how cynical you are, my lady!" the reporter replied with a smile like vinegar. "Though that is one possible interpretation of what you said. After all, I can't help notice that your donations tend to be, how shall I put it? *Abstract*. Why not give to something more *practical*, if you really want to put your money to good use?"

"What would you suggest?" asked Elizabeth.

"Say, the League of Women Voters? Or the Peace Pledge Union? Something for the immediate benefit of mankind...."

"Personally," said Perseus, sliding into the conversation. "I don't think people are on a level with horses. I think, taking all in all, that horses are far preferable. Particularly compared with the League of Women Voters."

Elizabeth turned to him with grateful surprise, while the reporter scowled.

"And who are you, sir?" asked the reporter with an air of wounded dignity.

"Only a barbarian from beyond the sea," he said with a bow. "Now if she doesn't object, I should like to borrow her ladyship for a moment."

Elizabeth nodded at the woman with elaborate politeness and allowed Perseus to draw her aside. "Thank you for coming to my rescue," she said. "I'd a hundred times prefer to be abducted by barbarians than preyed upon by reporters."

"She seemed abominably rude to me. Does she do it often?"

"Always," said Elizabeth. "That's Sarah Manning, society writer for the *Guardian*. Rather hot on the subject of the aristocracy and how it is 'a parasitical tumour upon British society,' I believe is how she put it. I suppose tomorrow I'll receive a double-dose of venom for your gallantry. But at least I can enjoy the look on her face tonight, and so for that I thank you, Sir Barbarian."

"My pleasure, your ladyship," he answered with a bow.

"I didn't catch your name," she said. She tilted her head, scrutinizing him closely. "And...pardon me, but have we met before?"

"We have," he said. "And I am glad to see that at least the sea monster hasn't gotten you yet."

Her hazel eyes widened and her jaw dropped. For a moment, all her good breeding and elegant habits were lost in astonishment, and the coltish school girl shone through once more.

"Perseus?" she said after a moment of such bewilderment that it left her without the power of speech. "Perseus Corbett? I...my goodness, I wouldn't have recognized you! You have...well, you've grown!"

"So have you," he said. "I suppose it happens over fourteen years, doesn't it?"

"Yes, yes it does," she stammered, as though hardly thinking what she was saying. "But where on Earth have you been? The last I heard you'd gone off to sea."

"You heard of that?" he said, surprised.

"Of course. Well, I tried writing to you from America, but you never wrote back, then I...I tried to look you up after we'd got back to England – after the war, you know – but all I could find out was that that you'd gone."

"Oh," he said. He felt thrown by the news. It had never occurred to him that she would do such a thing. "I'm sorry. I never got any of your letters. I suppose they got lost with all that was going on, and then my father was very ill for a time, you know. He died early in the war. Then afterwards, well, I'm afraid I had to start earning my fortune, you know."

"Oh, yes," she said. She seemed suddenly embarrassed and dropped her eyes, fingering her dress. "I mean, of course I realize that now. Rather silly of me not to think of it, I suppose."

As they spoke, he thought something else about her had changed. The quickness and energy that had marked her every move and expression in the past was gone. She seemed...slower. Warier. The spirited colt had been broken.

There was a somewhat uncomfortable pause. The things he really wanted to say to her could not be said, and Elizabeth seemed oddly reluctant to engage. She was fidgeting slightly with her hands and not meeting his eyes, as though something about their meeting made her unsure of herself. Meanwhile, he was trying to get a surreptitious look at her left hand, but she was holding it so that he couldn't see.

There was nothing for it; he had to ask. He had to know.

"So...you are a ladyship now?" he said, doing his best to hide the tension in his voice.

"Yes," she answered rather shortly. "I've inherited the title, you know."

"I did not know," he said in genuine surprise. "Then...Oh. I suppose that means your father has passed away?"

"Yes," she said, looking uncertain. "But didn't you hear about that?"

He shook his head.

"I haven't really had any news from England," he admitted. "Not since the end of the war. Was that...how it happened?"

"No," she answered in a dull voice that sounded jarring coming from her. "No, he made it through the war all right. But just after it was finished, some drunken fool ran him down in a motorcar."

"Oh, damn," Perseus said. "I'm more sorry than I can say!"

"Yes, it was rather horrible. Especially coming just then when we were all thinking we'd gotten through it."

Perseus shook his head sadly. "I always liked him. He was a great man."

"I know that," she answered. "But you really didn't hear anything about it?"

"No, nothing. I was...well, I was busy, I'm afraid. Sounds horrible, doesn't it?"

"No...no, I understand perfectly," she said. She looked very thoughtful, and Perseus imagined that he could detect a rapid series of emotions flashing behind her well-bred face.

For a moment, there seemed a danger of them sinking back into silence, but they were rescued by Lord and Lady Worthing.

"Lady Darrow! Do you know Mr. Corbett?" his Lordship asked.

Elizabeth seemed to rally herself.

"Oh, yes, we go way back," she said.

"Old friends," put in Perseus, watching to see what effect that might have on her. She gave no sign of either approval or disapproval.

"I am surprised you never mentioned him!" said her Ladyship. "Such a charming man."

Was it his imagination, or was there a twinkle in Lady Worthing's eyes?

"It's been some time since we've seen each other," Elizabeth answered, a little uncertainly.

"Then that explains your hasty departure, Mr. Corbett," said his Lordship with a smile. "Say no more! We shall leave you two to catch up." They bowed and drifted off.

"When did you become acquainted with them?" she asked

"About five minutes ago."

"Quick work."

He hesitated, then began, "I am frightfully sorry..."

"Oh, that's all right," she said hastily, with something like an imitation of her old manner. "It's all past; no help for it now. You seem to have made your fortune at any rate, haven't you?"

"Looks can be deceiving," he said, glancing down at his suit. He felt they ought to talk more on the subject, but he certainly wasn't going to draw her back to so painful a memory. Not yet at least. "As a matter of fact," he admitted. "I'm here on business."

"How tiresome," she said. "But tell me, what sort of business is it that you do these days? Nothing in London, surely."

"Not usually, no," he said with a grin, noting her renewed animation and following suit. "I have done...well, quite a lot. I was a sailor during the Great War, and a soldier in one or two little ones. I ran a tour boat on the Nile, I tried my hand at ranching for a bit, and I've hunted and trekked through most of the odd places of the world. Now I'm dabbling in a bit of field science."

"Wonderful!" she exclaimed, her lovely hazel eyes shining. "Then you've actually done it, haven't you? I mean, all those things we talked about as children that we wanted to do."

"I suppose I have," he said. "But I'm sure you've done your share as well, haven't you?"

"No," she answered. Her face fell once more and the light faded from her eyes. "No, I'm afraid I've turned into quite the boring, stay at home sort. The most adventure I have is the occasional hunting trip or riding party. And since the war I've never been farther abroad than Ireland."

"Really?" he said in genuine surprise. "Has something happened to Sangral?"

"Oh, no; it's taking in quite as much money as ever, and I've made an investment or two that have paid off handsomely. It isn't want of resources, more...want of opportunity."

"I see," he said, though he didn't. "And how is the old place?"

"Much it ever has been," she said. "Tredwell is still treading about, and your uncle is still keeping the grounds lovely. Mother sits home in her conservatory most of the time, and I go about the farms and such when I'm there, though naturally I'm in London quite a lot on business. It...it isn't *quite* the same, of course."

She seemed ready to falter again and caught herself.

"But I don't suppose you want to waste time hearing all my dreary news. And most of it is dreary. As I say, I've turned out frightfully boring."

"It can't all be dreary," he said. "Come now, no good news?"

He braced himself a little as she considered the question.

"Well, as you heard, I have some charming horses," she said. "And I have had a bit of a lark funding expeditions to interesting places. I never go myself, but at least I hear amusing stories from the people who do. As a matter of fact, I put a bit of money toward *this* trip, though don't let Ms. Manning hear that. She did a piece last year on how I only do it to keep my name in the papers. As if I want people to write horrible things about me! But there I go being dreary again. And it's really too dull for me to recite that sort of thing when I want to hear more about you. Do you still have that medal I gave you?"

"Of course!" he said smiling to cover the stab of guilt in his stomach. "I keep it very safe."

"That's a relief! I was just thinking that, with your running all over the world, getting into adventures, and being in the war and all...not that I'm suggesting you would be reckless with it," she added hastily. "Just that it is very precious and all."

"Quite, quite," he said, hoping she would change the subject. At the same time he noted the nervous, embarrassed edge to the question, with her perceived need to apologize for asking. Yes, she was definitely less sure of herself than she had been. He wondered what had brought the change.

"So, what is this business you're here about?" she asked after another somewhat embarrassed pause.

"Oh, that," he said. "That is...a little complicated." He really didn't want to have to lie to Elizabeth of all people. Yet here was an opportunity that he could not possibly pass by.

"The long and short of it is," he said, lowering his voice, "that I'm hoping to get a little expedition together to go take a look at a backwater of the Amazon. I've happened to hear rumours of there being unique species in that region. I was rather hopping to convince one of these scientist types to take an interest in it."

"Oh, is that all!" she said. "Why the whispering, then? I might be able to help you there; I know most of these fellows. And if it's money you need...."

"I couldn't ask you to do that!" he said.

"Whyever not?" she said. "I told you, it's practically a hobby of mine. I'd just as soon fund something for you as for a stranger."

"Well..." he said, hesitantly. "I certainly could use the help, I won't deny. Like I say, I haven't been in England since the end of the war."

"Come along then; we'll hash it all out," she said. "But not here. Don't suppose you want to talk with all these people about."

He nodded, and allowed her to lead him away.

"Damn, there's another reporter. We'll go this way..."

After a few more turns and detours to avoid certain guests, she led him out of the central hall and down one of the corridors. After checking one or two chambers and finding them occupied by other guests who had sought to escape the main party, she at last deposited him in the hall of reptiles beside a case of various stuffed snake specimens.

"Perfect," she said. "Now wait here a moment. I think I know just the man you want to see..."

She disappeared, leaving Perseus to gather his scattered thoughts. At least, he reflected, she'd seemed to come back to life a little.

A few minutes later, she returned trailing a thin, elderly man behind her.

"Professor Julius Illingworth, may I present my old friend, Mr. Perseus Corbett."

During one of his many adventures, Perseus had spent some time in a very old house in the southern United States. One room had held numerous taxidermied specimens of deer, bear, and other creatures, but the house had been abandoned for so long that they had all dried out and begun to fall in upon themselves.

Professor Illingworth reminded him forcibly of one of those creatures.

He was tall and very thin, with sunken cheeks and grey hair that was rapidly losing its war with destiny. He had a drooping kind of moustache and deep-set grey eyes with heavy eyelids that made him look a bit like an old dog. His grey suit appeared a trifle too large for him, as though it had been tailored when he had been more filled out and healthy. But the gaze that met his was sharp and cunning, and Perseus guessed that, however desiccated the old man might be, he had lost none of his wits.

"How do you do, sir?" said Illingworth, offering a cadaverous hand as he surveyed Perseus with his cold blue eyes. Perseus could almost feel the old man's gaze as it swept over his tan, his scars, and took the measure of his frame. "I understand that you have some sort of proposition."

"I do, sir," he answered. "I'm by way of being an amateur naturalist myself. Knocked around the world quite a bit..."

"Have you?" Illingworth interrupted. "Then of course you would have no trouble recognizing that specimen?" He indicated one of the taxidermied snakes under the glass, putting his hand over the label.

"Naturally," said Perseus smoothly. "Kanburi pit viper. Lovely creature, isn't it?"

"Magnificent," said Illingworth in a mechanical tone. "And are you familiar with its cousin, the Stejneger viper?"

"I have made its acquaintance, yes," said Perseus. "Not quite so attractive as this fellow."

"Not at all. And you must then have encountered the Carneddau viper in your travels?"

Perseus sensed the trap.

"I have not, I am afraid, nor have I read of that species," he said. "Some new discovery of your own, perhaps? The name suggests a Welsh variant."

Illingworth smiled, a thin smile that did not reach his eyes.

"It has been some years since I have been involved in field work," he said. "But there is no such creature, to the best of my knowledge."

"Ah, I see," said Perseus genially. "You were attempting to trip me up? To show me as a fraud and imposter?"

"It has been known to happen," said Illingworth. "Particularly where...." He glanced at Elizabeth. "Money is concerned."

"So it has. I could tell you a fair few stories from my travels."

"I am sure you could," said Illingworth in a dry tone. "Now, what is this proposal of yours?"

"As I was saying, I have been around the world quite a lot. I was in Portugal a short time back where I chanced to meet a retired fellow from the Brazilian army. Left when the empire was overthrown. Anyway, he had done a deal of work in the Amazon; helped get the telegraph started, among other things. Living out in the wilds, he got to know the locals quite well, and they told him tales of a certain tributary, way back in the beyond of beyond, supposedly the haunt of monsters. One day he got curious and paid some of the fellows to show him the way. Well, he told me, after a long journey, they started seeing queer things. Things he hadn't seen anywhere else in the jungle."

"Such as what?" asked Illingworth.

"He had a bit of trouble describing them to me," said Perseus. "He was a bit far gone, I'll admit; stumbled a little in his words. But I gather there were great snakes and huge birds, like the moa, you know. And a variety of large mammalian life. Like bears, he said."

"In the jungle?"

"Quite, that is what I thought."

"What was your friends' name, may I ask?"

"He said that it was Colonel Torres," said Perseus. "Though I confess, from things he let drop, I suspect that was an alias. He kept talking of enemies."

"This is all very entertaining," said Illingworth, in a tone that suggested he had never been entertained in his life. "But I still do not grasp what you want from us?"

"Why, I propose an expedition, sir, to travel up this river and document its wildlife."

"In fact, you wish us to pay you to travel to the Amazon based on the word of a man you yourself describe as both paranoid and senile, and who, for all I can see, may not even exist?"

"Not at all!" said Perseus. "I want you to send some of your own people to the Amazon, and I offer my services as a guide."

"It comes to much the same thing, does it not?" asked Illingworth.

"Indeed," said Perseus with a bow. "You, professor, are a very clever man I can see. You've got me in a nice little corner here. How can I prove my good faith on such a matter? I have no references in this country, save Lady Darrow here, and while I'm sure no man alive could doubt her good will or good sense, what can she really tell you on this matter when this is the first she is hearing of it as well? If I were to summon my partner to vouch for my story, you would only say that he is as much a crook as myself. What, then, do you suggest I do?"

"What indeed?" asked Illingworth.

"What are you going to do?" asked Elizabeth. She was watching him with keen interest; like a child watching a magician and waiting for the trick.

"Nothing simpler," he answered. "I will venture to forego all payment until the successful completion of the expedition. 'Satisfaction guaranteed or services free'. How will that do?"

Elizabeth's face broke into a radiant grin that nearly upset Perseus's air of nonchalance.

"That, I should say, will be most satisfactory," she said. "You might have had a career in advertising."

Illingworth, however, though he looked surprised, did not look satisfied.

"May I ask, sir, why this is so important to you?"

Perseus tore his eyes off of Elizabeth to look at Illingworth.

"An adventure," he said. "I am not particularly concerned with money, you see, but I do like adventure, and this seems a cracking good one: the chance to explore one of the few remaining really unknown places on Earth, to see things that perhaps hardly any men have ever seen before. That is worth more to me than any gold."

Illingworth surveyed him with dry skepticism.

"That may be so, sir, but I must say that I see no practical benefit to the museum in this proposal."

"No benefit?" Elizabeth exclaimed. "A truly unexplored and undocumented ecosystem?"

"In the first place, I have heard yet nothing to convince me that such a place exists," said Illingworth. "You have not even given the name of this supposed tributary...."

"The Rio Noite," Perseus said at once.

Illingworth checked himself in surprise.

"The Noite?" he said. "I...see..."

"You have heard of it, then?" said Elizabeth.

The professor looked a little uncertain.

"I do know that attempts have been made in the past to examine that particular tributary," he said.

"I don't believe there have been any *successful* ones," said Perseus. "Although I defer to your superior knowledge on the subject."

"Regardless," Illingworth blustered, rallying his faculties. "I am sure there are many such places in the world today, but an institution such as ours has better things to do with its time and money than go hauling around the world looking for them on bare and uncertain evidence. It would be a great expense with a very small likelihood of a reasonable return. Much as I care for the advancement of knowledge, the discovery of a few new species of butterfly or lizard or bird would not significantly impact our reputation or income one way or another, despite what the papers may say."

Elizabeth looked at him with an expression she might have used had she caught him burning the Union Jack. Then a mischievous glint came into her eyes, and she shrugged her slender shoulders. "Oh, well," she said. "I can certainly respect your feelings on the matter. We shall simply have to ask elsewhere."

"I beg your pardon?"

"Personally, I am convinced of Mr. Corbett's sincerity and good intentions. I, for one, mean to see to it that this river is at last documented. And so, if the Natural History Museum is not interested, I will have to go elsewhere."

Illingworth's cold, dry manner slipped a little.

"Lady Darrow, you surely are not going to waste your money on such a..." he glanced at Perseus. "*Uncertain* venture?"

She seemed to falter a little, glanced at Perseus, then rallied.

"Why not?" she said. "It is my money, after all, despite what some people seem to think. And I don't know that it is so uncertain. At any rate, I intend to fund this expedition as soon as I find a scientific organization that is more concerned with advancing human knowledge than promoting its own reputation."

Perseus had to bite his lip to hide his grin. He tried not to look at either of them for fear he would lose composure entirely.

"I...as to that..." Illingworth spluttered.

Perseus could almost hear the thought process going on in the old man's head. The Baroness Darrow was an important patron of the museum. Whatever the costs of the expedition, losing her backing would be worse.

"Not only do I intend to fund the expedition," Elizabeth went on. "I intend to accompany it."

Perseus's amusement vanished. "You what?" he said.

She beamed at him.

"Yes, I think, since I am making an investment, I ought to see what my investment will buy for once."

"Well, yes," he said. "But, you know, it's going to be quite dangerous."

"Of course I realize that."

She didn't, he could tell. No one ever really did until they were there.

He hadn't expected this. It was one thing risking himself in a quest for gold; risking Elizabeth was something else entirely. Especially when he had lied about what exactly they were looking for and why he was going. He felt hot, prickling shame in his stomach and a sensation like coming fever at the back of his throat.

But it was too late. If he admitted the truth now, there would be the end of it.

"Delighted though I would be to have you along," he said. "I strongly, *strongly* advise against it. We are going to be traveling in very rough country. There will be jaguars and venomous snakes and insects and disease and many of the tribes are very unfriendly to outsiders. That isn't even considering the hardships and lack of privacy and...."

He stopped. The more he spoke, the brighter her eyes became, and he realized he was only making her more resolved on going. He sighed. There was nothing for it.

"But if you really are determined," he said. "Then I suppose I can't stop you."

"No, you can't," she answered. "Now all we have to do is to find another museum to provide the scientific..."

"Oh, very well, very well," said Illingworth. "If you really mean to insist upon this venture, then I shall at least see that some good comes of it."

"You will back the expedition, then?"

"Yes, yes, I shall," he sighed. "I don't know what it will do to my reputation, but so be it. When do you propose we start?"

"The sooner the better, I should think," said Elizabeth.

"Very well. I shall have my assistant begin work on an itinerary. Now, where is that boy?"

***

While all this was going on, Martin had waited in the eastern wing of the museum, watching the party from the shadow of the portico with his keen eyes peeled for any sign of trouble. Underneath his stoic exterior, he was really rather anxious; he didn't like Perseus's scheme very much, and had only agreed to it because he hadn't been able to think of a better plan. But if he could not prevent it, the only thing to do was to be on hand to try to ensure it came off.

At the same time, he'd had an impish curiosity to see what happened when Perseus met Lady Darrow at last, as well as to see her for himself (it was partly for that reason that he had neglected to inform Perseus that she would be there). For though Perseus had never spoken much about her, Martin knew enough to guess at what he hadn't said.

He observed their conversation closely, unable to hear, but exercising his keen eye to judge their manners. Once they had disappeared into the west wing, Martin withdrew into the quiet corridors to consider what he had observed.

He rather liked what he saw of Lady Darrow. She was certainly a beautiful young woman and, what was rarer, she knew how to dress well. He perceived her to have perfectly good manners, but without affectation. A thoroughly charming woman, he concluded, though he detected an air of anxiety about her that he didn't quite like. He would have to keep an eye on that.

For all his sophistication, Martin Halritter really had a very simple soul. He was the quintessential servant; no talk of salary interested him, nor was he a company man or filled with national fervour. Personal loyalty to one particular man and his family was the prime mover of his heart. Many there are for whom it is so, and already at that time they were beginning to suffer from the want of such opportunity in a rapidly changing world.

Perseus Corbett was no gentleman, at least not by birth, but Martin had seen in him qualities that he thought could make for true nobility and so had attached himself to him. They spoke as equals, and Martin never used the word 'Sir,' yet in his mind he was a valet and Perseus was his gentleman. There was between them that deep, abiding love that is sometimes called friendship, other times simply loyalty, but stands in a class of its own; the peculiar love of servant and master that is in some ways akin to that of father and son, save that neither could say which held the greater obligation.

As he strolled softly up the corridor, he became aware of voices coming from the hall of fossils. Curious, he drifted nearer to try to catch what was heard. A combination of the training of a good servant and many years spent in dark and dangerous places had given him the power of moving quite silently when he wished. He did so now, gliding down the hall to see what was afoot.

Peering around the corner of the entry way, he beheld two young people standing amid the looming skeletons of ancient monsters. One was a big, amiable-looking young man with a thin moustache, the other a slender girl with long dark hair and an attractive, clever kind of face.

"Bill, this is ridiculous," the girl was saying.

"No, but really Frances, I *do* love you..."

"Yes, yes, you have told me many times, but why you dragged me in here to tell me that..."

"Why? You think it's odd that I should want to talk to you alone?"

"No, of course not," she said. "But why here?"

"So your father shouldn't catch us."

"Do you think I would mind terribly if he did?"

"Perhaps not, but I would, seeing as he's my employer. And how could I marry you without a job?"

"Honestly, Bill, I don't know that having you constantly worrying about what my father will think is much improvement over a life in the poorhouse."

"I don't *worry* about what he thinks, but I *do* respect him and..."

"And you are terrified of the idea that he may sack you," she said.

"I am not terrified!"

"Is that why you haven't told him yet? Is that why we're meeting here, in secret, away from everyone else?"

"No, I...well..."

He stumbled, fumbling for a way to deny the obvious. She sighed and shook her head.

"Bill, I do love you, but I don't know that I can go on like this. You simply have to tell him and take whatever comes. It'll do you good."

"It's likely to do me in."

The girl lost patience. "Perhaps it will, but I don't know that I care to marry a man who cannot even risk a harsh word from his employer."

"But Frances, darling..."

"No, listen to me, Bill," she said, recovering her temper. "A comfortable home and a sure income are not all. I need to know that I can rely on you."

"Surely my judicious caution proves that."

"No, Bill, what you call 'judicious caution' only shows that you can't stand unpleasantness. You always try to take the easy, safe way, and that makes me wonder whether you will be there for me if it ever becomes difficult. Do you see?"

He swallowed.

"I...no, you're perfectly right. I shall prove my courage."

At this point, Martin heard the quick, soft steps of an approaching servant and silently ducked into an alcove as a waiter strode past him into the hall.

"Mr. Little?" he said. "Professor Illingworth is calling for you."

"Oh, yes, of course," said Bill, hastily stepping away from Frances. "I-I shall be there directly."

The waiter bowed and withdrew.

"Will you tell him now?" she asked.

"I...perhaps," he said. "We'll see what he wants first."

He hesitated, then kissed her in a sudden burst of passion before dashing off. Frances stood stunned for a moment, then sighed, shook her head, and followed. Martin remained where he was, stroking his long chin thoughtfully.

Young people, he reflected, were really very silly. Especially young English people.

***

"There you are!" Illingworth snapped as Bill appeared. "I would remind you that you are not here for your personal amusement; this is work."

"Yes, sir," said Bill. Perseus thought he gave the distinct impression of a dog. A big, friendly, likeable kind of dog; say a Labrador or a retriever. But definitely a subservient character.

"I want you to begin work on an itinerary," Illingworth ordered. "It seems that I shall be going on expedition soon. You will prepare my schedule and be ready with my apologies once the dates are set."

"Expedition, sir?" asked Bill.

"Do you mean you're coming yourself, Professor?" said Elizabeth in surprise.

"I do. Since I shall be taking full responsibility for this...endeavour, I shall at least go along to ensure the work is done properly."

"Is that wise, sir?" asked Bill. "At your time of life?"

"Thank you, Bill, but I assure I am quite fit," said Illingworth sharply. "This will not be my first trip to the Amazon. I know perfectly well what to expect."

He drew himself up and seemed to flicker momentarily to life, like a dying fire under the bellows. "It will probably do me good," he added. "I've been cooped up in that draughty office for too long."

"Yes, sir," said Bill.

"What is going on?"

A girl joined them. She was short and slender, with long dark hair and wonderfully formed hands. Her pale skin was appealingly contrasted by her black dress.

"Your father is going on expedition to the Amazon, Frances," said Bill.

"You are?" she said in evident surprise.

"Yes, and don't you start about my age," Illingworth said, though in a different and much gentler tone than he had used with Bill.

"I wasn't about to," she said. "I think it's wonderful! It's been ages since you've gotten out and done any real work. You'll probably have a simply marvellous time!"

She glanced at Bill, who coloured a little.

"Ah, before we go any further, sir," he said, clearing his throat. "There is something I...that is to say..."

"Well, what is it?" Illingworth snapped. "Out with it man! There's work to be done."

"Only..."

Bill glanced at Frances, then squared his shoulders.

"Only that I should very much like to join you, sir."

Perseus saw Frances' face fall from controlled excitement to open disgust. Illingworth, however, merely frowned.

"Would you?" he said. "Have you any experience with field work?"

"No, sir," he admitted. "But that is just why I would like to come. It would be a boon to my career to be able to say I accompanied you on one of your trips, and I'm sure I would learn more in a few weeks in the field than I would in years in the classroom."

"That's true enough," said Illingworth. "Very well, then, you shall come. But I expect no complaints and no shirking of your duties."

"No, sir. Also, I would like to marry your daughter."

"You WHAT?!" Illingworth exploded.

"Quick, come away and let's start planning," said Elizabeth, seizing Perseus's hand and dragging him out of the hall. Her face suggested she was holding in her laughter with difficulty and wanted to escape before it broke free. Illingworth's shouts followed them, echoing through the stone halls. Indeed, as soon as they regained the main hall, she burst into quiet but heartfelt peals of merriment.

"Poor Frances!" she laughed. "What a way to have it come out! But at least now they can get on with it. The silly ass has been wanting to marry her for years."

Perseus affected to laugh as well, though he was too uncomfortable to feel much amusement.

"Elizabeth," he said. "About this expedition. Are you really going to insist on coming? I've been on many trips like this before, you know. It's very different from reading about them. And I...the last thing I'd want is for anything to happen to you."

"That is very gratifying, and very sweet of you," she said sincerely. "And I know it will be terribly dangerous and hard and I'm sure I'll probably look back more than once and think what a perfect idiot I was to insist on coming. But then, I'm even more certain that if I don't go, I will always look back and wish that I had. It's not fair that you should have all the adventures, you know. I'd like at least one."

"As you wish," he sighed. "And I can't deny that it will be pleasant to have you along for once."

"Thank you," she said. "Partners?"

She held out a hand. He swallowed and took it.

"Partners."

Chapter Five
The End of the Known

"You have no business with consequences; you are to tell the truth."
-Dr. Samuel Johnson

"It took some convincing," said Bill. "Quite an unpleasant scene, really. But we won him over in the end. He said, 'all right, Bill, we shall see how you acquit yourself on this trip. If you give satisfaction and show yourself a man, then you'll have my consent. If you don't, then I don't suppose she'll care to have you anyway.'"

"A glowing endorsement," said Martin.

"Well, it's better than I expected," Bill replied. "Can't think why I went and blurted it out like I did. Of course I've always had a reckless streak in me. Act first, ask questions later. Did I tell you how, when I was a boy, I went and jumped off the pier at Brighton? Twelve feet straight down, and April, so the water was damned cold. We were gone to seashore for Easter holiday, see."

"A curious thing to do. Had you a reason for it?"

"This other boy dared me to do it," Bill answered. "Just shows, doesn't it, what an impulsive chap I am. That's why I have to keep it all bottled up, you see?"

"It is certainly an illustrative incident," said Martin with just a hint a dryness in his tone. Bill, unfamiliar with the Austrian's moods, missed it entirely.

"But I am most impressed," Martin went on, "that you should show such concern to secure your prospective father-in-law's approval. Many do not in this day."

"Frances tells me I'm old fashioned," Bill agreed with a faint laugh. "But you see, she's very close to her father. They've been a bit of a team ever since her mother died, and I certainly wouldn't want to create a rift between them, what?"

"Admirable."

They spoke while sitting in wicker chairs upon the deck of a riverboat making its way up the Purus River. A comfortable passage across the Atlantic had been followed by an almost equally comfortable journey up the Amazon to Manaus, where they had remained a few days while purchasing the remainder of their supplies before taking another steamer up the Purus. It was the 'dry season,' so to speak, though the air was heavy with moisture and the rains still came almost every day, when great, heavy downpours, with raindrops the size of hailstones lashed the mighty river and its green banks. But these didn't last long and they certainly didn't cool anything off. Even simply sitting in the shade upon the deck of their riverboat was enough to make Bill sweat as much as he ever had in his life.

"I say," he said, fanning himself with his book. "You've been all around the world, haven't you?"

"I have travelled extensively with Mr. Corbett, yes."

"Is it always this hot?"

Martin looked at him with a faint expression of pity.

"When one is only ten degrees south of the Equator, yes," he answered. "Though, of course, the humidity contributes."

"Is it going to be like this the whole way?"

"Unlikely," said Martin. "In the thick jungle, it will be far worse. There will be no breeze, you see."

Elizabeth, meanwhile, stood at the rail and watched the ranches and villages of the Amazon basin pass by. She was soaked with sweat, felt feverish from the heat, and the heavy, damp air seemed to resist being breathed. She was smarting all over from insect bites. All in all, she was extremely uncomfortable, and it had been a very long time since she had been happier. She was in the Amazon Jungle; that great, untameable ocean of life spread across a third of a continent, where man was not and never could be master. She stood only upon the surface now, but soon she would plunge into those dark depths and then the adventure—oh, what a word that was!—would truly begin.

Overhead, the clouds gathered once again and growled with thunder, making the air feel even heavier.

"I thought this was supposed to be the dry season," she said to Perseus as he joined her at the rail. "If this is dry, I wonder what the wet one is like."

"Oh, there's no such thing as 'dry' in the Amazon," he said. "The rains don't alter much; you get a few more downpours per day in the summer than you do in the winter, that's all. The 'wet' season is so because that's when it rains in the Andes and all that water washes down here and makes the rivers higher and faster. 'Flooded' would be the more proper way to speak of it."

"I keep forgetting it's technically winter here," she said. "The word sounds rather funny under the circumstances, doesn't it?"

They had spent a good deal of time together over the past few days. Sometimes he would tell her tales of his adventures, or they would discuss what they might expect in the coming days when they left all civilization behind. But lately they had mostly spent their time simply standing side by side and watching the banks of the river pass by.

At first there had been far more settlements and signs of human activity than Elizabeth had expected on the Amazon; towns, villages, and even cities on the banks and innumerable boats passing up and down the river. As they drew deeper into the basin, the signs of humanity became fewer and smaller, though they still floated past pretty often, usually in the form of small villages full of people of every hue and colour, who paid little attention to the familiar sight of a passing riverboat.

Here and there they passed great farms and ranches cut from the living jungle, with big, fine houses, some so grand that they made Elizabeth think of her own family estate. These sometimes sparked architectural discussions as they admired or critiqued the taste of the buildings: "What a hideous monstrosity!" "That one is charming; look at the latticework." "Now there's a house; classic Spanish style. Wonder how old it is?" "Good Lord! They brought all that paint this far into the jungle to give it *that* colour scheme?"

But these became fewer and fewer as they travelled up the Purus and the jungle closed in as a solid wall of green about them. Birds of every colour imaginable filled the trees, calling to one another with the sharp cries of the jungle. Monkeys gambled about in the trees, paying little or no heed to the boat unless there seemed a chance to jump aboard and steal food (which happened once or twice during the journey). The banks of the river were high, with vast expanses of mud crisscrossed with fallen trees, and in many places they saw fat caiman basking in the sun, reminding Elizabeth of sunbathing tourists, the thought of which made her laugh. At one point they saw a big, long-nosed tapir drinking in the shallows, though it took off into the jungle as they drew close. More often they saw small red deer coming down to the water to drink and watching the passersby with big, innocent eyes.

Professor Illingworth spent most of his time in his cabin, going over books and making notes in his journal. On the occasions he joined them on the deck, he would give extraordinarily dry lectures on the wildlife they saw ("*Caiman crocodilus*, commonly known as the spectacled caiman or white caiman. There are currently four recognized subspecies...") Or else he would expound a little on a few pet theories of his own ("The evolutionary history of this region very clearly demonstrates the principle of..."). And, when he had nothing better to do, he would entertain himself by yelling at Bill.

In this way they proceeded up the Purus for several days until they reached their destination. Here, at the very end of the civilized world, the Brazilian government had long ago established a telegraph station, guarded by a small contingent of soldiers. A trading post naturally grew up around it, along with a church, and a few small farms. And so, eventually, the small village of Pordesol was born.

Here goods were brought in from down river and sold among the villagers and soldiers, or shipped to the ranchers and rubber men further up river. The turn off for the Rio Tardas, from which they hoped to find the outlet of the mysterious Noite, was about three or four miles below the village. As far as anyone knew the only men who lived along the Tardas were the Catauxi tribesmen, who were generally friendly enough, but not keen on making contacts.

Perseus had known about Pordesol and its telegraph from an earlier trip he had taken into the interior, though he had never been there. This was how he had come to concoct his story of the imaginary Colonel Torres. Early on in their plans, however, he was surprised to discover that Elizabeth knew of it as well. An old friend of her father's, Colonel Newgate, had retired from service and left England shortly after the war, eventually settling down to take over the trading post of this little village on the extreme edge of the unknown.

Elizabeth had sent word of their coming ahead up the river, and so they found him waiting to greet them when the steamer pulled up to dock. Elizabeth alighted first and he embraced his friend's daughter with warm affection.

Newgate was a muscular man of middle height, with a square, expressive kind of face that held a slightly elfish quality about the eyes, suggesting an Irish ancestry. His greying hair was beginning to recede a little, and his clothes were simple, but clean. Elizabeth introduced him to her companions, and he greeted them with well-bred politeness tempered by the ease of a man used to living far from society.

The trading post and general store that he ran fronted upon the docks, and his long, comfortable home extended out the back, running parallel to the riverbank. He gave a few quick orders to the *comaradas* who were handling the receipt of goods from the steamer, then led the expedition onto a shaded veranda overlooking the Purus. Drinks were provided, and they sat in perfect comfort while the breeze blew in off of the waters.

"I can't tell you how surprised I was to get your telegram," he said, leaning back in his chair and looking at Elizabeth with a warm smile. "I really thought my days of receiving old friends were over."

"I had thought of simply surprising you," said Elizabeth. "But then I wanted to be sure you were still here."

"Where else should I be?" he answered. "I fully intend to die out here. It's a good life; the people are pleasant company, there's enough work to keep me occupied, and the scenery can't be beat."

"What made you decide to come all the way out here in the first place?" asked Illingworth. "Pardon me, but it seems a strange place for a British officer to retire to."

"Not at all," said Newgate. "After the war, I'd had quite enough of civilization and looked about for the most isolated place I could go. I considered Tibet for a while, but eventually settled on the Amazon as I prefer the heat to the cold. Here, at least, no one tries to blow each other up. And I'm two weeks behind the times, so when I do hear news of trouble, it's most likely already over."

"Sounds most appealing," said Perseus. "You don't find the weather a trial?"

"Yes I do, but it is quite worth it. Now tell me, what are *you* all doing here? Your telegram didn't quite say. Some scientific survey, was it?"

"Yes," said Elizabeth. "A survey up the Noite. Perseus here says that he met an old colonel from the Empire days who I suppose must have been stationed in this very spot, right?"

"I believe so, yes," said Perseus. He spoke lightly, but inside he was tense. They had reached the point where the truth would soon have to come out, and he only dreaded its being discovered too soon. It suddenly occurred to him that people who lived at this station likely knew that there had never been such a man as the supposed 'Colonel Torres' here.

Newgate added to his unease by shooting a quick, cunning glance at him, but he allowed Elizabeth to continue.

"Supposedly there are some very interesting species to be found along the Noite," she went on. "We're going to document them."

"I see," he said. "But, forgive me, what are *you* doing here, Elizabeth?"

"I'm funding the expedition," she said, with just a hint of defensiveness in her voice. "Thought I ought to know what my money was being used for."

"Really?" he said. "Is that all?"

She smiled a little embarrassedly.

"I confess, no. I've always wanted to go on a trip like this, and I didn't know when I would have another opportunity."

"I see," he said, frowning a little. Perseus guessed that, like him, Newgate saw that Elizabeth really had no idea what she was in for. But he said no more and instead began inquiring after their mutual friends in England.

After they had sat and chatted for a time, Newgate showed them over his house and store, which was remarkably comfortable and well-furnished for being so remote. He gave them a regular tour; showing them his wares, his comfortable, book-lined rooms, his shining rifles upon the wall, and his photographs of old friends from England, whom Elizabeth wasted no time in examining.

"There's father, of course," she said. "That was during the war, wasn't it?"

"Yes, just outside of Toutencourt. Right before the Somme, I think it was.

"That's what's his name, Lieutenant..."

"Lieutenant Herbert. Surprised you remember him. He got blown up a few days later.

"I remember father writing me about him...and that's Colonel Blunt, right? He used to come down for shooting parties before the war. You met him, Perseus."

"Oh, yes. He complimented my flower border. Whatever happened to him?"

"Survived the Somme. Died at Passchendaele," said Newgate.

"Hard luck, that," said Perseus.

"What about this one?" asked Elizabeth, pointing to another photo that showed Newgate and a much younger man.

"Don't suppose you ever heard of him. Sergeant Allenby. Good chap from Birmingham. Invalided out with shell shock and cut his wrists in hospital."

"Have all these people died, then?" asked Bill.

"Most of them," said Newgate sadly. "They're useful reminders in case I ever get the urge to go back to what is called civilization. I think your father and I, Elizabeth, were the only ones pictured who survived the war, and then, of course, that damned motorcar...except this group shot; some of those boys made it, I think. Oh, and you of course."

Perseus, who had been examining the group shot, turned eagerly to this last photo. He recognized the setting at once: the back porch at Sangral House. There were Newgate and Lord Darrow in their dress uniforms, sitting in wicker chairs. And there, standing beside her father, was Elizabeth, just as he remembered her; all arms and legs and tangled hair, with her arm around her father as though she wanted to show him off, wearing that look of unrestrained happiness that he'd once known so well.

"I remember when that was taken," she said. "Just before we left for America. You came to stay for the weekend and wish us a good trip."

Then it was only a short time after he had left. He looked at the girl in the photo and smiled to himself. That was how he liked to think of her, with that radiantly expressive, hold-nothing-back kind of smile.

He had yet to see that look on her present face. His eyes shifted from her to the man beside her in the photograph and he thought he understood why.

They were treated to a delightful supper on the veranda, while the usual afternoon downpour rattled outside. As they ate, Illingworth turned the conversation back to the purpose of their journey.

"Have you heard any rumour of these supposed strange beasts on the Noite, Colonel?"

Newgate leaned back in his chair and looked out on the misty river and the jungle beyond.

"One hears many strange stories out here," he said. "The Noite holds a certain reputation among the natives. The Catauxi will not travel upon it, and the other tribes regard it as unlucky."

"What for?" asked Elizabeth.

"It is said that the river marks the path to an evil place, a forbidden place. Some say it is only a part of the jungle, others say it is a great pit or cave in the earth. The legend goes that it is both an abode of monsters and the treasure house of the gods."

Perseus flinched a little. They were getting very close to the mark. He wondered suddenly whether details of Professor Applegate's expedition had reached Newgate's ears, for surely they must have passed this way.

"Do they say what manner of 'monsters'?" asked Illingworth.
Newgate smiled.

"Cuangi is said to dwell there."

The rain seemed momentarily to grow more intense and the sky grumbled with thunder.

"What is 'Cuangi'?" Elizabeth asked.

"A native superstition," he said. "Most of the tribes of the southern Amazon have one version of him or other. Some say he's a spirit, others a great beast, and others something in between. The only common thread is that he's monstrous and all-powerful."

The rain rattled upon the roof, and a fork of lightning lit up the sky. The expedition members had fallen silent.

"And he's said to dwell along the Noite?" asked Perseus.

"Yes, or in that forbidden place I mentioned. One version of the legend has him the guardian of the gods' treasures. Sort of a demonic watchdog. There's a story that goes along with it."

"Oh, tell us!" said Elizabeth.

"Ah, well, I only know the one version," he said. "But it goes something like this. There once was a great warrior of a certain tribe. He was chief and the mightiest hunter the world had ever seen. He was betrothed to the most beautiful maiden in the tribe and, as is said of many a promising young buck, had everything in his favour.

"One night, while performing the sacred rites – for he was also well-versed in the spirit realm – he received a vision. A great spirit spoke to him from the smoke of the ritual fire. The spirit said 'thou art great, but shall yet be greater. Take thy betrothed and walk into the forest for seven days and seven nights. Then thou shalt come to a great wall. There thou shalt possess the treasures of the gods.'

"So the chief took his betrothed and walked through the jungle. They didn't need to fear anything, as he was the greatest hunter in the world, and the jaguars and snakes and such all knew to fear him. He came to the great wall of stone, and in the wall was a gate, and at that gate stood mighty Cuangi. They bowed and made obeisance before him, and the chief said, 'Oh, mighty Cuangi, it has been given to me to possess the treasures of the gods.'

"But Cuangi answered and said, 'None may pass my way without an offering.' So the chief asked what he would have, and Cuangi said, 'If thou wouldst possess the treasure of the gods, then thy betrothed is the price. Give her to me, or go back the way ye came.'

"And so the chief took hold of his betrothed and gave her to Cuangi, who ate her in one bite..."

"He did *what*?" Elizabeth exclaimed.

"Not very nice, was it?" said Newgate, laughing. "Our friend is not a hero by English standards. But that is not the end of the story. After he had offered his betrothed to Cuangi, he was permitted to pass and to enter the great treasure house. There he outfitted himself in the raiment of the gods, took their treasure for his own, and set off to claim his place among them.

"Only, when he tried to pass through the gate again, Cuangi again prevented him, saying that if he would pass, he must offer a *second* gift, equal to the first. But of course, he only had one betrothed and had already offered her. He protested and said that he had been promised possession of the gods' treasures. 'Yes,' said Cuangi, 'Thou wert promised to possess them. But thou dost possess them. Thou wert never promised that thou shouldst bear them away.'

"And so, the great chief simply had to sit there in the god's treasure house, bedecked in marks of power that he could never use to command and holding weapons he could never hunt with, until he grew old and rotted where he sat."

"Overall," said Perseus after a brief silence. "That is not an edifying story."

"I'm glad the chief got his comeuppance at least," said Elizabeth. "Serves him right!"

"Hear hear!" said Bill.

"Let us not be too harsh in judgment," said Martin. "He merely did what most of us do."

"What do you mean?" asked Bill. "You're not saying most men would feed their fiancée to a monster to get his hands on a lot of treasure?"

"After a fashion, yes," he answered. "Most of us are all-too quick to sacrifice the real good at hand for the mere promise of a better one."

"I don't know," said Newgate. "I'm more inclined to think men too ready to cling to goods that they know, even it means they and others must suffer for it. We are altogether far too conservative a species."

"I quite agree with you, Colonel," said Illingworth. "Surely obscurantism is the greater danger. A certainty of the continuation of the evils of the past must be outweighed by the possibility of a better future."

"But the evils of the past are known and we can, in a sense, manage them," Perseus argued. "The potential evils of future novelties must be unknown and, for that very reason, must be worse."

"I think there's something to be said for both sides," said Elizabeth. "We can't stop all progress, even at the cost of losing something we love. But then, we can't simply throw everything onto the chopping block, or else what would be the point? The trouble is knowing where to draw the line."

"I certainly hope we all agree that it is somewhere on this side of 'feeding beautiful young ladies to monsters,'" said Perseus.

"Only beautiful ones?" asked Elizabeth. "What about the plain young ladies?"

He shrugged.

"As you say; we can't stop all progress."

She laughed, and so did Bill. Newgate, however, did not laugh. He was watching Perseus with a thoughtful expression.

After dinner he showed them their rooms. The trading post also functioned as an inn for the rare few visitors who came that way, and he had two small, but comfortable spare bedrooms made up. He insisted on giving up his own room for Elizabeth's use and promised that he would be quite comfortable in his study, as he often slept there when he was obliged to work late.

Before they retired, however, he beckoned Elizabeth to join him on the now-empty veranda. She went willingly, not feeling the least bit sleepy. It was just after sunset, and the forest across the river was like a sharp black shadow against the pink sky, both doubled in the river. The rain had cleared and left the air cooler, and the insects sang from the shadows. Elizabeth once again felt a shiver of delight at the thought of where she was.

Then Newgate began without any preamble. "Elizabeth, how much do you know of this man, Corbett?"

She looked at him in surprise. "I've told you, he worked for us for two years before the war."

"Yes, I know that. Have you had any contact with him since?"

She flinched involuntarily at the reminder. "No," she said. "Not until a few weeks ago when we got this all together."

"I was afraid of that," he sighed. "Now listen. I am going say something that I know you are not going to like, but I owe it to you, and to the memory of your father. I know men like that; that sort of devil-may-care, vagabond type who travels the world doing this and that and never settling to any honest trade. You see them all the time around here, and there were more than a few the in the army. They're devilishly charming and handy in a tight spot, but you *cannot* trust them. They always are after one thing and one thing only: money."

Elizabeth looked at him in shock.

"Thank you for your concern," she said slowly. "But you're quite wrong about him. Perseus isn't like that at all. He has travelled about the world a good deal, but he isn't in it for money. Why, just to give you an idea what he's like, he's the boy I gave that Charles the First medal to, you remember? He still has it. You can't tell me a mercenary personality wouldn't have sold that thing long ago."

"You're sure he still has it, are you?" he said.

"I...yes, I'm quite sure. But besides that, he isn't even charging us! Says he'll take his salary upon delivery."

"He is taking you into the jungle and not even asking to be paid?"

"Yes. So that shows, doesn't it, that he's acting in good faith. It isn't the money he cares about – it's the adventure."

His face did not relax. "Why would he need to make such a gesture of good faith?"

"Because we did, after all, only have his word for it. Like I told you, he happened to meet an old colonel – Colonel Torres, I think it was – who used to be stationed here in the empire days and learned about the Noite from him. So, to prove that he was telling the truth, he volunteered to defer payment until his story was verified."

Newgate looked at her with something approaching pity. "Elizabeth," he said. "This station wasn't started until after the empire."

"Oh," she said, taken a little off guard. "Then it must have been another site. What does it matter?"

"Didn't you hear what I told you about the Noite, and the legends around it? The treasure house of the gods?"

She felt suddenly uncomfortable as she realized what he was getting at. "You think *that* is what he is after? But that's just a legend, isn't it?"

"All legends have a basis in truth," he said. "In any case, I can much more readily believe him willing to go after a legendary treasure than I can believe a man like that would have such a disinterested love of science that he would propose and undertake a trip like this simply to discover a few new insect species."

"No, no," said Elizabeth. She was beginning to feel faintly desperate as she realized the plausibility of his words. What was worse was that she had no answer to them. "He...he said that he was only interested in an adventure. The chance to see one of the few unexplored places left on Earth."

"Of course he would say that," Newgate sighed. "Just the thing to get you hooked. Elizabeth, he is using you! Can't you see that? He knows what kind of person you are, so he shows up with just the right story to pique your interest."

"No, you don't know him!" she said furiously. "He wouldn't do that sort of thing. He...he can't have changed that much."

He gave her an odd look.

"Need he have changed at all?" he said. "You were children, remember, and he was poor. Your friendship benefited him. Just as it does now. Tell me honestly; can you recall a time, even once, when he was not the beneficiary?"

Like a dormant spectre, the memory of those days and weeks immediately after her father's death floated before Elizabeth's mind, and a pain like an iron hand touched her heart.

"You will please not suggest that again," she said in a tight voice.

"Very well," he said. "I'm not trying to make you unhappy, Elizabeth. I'm only trying to keep you safe. I know something of men like that, and I do not think you ought to go off into the jungle with him."

Elizabeth was too sensible not to see the reasonableness of his request. It was all horribly plausible, and against it she only had her own knowledge of and affection for a man whom she had not seen in many years. Her head told her that Newgate was perfectly right, and those old, painful feelings of her own shouted in his defence. But her heart rebelled against the idea that Perseus was the kind of man he had described. It *must not* be so.

"No," she said aloud. "I don't care what you say, I *know* him. And Perseus would never lie to me. I'd swear to that."

"All right, all right," sighed Newgate. "I won't badger you. But please, Elizabeth, think hard about what you're doing. This will be your last chance to turn back."

"I most certainly will *not* turn back!" she said. She drew a deep breath, summoning all her self-control. "I know, Colonel, that you mean well, and I thank you for you concern, but I...I know what I am doing."

He shook his head. "I hope so," he said. "I really do."

Elizabeth turned away from him and hurried into the house. She felt something like hatred for Colonel Newgate; hatred of the fact that he had planted such seeds of doubt in her mind, which she could neither accept nor get rid of. She wanted badly to speak to Perseus, and she was just resolving to go seek him out when he stepped into the hall from the study.

"Elizabeth?" he said. "Can I speak with you a moment? In private?"

"Certainly," she said, endeavouring to appear as herself. "I was just coming to see you in fact."

"I thought you might be," he said.

They went into the store, which was closed up and deserted. Elizabeth waited for him to begin.

"I...I have something of a confession to make," he said. "Which I probably ought to have made earlier, but I beg you to hear me out before you judge me."

"What do you mean?" she asked. The suspicions so recently and unwilling sown in her mind sharpened.

"It isn't easy to have a private conversation in a country where the windows are always open," he said with a grimace. "I heard what Colonel Newgate and you were saying."

"Oh!" she said, colouring. "I'm sorry. I hope you didn't take offence or..."

"No, no, nothing like that," he said hastily. "Newgate's an astute man, and he clearly cares for you. My confession is that he is...he is not entirely wrong."

There was a heavy silence.

"What are you talking about?"

He reached into his shirt and drew out a leather bundle. He unwrapped it and handed her the torn notebook.

"*True Narrative of Certain Events in the Brazilian Jungle, by Robert Cooper*," she read aloud. "What is this?"

"An account of the Applegate expedition from 1911," he answered, and he gave her a summary of the journal and its fragmentary account of the Forbidden Valley.

She stared at him. "Then...that is where you mean to go?"

He nodded, and in answer to her further questions told the whole story of how the book had fallen into his hands and of Byron's attempt to first buy it and then to steal it.

"I got the better of him," he concluded, "but from what he let slip I realized that there was some sort of organization after the book. I don't know how they knew about it, or how they knew I had it, but they were clearly willing to do anything to get their hands on it. So I thought it best to keep its existence a secret and to not let our real object be known, just in case they were on the lookout. I don't mind being shot myself, but I hate having my friends shot at."

She did not smile. "Then, that story you told us, of the Brazilian colonel..."

"Was just a story," he admitted. "I needed a plausible alternative that would take us up the Noite. But I tried to make it as true as possible; we *are* going to an undiscovered ecosystem off of the Noite. I only left out a few details about its nature and location.

Probably would have been easier to convince Illingworth if I'd told him everything."

"In short," she said slowly. "You lied to me."

The words landed like blows.

"I am sorry," he said. "When I decided on that story, I had no idea you were the one I would telling it to. And I only did it to try to keep you safe."

"You might have told me afterwards," she said. "You could have trusted me to keep quiet about it, couldn't you?"

"Oh!" he said. "I...yes, I could have. I...I am afraid I didn't think of that."

She looked from him to the book in her hands, then back to him. Her face was very red and her eyes were hard and angry.

"Tell me honestly," she said. "*Do* you still have that medal?"

He opened his mouth to say 'yes,' but the word seemed to stick in his throat. "It's safe," he said.

"What does that mean?"

"I...we spent the last money we had coming to London. I needed some to start putting this together, and I needed it quickly, owing to those people being after us..."

"You sold it."

She said it in a quiet, almost a childlike voice. The realization of what he had done seemed to take everything from her.

"Pawned," he said. "And I'm making him hold it for a year. It's only temporary, and it's as safe as can be. I swear to you, I *will* get it back..."

"What are you really after?" she snapped, cutting him off.

He blinked. "What are you talking about?"

"You didn't drag us all out here for a mere lark," she said. "You expect to find something in that valley, don't you? That's why you're so set on it, isn't it?"

There was a commanding expression in her voice. It was the voice of one who was used to giving orders and having them obeyed. The cheerful, exuberant girl had faded, and the feudal lady of the manor had risen to the surface.

"Yes," he admitted. He pointed to the wall. "But whatever he says, I am *not* using you, and I never would!"

"No, you're just using my money, aren't you?" she spat. "Like you used my medal."

"It isn't like that!"

"Isn't it?"

He looked at her. "Do you really think it is?"

A kind of painful cramp was growing in her heart as she met his gaze.

"A few minutes ago, I swore that you would never lie to me," she said. "Yet here we are. So I don't know *what* to think."

Elizabeth began to ask another question, but the words stuck in her throat. It was a subject that she couldn't stand to bring up now. And anyway, it wouldn't matter what he said, would it? For several minutes they simply looked at each other, both breathing rather hard.

"If you don't think you can trust me," he said at last. "Then it probably would be best if you were to return home. We are going to be going into very dangerous territory, and I would much prefer if you were not exposed to it."

"First you lie to me, now you try to humiliate me," she said. "Send me home to be jeered at for spending all this money and then running off when it gets difficult?"

Her vehemence took him off guard.

"I would rather have you embarrassed and safe than otherwise," he said. "Elizabeth, you really ought to take Newgate's advice and go home."

"I appreciate that advice, *Mr.* Corbett," she said. "And I thank you for at least telling me this now. I only wish that you had done so while there was still time for me to fire you!"

So saying, she turned and marched back into the house, slamming the door behind her. She fairly ran to her own room, threw herself down on the bed, and began to cry.

Chapter Six
Excerpt From the Diary of Bill Little

"That Cheyne boy's the biggest nuisance aboard. He isn't wanted here.
He's too fresh."
-Rudyard Kipling, *Captain's Courageous*

August 9th

My Dear Frances,

As we at last leave the final vestiges of civilization behind us and venture into the unknown, I find myself torn. I long to see you and would rejoice to have you here with me, and yet I would not wish the dangers and hardships that we face on any woman (or man for that matter). Being able to dedicate these diary entries to you, my love, is a great comfort, as it allows me to imagine you are with me without the worry that must have attended your presence. I fear that Lady Darrow is already beginning to realize the folly of her insistence on accompanying us, and I intend to make it my duty to see to it that she is as safe and comfortable as possible.

This resolution has become all the more important given a recent development. Last night, when we were preparing for bed, Corbett summoned us all – save the Baroness, whom it seems he had confided to privately – to inform us that he had, in fact, been lying this whole time about our destination. It was not, as he had claimed, a simple matter of an unexplored tributary described by a Brazilian army officer. Rather, he intended to follow the course laid out in a tattered old book that supposedly would lead us to a legendary lost valley. The very same one, in fact, which features in some monstrous native superstitions.

Well, as soon as he told us all this, I naturally assumed that the Old Man would cancel the whole affair. Indeed, I really believe that he intended to at first. Corbett is a clever scoundrel, however. He argued that there was no *practical* difference in the purpose of the expedition, save that our destination is now both more specific and more likely to yield profitable results than was previously believed.

"If this valley does exist, then it will be a thoroughly isolated environment, and you don't need me, professor, to tell you what that might mean for the museum," he said.

He kept at it in this vein for some time, and the Old Man gradually softened. It seems that the Professor Applegate who had led and died upon that earlier expedition had been an acquaintance of his, and he remembered hearing something of the event. This, combined with the evidence of the journal itself, at least led him to believe that this new story was more credible than the old. By the end he was, if anything, more interested in the journey than ever before. Such is the power of a clever tongue attached to an unscrupulous mind!

Personally, I was much more struck by the fact of Corbett's dishonesty than by an interest in any lost worlds. I tried to point out the madness of following a man whom we now knew to be a liar into the trackless wilderness. Corbett's excuse was that certain people wanted the book and wouldn't have stuck at murder to get it, and that his intention was to protect us. I thought that a most melodramatic and unlikely tale and said so.

It was then that Corbett had an unexpected ally in the form of Colonel Newgate, who said that such things were perfectly likely, especially if the legends of the valley were at all true. He was also able to further confirm the story of the journal by saying that some of his friends at the telegraph station had already told him of the expedition's passing through that way in the years before the war.

In any case, the Old Man opted to go on, and when I applied to her this morning, Lady Darrow proved equally determined to continue.

"We have already come too far to turn back without anything to show for it," she said. "Besides, I don't see why the whole journey should be ruined merely because one of our members has failed to behave with honour."

I think this is sheer madness, but no one asked my opinion. Though I will say that Lady Darrow at least seems to have taken Corbett's perfidy to heart and is refusing to speak with him. She is indeed quite the fine lady, and I cannot help feeling for what she must suffer.

So we set out early this morning in two canoes; the Old Man, Corbett, and myself in one, the Baroness and that Austrian fellow in the other, along with most of the baggage.

(Incidentally, I must mention that Lady Darrow has been obliged to adopt the habit of wearing trousers at all times. Though this is undeniably practical given our situation, I must think it a humiliation that so fine a lady should be forced to adopt so vulgar and masculine a style of dress. This is yet another hardship that makes me thankful that you, Frances, are safe at home.)

We also hired two of Colonel Newgate's men – '*comaradas*' they are called – named Gomez and Costa. They're great strapping fellows of mixed blood, I believe, but tending more to the Hispanic or Portuguese side, with black hair, dark eyes, and olive skin. Gomez is the larger of the two and speaks the most English, while Costa is more of a compact, square kind of creature. Gomez served as the paddler for our boat, Costa for the baggage canoe. They seem quite good fellows in their way; perfectly friendly and accommodating, and I must say that they are as deferential and respectful to her Ladyship as one could possibly wish.

Corbett and the Austrian help in the rowing most of the time, and even I am obliged to take a turn now and again, for our journey will be entirely upriver. The current is sluggish, this being the so-called dry season (a mockery of a term in the Amazon, as it rains heavily at least once a day), but it is still difficult work. We proceed by zig-zagging across the river, catching the counter-flowing eddies that form along the banks and using the extra momentum to help push the canoes against the main current, then driving across the stream to do the same from the other side. In this way we made about twelve miles along the Rio Tardas on our first day.

The Tardas is far less settled than the Purus. We passed a village or two, and a handful of ranches, but the villagers didn't appear anything like as friendly as the ones we passed in earlier days. When we passed, they would stop what they were doing and glare after us, as though saying we should keep going if we know what's good for us. The ranches were smaller and wilder looking than on the other river. Now and again we saw the outlines of abandoned houses that had been reclaimed by the jungle; hollow shells of man's efforts being eaten alive by the greenery. As, I suppose, all our works shall be one day in the future. If there is one thing my training so far has taught me, it is that, disguise it as we will, it is nature, nature rules us still. But I fear I am growing morbid; it is an effect of the jungle atmosphere.

We stopped for the night, and Corbett, the Austrian, and the two *comaradas* cleared a dry-ish spot on the bank to make camp and prepared a fire. After so many hours cramped in that canoe it was a relief to stretch my limbs and have the prospect of a decent cooked meal. The Austrian disappeared for an hour or so then returned with a *jacu*, which is a bird rather like a pheasant. It was quite good, and

Corbett explained that they meant to conserve our stores at present by hunting or fishing wherever possible.

"Martin and I were on a trip in Africa once where we ended up lost and wandering the jungle for four weeks," he said. "Only things to live on were what we could trap or gather ourselves."

"Have you often become lost on your trips, Mr. Corbett?" asked Lady Darrow. Her words were polite, but her tone was acidic.

"A few times," he said stiffly. "It does happen in the jungle."

"Ah, that is yet another fact I would have liked to have known before engaging your services," she said. "Though I'm sure you will say that you would not mind being lost yourself, only losing other people."

"I wasn't going to, but that is very much my opinion."

"Mine as well," she answered. "I too shouldn't mind your being lost, only losing other people."

Corbett did not reply, though I thought he was annoyed with her. It was a most uncomfortable conversation to be present for, but I must say I think he entirely deserved it.

All in all, it was not a very pleasant evening. The Professor took over the conversation by delivering one of his tedious lectures on the species he had observed during the day. This mostly consisted of a few birds and monkeys, and a number of fish glimpsed through the clear waters. Dull as it was for me, whom am a naturalist by trade, I can only imagine how the others bore it. I don't suppose they listened much. Lady Darrow spent the whole of it gazing out at the river, and Corbett in cleaning and sharpening his machete.

Now it is almost time to turn in, and I really must end. All in all, I would not call this an auspicious beginning to our venture.

August 10th

Spent a truly horrible night. We sleep in two tents; one for the Baroness, as is proper, and one for the Professor and myself. Corbett, Halritter, and the two *comaradas* sleep under a light canopy on hammocks. The insects were simply intolerable. Even sleeping on a raised cot and under netting I was fairly swarmed. How the others could sleep, I will never know. I woke up three times to find myself literally crawling.

Not a word of sympathy from the Old Man either. He simply snapped that it was the jungle and this was to be expected and told me off for waking him. I am covered in bites and my netting is quite eaten through. I tell you, Frances, this trip really is the limit.

When the dawn finally came, however, the Old Man insisted on a survey after breakfast. I was exhausted from lack of sleep, but of course I had to give in.

"I suppose we all might do with a walk," said Lady Darrow, in what I thought was a very kind manner.

"This is no pleasure excursion, your Ladyship," answered the Professor. "It is a serious scientific survey to sample the fauna in this region. There will be a good deal of tedium and some danger."

"Of course," she said hastily, blushing a little. "I quite understand that. I only meant that at least you and Bill will be able to stretch your legs a bit in the process."

Corbett came with us, I think as much to get away from her Ladyship as anything, and we plunged into the jungle.

It was not at all like going into the woods in England. It was like plunging into a sea of living things; a dense, tangled green mass that seems to close in about you. The air was close and thick with moisture, and fragrant with the smell of mud and wet, decaying leaves. Insects were everywhere; cut through a tangle of brush, and wasps flew out. Grasp a branch overhead and stinging ants drop down onto you.

I was exceedingly glad that Lady Darrow had not insisted on coming with us, both because of the roughness of the terrain and, I confess, because it prompted me to certain exclamations that I would have been quite ashamed for her to hear.

Yet, the forest was largely silent and empty, apart from the insects. We heard no bird calls and saw very few creatures. Two hours' work led to the discovery of a handful of geckos, a *mussurana*, a *jararaca*, and a single group of *paca* rats, all of which were duly recorded by your humble servant. I was surprised by the dearth of specimens; I had thought for sure that the jungle would be teaming with such creatures.

"It is," said Corbett when I mentioned this. "Only, you see, there is quite a lot of it, which means many, many places for them to hide. I've no doubt there were many more all around us, but we never saw them. It's often that way in the deep jungle."

We returned to camp under the direction of Corbett's compass. Lady Darrow had taken our absence as an opportunity to wash in relative privacy and was just putting her damp hair back into place as we returned (she continues to wear it done up as a matter of course, which I think is very sensible and becoming in this environment). I carefully preserved the specimens in jars of alcohol and we resumed our journey up the Tardas.

Today's journey was much the same as yesterday's; very uncomfortable, though at least the swarms of mosquitoes and biting flies do not come out into the stream. The water is remarkably clear. When the sun is overhead, one can almost see straight down to the bottom in places, and I was thus able to observe many species of fish in the depths. The river averages about sixty yards across, I should say, and the banks on either side are thick with tangled jungle, save for here and there a burned-out patch shows where the natives have had a field of crops.

We made perhaps seven miles today, owing to our late start. I am writing this as we sit around the fire, eating a large fish that one of the *comaradas* caught. Corbett says very little and seems to be absorbed with a book he has brought. I have just glanced over at it and find that it is *Poems of Rudyard Kipling*. Most appropriate, I must say.

After writing the above, Lady Darrow, to my great delight, came and sat beside me. She looked very tired and unhappy, and no wonder. But she affected an easy manner that wouldn't have been out of place in a drawing room. Such are the fruits of good breeding.

"You know, Bill, I suddenly realized that I don't actually know very much about you," she said. "Where do you come from?"

"From Devon, your Ladyship," I answered.

"I don't think the 'your Ladyship' is really necessary in the jungle," she answered with a quite disarming smile. "At least, I won't insist on it from you."

"That is very kind your...um, ma'am," I said.

"Oh, never mind," she said, laughing a little. "Where abouts in Devon are you from?"

"A place called Evensbrough, ma'am. Little country village of no importance at all. My father is a doctor there."

"How lovely. I've known quite a few country doctors in Limstock. Very good people. That's the village near Sangral, you know. Or maybe you don't."

I couldn't honestly say I did, never having been to Kent.

"Well, I remember fat old Dr. Gloster, with his great thick glasses. I always thought he looked like a toad, but he was very kind and knew his job quite well. Always came by when I was ill as a girl, or had had some scrape. I..."

She stopped abruptly and glanced at Corbett. She seemed embarrassed, though why, I couldn't imagine.

"Forgive me, I was supposed to be asking about you. Does your father still practice?"

"Certainly. He knows his job very well and is as sharp as he ever was. His patients are very fond of him. My brother is preparing to take over the practice."

"Oh, you have a brother?"

"Three, actually," I admitted. "I am the youngest. Gerald, the next elder, is the one I mentioned. Charles went to London and is working at a bank – doing rather well for himself – and poor Henry died at Antwerp."

"I'm very sorry," she said.

I did not want to talk about Henry, and I'm sure Lady Darrow didn't want to hear about him, so I changed subjects.

"Yes, I'm a bit of a disappointment, I'm afraid; going in for zoology. Not much of a future in that, what? At least that's what Charles tells me. Rather a silly field, though Gerald says he thinks it quite a good career, and that there are many sillier things I might do."

"I don't think it's silly at all," she said. "I think it's marvellous! Adding to the stock of human knowledge. Not to mention the chance to go to beautiful places like this and work with fascinating creatures."

I didn't see what was beautiful about the jungle myself, but I certainly wasn't going to contradict her. It felt wonderfully encouraging to have my life's ambitions approved by her Ladyship. Though I deplore what I can only describe as the thoughtlessness that led her to come on this trip, I cannot help but be grateful she is here. It is like having a little bit of home constantly with us. One smile from her is as strengthening as a good night's rest.

I am sure, Frances, you will not begrudge my saying these things. Lady Darrow is a beautiful, kind, and elegant woman, as you probably know better than I, and I admire her greatly, as all right-thinking men must do.

We spoke a while longer, and I told her of how I had become interested in zoology, of my ambitions, such as they are, and, of course, of you, Frances. Though I was obliged to temper my praise of you, as your father was sitting nearby. I don't think he quite approves of our plans yet.

We even touched on the subject of Cricket! It seems her father was an avid follower of the sport and she was most interested to hear I had qualified for the Devon Cricket Club.

All in all, it was the most delightful evening I have yet spent on this accursed trip, and gives me hope, as I close my eyes, that perhaps it will not be as horrible as I have feared.

August 11th

Another horrible night. The insects were not so bad as they had been (Corbett gave me some 'fly dope' which, applied to the skin, keeps the insects at bay, at least for a time before it is sweated off), but there was a most alarming and, it must be confessed, shameful incident. I shall duly record it as penance, and shall hope that by the time I see you again, Frances, I may be able to laugh at it.

I was obliged to get up in the middle of the night to answer the call, as it were. As I didn't want to wake the Old Man, or anyone else, I slipped out as quietly as I could. The jungle is absolutely black at night, you should know, and a very short distance beyond the light of our fire sight becomes impossible. I slipped around the tents, away from the hammocks, and on the opposite side from the fire.

I had just finished and was starting back to the tent when I became aware of a soft, wet sound; like something slipping out of the water. I looked toward the river, which was about twenty yards away to my right and slightly luminous in the moonlight.

I should explain that there is lightning almost every night in the jungle, even when the sky overhead is clear. The weather is so volatile and the air so heavy that there is almost always a storm happening somewhere in the Amazon. Well, as I was looking toward the river, there was a flash of lightning. By its light I saw a large, low-slung shape beside the river, and caught a flash of luminous green eyes, which seemed to linger when the darkness had returned.

Though I had not yet seen one on this journey, I knew at once what it was; a jaguar.

Naturally, or so it seems to me, my first thought was to prevent its noticing me. Surely that is what any sensible man does when he realizes he is in the presence of a large predator? I ducked down to the ground, trusting to the darkness, and began to crawl slowly back to the fire. I could hear a very faint rustling in the undergrowth as it moved; too faint to be sure where it was or where it was going. I prayed that it hadn't seen me, and that it was going to pass by into the jungle, after a peccary or something.

As I crept back toward the fire, my foot landed on a stick, which snapped with what seemed to me an extremely loud sound. I bit my lip to stop myself from crying out. The sounds of the jaguar had stopped, or so it seemed; it was hard to hear over the noise of those damned insects.

Then, all at once, a light blossomed around me. Those green eyes glowed in the darkness not ten feet away, looking straight at me. I was so startled that I actually cried out and scrambled backwards.

"Get up," Halritter snapped. "Get up at once."

It was he who was holding the lantern that showed the big cat. He thrust it into my hands as I stumbled to my feet, then raised his rifle. The jaguar showed its teeth and snarled.

"Shoot it!" I gasped. "Quick!"

But he didn't. He simply stood, rifle at the ready, while he and the big cat looked at each other. I had a sudden impression that I was witnessing a battle of wills; the man and the beast each striving to conquer the other with their eyes alone. On one side the fierce green eyes of the snarling jungle cat, on the other the calm grey eyes of the stoical Austrian.

The standoff lasted for about a minute (though it felt like an hour). Then the green eyes blinked out of sight, and I heard the soft sounds of the big cat slinking away into the forest.

I let out a long, slow breath. "Why didn't you shoot it?" I asked.

"I would have, if I had needed to," he answered. "But I find it is not often so. It is enough with most beasts, and most men, to show that you see them and are willing to face them. Most are not looking for a fight."

He turned those cool grey eyes on me with a stern expression. "Why did you not sound the alarm?"

"What do you mean?"

"You saw there was a jaguar near the camp. Did you not think that something we ought to know?"

"I..." that had never occurred to me. "Well, I didn't want him to notice me."

"You thought you could hide from a jungle cat by cowering in the shadows?"

"I shouldn't put it that way..."

"But that is what you did," he said. "And suppose it did miss you in the dark. Would you have been content for it to take the Professor? Or Lady Darrow?"

What was I to say to that?

"I...didn't think of that," I confessed.

"No," said Halritter. "I would not wish to be so uncharitable as to suppose you did. But kindly try to think of it next time."

I don't think I have ever felt so ashamed as I did at that moment.

Chapter Seven
The Hitchhiker

"An animal may be ferocious and cunning enough, but it takes a real man to tell a lie."
-H.G. Wells, *The Island of Dr. Moreau*

Despite his devotion to Frances, two days of discomfort and two nights of little sleep caused Bill to fail in his writing for a time, and so we must leave his contribution for now.

For Perseus, these first few days were some of the most uncomfortable and discouraging he had ever experienced. Elizabeth hardly ever spoke to him, and when she did it was only to vent her anger with a cutting remark. He knew that he had no cause to blame her for her anger; he had brought it on himself by his thoughtlessness. Yet it annoyed him nonetheless, all the more so because it came with the pain of knowing she now thought so ill of him. Being angry with Elizabeth hurt as much as having her angry at him. Taken on top of the normal discomfort of jungle travel – the heat, insects, and strain of rowing – and it took all his self-control to remain in a tolerable temper.

His only hope was that Elizabeth's anger would cool with time and that, before their journey ended, she might be prevailed on to forgive him.

The expedition continued up the Tardas for several more days, with Professor Illingworth making a morning or evening survey every other day. The jungle remained much as it had been on either side; a towering wall of green, sometimes festooned by brilliant, fragrant flowers, sometimes by equally brilliant tropical birds. Families of monkeys watched the boats from their treetops with pointed disinterest, and very occasionally they would pass villages where the people watched with much the same expressions.

The marks of civilization soon vanished entirely, and apart from the occasional native village or the remains of a field, signs of humanity disappeared as well. They were entering the deep jungle, where nature held undisputed sway and the teaming, swarming fecundity of life reached its peak.

Elizabeth wondered at the way every plant and tree, every vine, every fungus seemed to be fighting and struggling for its small patch of life. She had thought she loved forests and wild places, but that was in England, where the cooler climate left the green, growing things half asleep and content to take what they could find.

Here they were fully awake and clawing, biting, tearing at one another to survive. As each grew, it pushed against everything around it, greedily sucking up as much as it could, while its neighbours did the same to it, resulting in an endless slow-motion battlefield of each against all and all against each. They were in the midst of the wet, torrid fever of the earth in which her children tormented each other like the souls in Hell; the workings of nature stripped bare.

For all she had spoken and thought of 'wild places,' Elizabeth had never realized just how frightening those wild places could be once you were in them. More than anything she felt horribly exposed, almost naked, as though barriers she had been used to all her life had been stripped away, leaving only her and the unfiltered jungle to face each other.

This was brought home to her one day when, tired and bored, she let her hand trail into the water. Martin, who was sitting behind her, snapped with uncharacteristic vehemence, "Take your hand out!"

She jerked it away from the hot, clear stream at once, looking back in surprise.

"My apologies your Ladyship," he said, doffing his hat. "But that is not safe. There are piranha in these waters. I have known men to have fingers taken off."

"*Si*," said Costa, the boatman, from the stern. "I too. My brother, Santiago, he lose three toes! Take bath in wrong place. Bitten many times."

"Thank you for warning me," said Elizabeth, unconsciously wringing her hand as if to make sure every slender digit was in its place. "I was more worried of crocodiles myself."

"Black Caiman," said Martin. "The Professor could tell you about them. They are also to be concerned about."

"They wouldn't tip over the boat, would they?" she asked, struck by the sudden thought.

Martin shook his head.

"Not nearly aggressive enough for that," he said. "They are ambush predators. Lay in wait, then spring. I have never heard of one attacking a boat directly. Have you, Costa?"

The boatman shook his head.

"That's a relief," said Elizabeth, eying the water with renewed unease.

It was so clear that she could see straight down through it, all the way to the bottom in places. It was a maze of rotting logs and branches from countless trees over untold years, and often teamed with fish. Some were so large she thought they must be a species of shark, but Martin assured her they were, in fact, catfish.

"No less dangerous for that," he warned.

Woman-eating catfish. That was one nightmare that had never previously occurred to her.

Yet there was beauty here as well. The fish swimming below included gloriously coloured species like living jewels. Once, a flight of brilliant tropical birds took off right in front of them, briefly turning the scene into a rainbow of feathers. Another time she saw a series of pinkish backs cresting some dozen yards off, in the middle of the stream. She thought they were some large fish, or perhaps turtles, until one of them blew forth a spout of air.

"Dolphins!" she exclaimed in wonder.

"River dolphins, your Ladyship," said Martin. "Here, the Yellow River, and the Ganges are the only places you will find them in the whole world."

So the days rolled away along with the river, until at last the river forked. To the left, the bright, clear Tardas rode on. To the right went the murky waters of the Rio Noite. The difference was startling; here were waters so clear that one could see straight down to the bottom, then right alongside it, almost in a straight line, were waters so thick with black mud that they were completely opaque. It was like two lines of paint run side-by-side. They turned down the broad black river and paddled on.

At first, there was little difference in the journey, save that now instead of gliding over a world of fallen limbs and darting fish, they skimmed over the surface of a black mirror. The jungle was as thick and tangled as ever, trees towering overhead and birds screeching from the branches. They paddled on, making better progress on the slower Noite than they had on the Tardas, and they had little trouble finding a relatively clear spot on the bank to make camp.

The second day, however, brought a slow, subtle change. So Elizabeth thought, at least. The air seemed more still, and the jungle unusually quiet. They saw no monkeys beside the river, nor or any other wildlife, save the occasional bird. Even the humming of the insects was more subdued than it had been. The trees seemed to her to have darker leaves and to crowd closer to the banks, which grew steeper. The sky was thick with clouds, so that even the tropical sun could hardly pierce them.

The very air seemed to sit heavier than ever upon the expedition, so much so that Elizabeth almost found it difficult to breathe.

Worst of all was the inescapable sensation of being watched. The stillness of the jungle made one feel that all that riot of life was waiting for something, glaring down at the people who had dared to penetrate its domains. She felt as she had sometimes felt when in a room with many progressive-minded people; the impression that they disliked her on principle and were only looking for reasons to dislike her more

Their third day on the Noite dawned as oppressive as the day before. The air was hot and thick with moisture. The usual growls of thunder had a more aggressive, hungry tone, as if stirred to anger.

Perseus took one glance overhead and knew they would be in for a rough time. They packed hurriedly and took to the river, tying their skin coverings in place straight away.

They hadn't been on the river more than an hour when the storm began. It was not the usual daily downpour, but a violent assault from the skies, hurling vertical sheets of water down into the Amazon basin. These were accompanied by an artillery of lightning and thunder that seemed to crack the sky. The trees buckled and twisted in the storm as though they were frightened animals, straining to escape their harnesses, and the river seemed to boil under the assault.

The expedition paddled on through the pouring rain. They were soon soaked to the skin, and despite the skin coverings the passengers still had to spend a good deal of time bailing out the canoes.

It was getting on late afternoon, and the storm continued unabated. The clouds were so thick that it was getting hard to see, and Perseus signalled to the others to keep an eye out for a place to camp. But with the banks averaging six feet on either side, nothing appeared.

As they paddled on, Perseus's quick ears caught a sound on the air; a sound that wasn't wind or rain or thunder. It was the unmistakable tone of a human voice; a voice calling for help. A moment later, they rounded the bend and he saw the dim outline of a fallen tree lying half-in the river against the bank. A figure stood in its branches, waving a lantern as he clung to the tree.

"Help me!" the man called. "I am stranded! Help me!"

"Hello!" Illingworth shouted, squinting into the rain. "Someone's on the bank!"

Perseus rapidly considered their options. He didn't like the situation; a man, apparently alone, stranded by the side of the river in the middle of the jungle. He was experienced enough to know what sort of man they were likely to find out here, and of all the many, many dangers that might be involved.

But he also knew that no decent man, let alone any gentleman, would leave a man stranded in such a place simply out of fear.

"We see you!" he called back to the stranded figure. "We'll come alongside! Gomez, pull alongside that tree, carefully. Bill, get ready to take down the covering, but don't do it until I say."

Bill took hold of the covering and waited as Perseus and the *comaradas* steered the boat alongside the tree.

"Watch out!" the man warned. "There are sunken branches! Can puncture your boat!"

With expert hands, they evaded the hidden menace and drove close enough for the man to come aboard. Perseus gave the word to Bill, and the covers opened up. The rain immediately dropped a puddle into the centre, but the man stepped nimbly from his tree into the middle of the boat, bringing a tattered old knapsack with him.

"Thank the Lord for you people!" he cried as he sat down and hastily helped to pull the skins tight again. "Thank the Lord!"

"Are you all right?" Illingworth asked, twisting in his seat to look at their new companion.

"My canoe, it ran against a tree," the man answered, shouting over the rain. "Poked a hole straight through! Had you not come, I would soon be dead!"

Martin drew alongside them.

"What is going on?" Elizabeth asked.

"Man stranded," Perseus called back.

The hitchhiker turned to Elizabeth. Perseus, seated in the stern, could only see the side of his face, but he did not like the expression on it at all.

As though he sensed Perseus's disapproval, the man turned all the way around to face him, smiling broadly. This gave Perseus his first opportunity to see him properly.

He was pale – much paler than one would have thought to find a man in the jungle – with thin, lank, greying blond hair. His eyes were bright and icy blue, and his face had a curiously rubber quality, as though his muscles pulled his skin further than its natural extent with every expression. He was dressed in a simple grey shirt and trousers, and had a broad-brimmed grey hat set upon his head. Despite the somewhat unhealthy look of his skin and hair, Perseus could see the great, powerful muscles evident beneath his shirt.

The man's expression changed slightly as he and Perseus looked at each other. He was still smiling, but something like recognition came into his eyes, almost as though the two men were old comrades from way back. It was the recognition of a man for his like; someone who knew the things he knew and had experienced the things he had. It was a kind of kinship born from being of the same breed, but not the same blood. Perseus felt it too and did not like it.

"My thanks to you, friend," the man called over the storm. He had an unusual accent; sharp and keen, with an almost Germanic edge to the Hispanic. Not a native Brazilian, Perseus judged.

"Don't mention it," he answered. "Only common decency."

They continued looking at each other, sizing one another up for a few moments. The longer Perseus looked, the less he liked what he saw. There was a cold, almost reptilian quality to his eyes, and the smile he wore did not reach them.

And there was something else; something Perseus had learned to recognize over his many adventures. A faint twinge of the expression, the smallest upturning of the face and hardness of the eyes. It was the mark of one who is all things to himself and for whom love and empathy are as classical music to an ape. Perseus had seen that kind of face on gangsters in America, revolutionaries in the Caribbean, and Commissars in Russia.

This, he knew, was a dangerous man.

There was nothing more to be said until the storm passed; conversation was too difficult. The stranger turned back to face forward and called something to Bill, who seemed uncertain how to answer.

The rain finally let up near evening, just as they at last found a spit of level ground on which they could land and pitch their tents.

"What's your name, friend?" Perseus asked as they pulled ashore.

"Silva," he answered, helping Gomez secure the canoe. "Paul Silva."

"I'm awfully sorry, Mr. Silva," said Elizabeth, stepping out of her canoe. "But I don't think we can take you back. We're going upriver, and it would take much too long."

"I understand," the hitchhiker answered, inclining his head without taking his eyes off of her. "I understand completely. It is no worry. You people saved my life. What you decide is what I do. Besides," he added with a slight laugh. "I am not expected anywhere."

Wanted somewhere though, perhaps, thought Perseus.

"You, uh, you seem a strange party to be traveling in jungle, if I may say so," Silva went on, glancing about the group before returning his eyes appreciatively to Elizabeth. Her beauty was evidently not lost on him. "Where do you think you are going?"

"We are a scientific expedition," said Illingworth. "Documenting local species. We particularly hope to find a certain sunken valley that supposedly exists somewhere along this river."

Silva's eyebrows lifted slightly and he laughed. "The Forbidden Valley?" he said.

"Yes," said Perseus. "You've heard of it?"

"Oh, yes," said Silva. "Most men who travel this river hear of it sooner or later. But no one has ever seen it."

"You don't think it exists, then?" asked Bill.

Silva shrugged. "Maybe, maybe not. Who is to say? The jungle, it has many secrets. I only say that this is one no one has found yet."

"Some people did, not many years back," said Perseus. "Professor Applegate and his party."

"Is that so?" said Silva. "These men, they found the valley, did they?"

"Supposedly," said Elizabeth. "Though our source is not as reliable as could have been hoped."

"We are following their directions," put in Martin.

"*Dios mio*, how curious," said Silva. "Well, I shall be happy to give whatever help I can. I am a hard worker, a good shot, and I know the jungle. Maybe you will be happy you found me, eh?"

Unlikely, thought Perseus. His annoyance with Elizabeth's bad temper left him in no mood to be charitable.

They made camp, Silva helping to clear the brush and set up the tents. The sun sank toward the west, and the deep jungle shadows turned coal-black around them while the sky glowed deep gold overhead.

"Where are you from, Mr. Silva?" asked Illingworth over dinner.

"Paraguay," came the answer. "I started out studying for the priesthood in Concepcion. But, ah, I soon realized I did not have what they call a 'vocation'. But it was not what you might think," he said, raising a finger as his eyes once again turned to Elizabeth. "Women, I can take or leave. But the books and the Latin and up at the same time and down at the same time, it was not for me. So, I went to see the real world. I've been to the United States, Africa, Europe. All over. Tried many things. In the end, I wound up in the jungle. Heh! I seem to fit."

"And, uh, what do you do in the jungle?" Bill asked.

Silva winked at the boy.

"Oh, this and that. A bit of hunting, a bit of transport, a bit of guiding. Whatever people pay me to do, I do. You can always find work in the jungle, remember that."

In other words, Perseus thought. *He's a poacher and smuggler.*

He looked at Martin, who showed by the faint crinkle in his brow that he shared Perseus's conclusions.

"Martin," he said. "I want to double-check some of the baggage. I think it may have gotten waterlogged."

"Right," said the Austrian, setting down his plate and getting to his feet. The two men withdrew to the boats and bent over the baggage canoe.

"What do you think?" Perseus asked in a low voice as they worked.

"I think that we have a snake among us," came the answer.

"My thoughts exactly. Only question is, does he mean to bite us, or is he just a dangerous animal in dire straits?"

"Quite so."

"I don't like it," said Perseus. "It seems a bit much of a coincidence that he happened to be out there."

"Perhaps. Though coincidences do happen."

"Yes, but when they happen when you're carrying a book that you know some people would kill to get hold of, they rather stand out."

"Do you suggest that this Silva is connected with that?"

"I don't see how he can be," said Perseus, shaking his head. "But I don't like it all the same. And here's another thought: if we *do* find the valley, what then? Supposing there *is* gold or treasure of some kind there, how do you suppose he'll react?"

Martin nodded. "I see your concern," he said. "But what do you suggest we do about it?"

"That is the trouble," sighed Perseus. "Because there doesn't seem a damn thing to do but to lump it and bring him along. I mean, we can't just shoot him, can we?"

"Indeed."

"Well, he won't be the first snake we've had on a hunt. May even prove useful."

But he was frowning, for on this trip there was a complicating factor. Perseus didn't really object to having a man along whom he wouldn't trust an inch further than he could see. He had worked with worse men before, and there really was nothing *definitely* threatening about Silva.

He did, however, object strongly to having such a man in perpetual close contact with a beautiful young lady.

Around the fire, Silva sat talking with Illingworth and Bill, apparently enlarging upon some anecdote. Elizabeth, however, had risen and was standing a little apart, looking out over the dark river as it began to shed the last remnants of reflected light from the setting sun. Perseus sent Martin back to the fire while he went and joined her.

"Lady Darrow," he said. "May I speak with you a moment?"

"Certainly, Mr. Corbett," she answered in the same cold, aloof tone she had used since their departure from Pordesol. He flinched a little, but now was not the time to worry about such things.

"Let us pretend, for a moment, that you have no personal animosity toward me, and that I am merely an expert in the ways of the jungle whom you have hired to guide and advise you on this trip."

She stiffened slightly, but nodded.

"Very well. Let us pretend."

Perseus glanced back at the camp, then turned his face to the river.

"I have met men like this before," he said in low voice. "The kind of men who choose to live in wild, uncivilized places, plying dubious trades..."

"That sounds familiar," she said.

"This is what you brought me for, so pay attention please," he said sternly. "I don't know whether he really is just stranded or whether he has some larger plans afoot, but I do know this: you will meet nothing in this jungle that is more dangerous than he."

The seriousness of his tone caused her to forget her affected coldness.

"You don't think he means us harm, do you?"

"I don't know. Probably not, but only because there is, at present, no possibility of sufficient gain for him. If he ever thought there were, I think he would do just about anything. And I don't think he will ever be famous for his self-command, whatever he says. So listen to me very carefully: do not *ever* let yourself be alone with him. Do you understand?"

"Why ever would I be?"

"I don't know, I am just warning you *not* to let it happen."

Elizabeth looked back at the camp, where Silva was laughing over his anecdote. She shivered a little, despite the tropical heat.

"Surely," she said in a vain attempt to push her discomfort aside. "You don't think he would...well, try anything?"

Perseus shook his head.

"Elizabeth, this is the jungle. The only law here is that of survival. Anything further is a question of what's in your own heart, and that man, I should say, doesn't have much inside him. When it comes to taking something he wants, there is absolutely *nothing* he would not do if he thought he could get away with it."

She folded her arms and hugged herself tight. He could see that this first realization that she was in the presence of a man who might be willing to do her real harm was profoundly disturbing to her. Fear made her angry.

"And what laws are in *your* heart?" she demanded.

"This is not the time for that," he said sharply. "Hate me all you like. Just promise me you will not give him the chance to harm you."

"All right, all right, you've made your point," she said. "I understand, and I promise."

"Thank you," he said.

They looked at each other for a moment. The light of the setting sun gleamed on the fiery crown of her hair and the smooth lines of her face, making him feel as though his heart were being twisted like a rag. Then she turned and rejoined the others, affecting a cheerful smile. Silva, he saw, was watching her intently.

He wondered, briefly, whether he ought to inform Silva in no uncertain terms that there would be consequences to his trying anything. But no; that would only be seen as a challenge that would make her all the more enticing a target, and Silva no doubt was cunning enough to understand this without being told. The best thing he could do, Perseus decided, was simply to watch the man; to watch him like a hawk.

Elizabeth, for her part, soon retired into her tent. She felt badly shaken and angry with Perseus for giving her such a fright, though she did not doubt the accuracy of his words. She made sure her revolver was close at hand and she didn't undress or even take the knife from her belt as she huddled down on her cot, eyes watchful.

She had never felt so horribly conscious of her own sex. She seemed more aware of her own body than she ever remembered being, and every nerve felt awake and on the watch, as though she were anticipating a blow at each moment.

Back home she had sometimes enjoyed listening to women speakers who had loudly declared against the term 'the weaker sex', proclaiming that men and women were no different from each other save where sex itself was concerned. It had seemed an admirable sentiment in London, under the protection of age-encrusted laws and customs. In the jungle, amid the raw battle of life against life, it was as comforting as a damp newspaper. She thought of Silva's thick, muscular arms and imagined what they could do to her.

At Sangral House there had, for a long time, been a delicate china shepherdess standing upon the top of an end table. She always wondered at it, thinking how easily it might be knocked over and shattered with a single careless gesture. When she was grown up, one of the first things she did was to pack the little shepherdess safely away inside of a glass cabinet.

Elizabeth thought she knew just how that little shepherdess had felt, being at once exposed and horribly fragile. Except in this case it was worse, for there was no cabinet for her to be packed away in. She was in the wild, far, far from any help or safety, and there was nothing she could do about that. For a moment the wild idea of cancelling the whole expedition and demanding to be taken home crossed her mind. Perseus would certainly do it, she thought. But no; that was a coward's way out. She had insisted that she was willing to take the risks, and now – well, it was time to make good on that.

The thought of Perseus brought a little comfort. After all, she was not alone. She had her friends. Perseus had all but told her that he would not permit anything to be done to her, and he, she thought, must be at least as dangerous as Silva. She could rely on him, couldn't she?

The doubt she felt on that point opened up the old wound in her heart, and she gripped the edges of her blanket in frustration.

But even apart from Perseus, there was Martin. Steadfast, reliable Martin. And Bill: a silly boy, but perfectly decent and game for anything. Even Illingworth would stand by her, she knew. Yes, as long as she stayed with them – and again, why should she not? – she would be safe. Or at least, no less safe than she had been up until now.

She told herself this over and over, until exhaustion overcame anxiety and at last she slept.

Chapter Eight
The Lord of Serpents

"They strike, wrap around you, hold you tighter than your true love, and you have the privilege of hearing your bones break before the power of the embrace causes your veins to explode!"
-Sarone, *Anaconda*

Perseus was on the last watch that night. As the sun rose and turned the humid night air to mist and vapour, he sat poking at the watch fire, rifle on his lap, his sharp eyes brooding over the chattering embers. The jungle was surprisingly quiet in the morning; far quieter than an English forest would have been. Here no songbirds rose to greet the dawn. Even the long screech of the insects faded with the coming light, leaving no sound but the crackling of the fire and the gentle motion of the river.

He had long since acquired the skill of not worrying overmuch. He recognized the many potential dangers that Silva's presence represented, on top of the ones that they were already bound to face in the coming days. But having identified these dangers and decided what, if any, precautions he could take, they ceased to occupy his mind. He was thinking, as he had always done at such times, of Sangral House. Though these days the memory gave more of pain than of pleasure, it never occurred to him to try to think of something else. No amount of regret or shame or annoyance could possibly be worse than to think that he could no longer dream of the dear old place; that it was closed to him even in his own heart.

Perseus's eyes snapped suddenly towards the shelter. Silva was coming to join him, moving as softly as a jungle cat.

"Good morning, friend," he said.

Perseus returned the greeting. He felt in his pocket and found his cigarette case. He was nearly out. He took one himself and offered one to Silva.

"Thank you," said the poacher, accepting it. "A rare luxury, this." He took a brand from the fire and lit it with relish, then leaned back, surveying Perseus with a practiced eye.

"This is not your first trip up the river, I think," he said.

"Quite right. I've been in the interior more than once over the years."

"Hunter?"

"Occasionally."

Silva puffed on his cigarette and blew a smoke ring into the air.

"None of my business, of course," he said. "But you are a strange party. You, your quiet friend, the old man and the boy, and the ladyship." He grinned. "A very strange party. Something new, and I don't see many new things in the jungle."

"We're a bit haphazard, I admit," said Perseus noncommittally.

"And you seek this Forbidden Valley, eh? What do you think you will find there, I wonder?"

Perseus looked him in the eye for a moment, but those sharp, cold orbs gave nothing away.

"I haven't the least idea," he said. "That's what we're going to find out."

Silva bowed his head as though to concede the point and the two men said nothing more until the camp began to stir.

For her own part, Elizabeth's first thought upon rising from a troubled sleep was that, danger or no danger, she was never going to sleep with her knife and boots on again. A night's rest had dulled the edge of her fears a little, and she was able to dress and wash and join in the morning company as something like her usual self. She was also beginning to feel a little ashamed of her anxiety of the night before.

After breakfast, as the others were loading the boats, Elizabeth stood watching them, savouring the few remaining minutes when she could stretch her legs and reflecting on the situation. Once again, she reassured herself that nothing could possibly happen. If worst came to the worst, the others would see that she was safe. There was no sense at all in overreacting the way she had.

As she was thinking this, Elizabeth abruptly became aware of someone approaching from behind. Turning, she found Silva carrying a last bit of a baggage lightly under one arm and less than foot away from her. She started back instinctively.

"Excuse, ladyship," he said, his rubber face breaking into a grin. His teeth were yellow and seemed to turn inwards toward his throat.

"Don't sneak up on me like that!" she said, in a much sharper voice than she had intended.

"Your pardon," he said, bowing his head. "I have bad manners, is true. It is so rare for me to meet with a great lady in the jungle. I mean no harm."

Elizabeth flushed a little, embarrassed by her momentary alarm.

"Of course," she said, summoning all her own good breeding to try to cover for it and forcing a smile. "I am very sorry. You startled me is all."

"Apologies. You people save my life, and all I do in return is frighten you."

"Oh, you don't frighten me," she said without thinking.

"Thank you," he said with a bow.

He winked coarsely at her before continuing on to the boat. Elizabeth inwardly flinched but pretended not to notice.

What on Earth did I say that for? She thought to herself. *Fellow's going to think I* am *frightened of him. And he's right. Oh, bother! I wish I'd never come on this trip!*

***

The storm of yesterday had broken the oppressive atmosphere. The normal heat and humidity of the jungle was almost comfortable by comparison, and they made fairly good progress for the next several days.

Meanwhile, Silva proved a helpful, willing companion. He took his turn with the paddles, letting Gomez or Costa rest, and lent his aid to setting up camp every night, where he regaled them with colourful tales of his many adventures. The *comaradas* seemed to develop a rapid respect for him, and he settled easily into acting as a kind of leader and companion to the two men.

As the days went by, Elizabeth's fears were further eased by sheer familiarity, and she began to wonder whether Perseus hadn't been overly concerned and herself too quick to judge. The idea, both foreign and unwelcome that Silva actually might do her harm was willingly allowed to fade, and she soon adopted much the same habits that she had before. She did not forget her promise to Perseus, but as no occasion for breaking it seemed likely to occur on their voyage it ceased to prey on her mind.

One positive effect of her fright, however, was that it neutralized her anger. She had not reconciled with Perseus, and she wasn't sure what she felt towards him at present, but she did stop sniping at him and made no objection to his sometimes taking Martin's place in the baggage boat. They didn't talk much on these occasions; nothing beyond simple comments on the river and the jungle. But it was, at least, a softening of feeling, and they both felt better for it.

One afternoon, about five days after meeting Silva, when they had once more made camp for the evening, Illingworth announced it was time for another survey. The storm had thrown them off their schedule and it had been nearly a week since their last one.

"Bill," he ordered. "Fetch my notebook and my specimen kit."

Bill, who looked exhausted (he had taken a turn with the paddles), grumbled something under his breath.

"What was that?"

"Nothing, professor," he said, moving to obey.

"I'll come with you," said Perseus, picking up his rifle.

"I will come, too," said Silva, unexpectedly.

Perseus eyed him appraisingly, and Silva met his gaze seemingly without a care. "As you like," he said after a moment.

Silva shouldered the rifle they had given him and then leant conspiratorially to Perseus. "Between us," he said in a low voice. "I do not think your friend likes me."

He jerked his head back at Martin, who was seated beside Elizabeth with his rifle on his lap

"I don't think so either," said Perseus.

Silva chuckled. He had a low, hissing kind of laugh, as though he wished to share his mirth with none but himself.

"Good luck!" Elizabeth called after them. "Be careful!"

The jungle here was thicker than most of what they had passed through up until now. In places it seemed almost to be a solid, tangled mass of leaves, vines, shoots, and branches. Their going was slow, with Perseus having to chop their way through with his machete while Silva brought up the rear, guarding their backs.

Bill, worn down, reached out a hand to lean on a tree. Quick as thought, Silva reached out and caught his wrist.

"Watch yourself," he said, and nodded to the tree. A large, blue-black wasp stood motionless on the trunk, just where Bill had been about to put his hand. "If he stung you, you'd be paralysed with pain for two whole hours at least," the hunter said with a grin.

"God!" Bill exclaimed, scrambling back. "Isn't there anything in this damn jungle that isn't trying to kill me?!"

Silva laughed as he released him. "No," he said. "There isn't."

Illingworth took a closer look at the wasp with interest. "*Synoeca*," he said. "Warrior wasp. Well-documented, of course. Still, mark that down Bill."

Bill compiled, casting resentful looks at Illingworth, Silva, and the wasp. The latter took off suddenly, nearly causing Bill to drop his notebook.

"Careful!" Illingworth barked. "We can't have the whole evening's work spoiled because of a little insect."

Bill ground his teeth but said nothing. The journey was wearing hard on him, and his patience was nearly exhausted.

They went on for some time, until they came to a place where the ground rose slightly and the undergrowth wasn't quite as thick. It wasn't a clearing, but after the wall of undergrowth it gave something of that effect. Illingworth seemed pleased with it and began to study the ground, peering at it rather as a different sort of old man might peer at a stamp collection. "Here, would one of you fellows mind just turning some of this ground cover for me?" he said.

Silva cheerfully obliged, turning the leaves over with the flat of his machete. The effort unveiled several beetles, a number of large ants, and a small lizard with bright blue scales and a green head, which was soon caught and obliged to make the ultimate sacrifice to the advancement of science. Illingworth thought that it might be a new species and dictated a careful description to Bill before depositing it into a jar of preservative alcohol from his pack.

While this work was going on, Perseus stood close by, rifle in hand, his sharp eyes scanning the jungle for any signs of trouble.

Suddenly, a great commotion rose from overhead as a troop of monkeys began hooting and howling and scampering through the branches.

"What's that all about?" Bill demanded.

Silva looked up and grinned. "That is a warning," he said. "They know death is near."

"Watch yourself, Professor," Perseus called to Illingworth.

"Jaguar, you suppose?" Illingworth answered.

Silva's eyes swept the jungle. His grin did not disappear. "Much worse than that, I think," he said.

"Worse?" stammered Bill. "What's worse than a jaguar?"

Perseus cast a sharp look at Silva, then back to the jungle. He had felt it too; that instinctual sense of being hunted. There was no doubt that Silva was right, and some kind of predator was watching them from the forest.

Then he saw it.

"Professor!" he shouted. "Get back!"

Illingworth jumped and took a few steps back, but then stopped. A big, triangular head was drifting through the undergrowth, held about three feet off the ground. It was black on top, with a deep red underbelly. As more of its body emerged, they saw it had red markings all down its back as well, rather like those of a jaguar. A forked tongue flickered in and out of its mouth, and its unblinking eyes were fixed on Illingworth.

"My God!" said Illingworth, who stood back from the enormous snake, but not far back. "An anaconda. But I've never heard of one of this colouring..."

"I would not get too close, Professor!" said Silva.

"No need to worry," said Illingworth, holding up an admonitory hand without taking his eye off of the snake, which now stood quite still, looking at him. "A snake this size won't be very fast, especially not on land."

"You are so sure about that?" said Silva.

"Mr. Silva," said Illingworth, turning to him. "I'm sure you know quite a lot about hunting in the jungle, but..."

He never finished. As soon as he took his eyes off of it, the snake struck like lightning. It clamped its jaws down on Illingworth's shoulder then wrapped around him, winding itself back into the undergrowth like a fisherman pulling in a catch or like a smaller snake seizing a mouse. It was so fast that neither Perseus nor Silva could get a shot off.

Bill screamed. Perseus swore and plunged forward into the jungle after the snake. The anaconda had not gone far; only far enough to wind Illingworth down to about the middle section of its body, where two great loops of black scales were coiled about his trunk, squeezing tight. The professor's mouth was open wide in a silent scream. His eyes were popping.

Perseus, coming suddenly upon it through the undergrowth only caught a brief glimpse before the snake was on him. Still holding to its prey in its coils, its head darted forward, snapping at him. Perseus only just managed to dodge the attack by diving to the ground.

Bill, white but game, came rushing in after him. The snake turned on him and drove its head into the young man's stomach with enough force to lift him off his feet. He landed in a crumpled heap; all the wind knocked out of him.

From the jungle floor, Perseus raised his rifle, but as though it sensed the movement, the snake's great tail lashed out. He had to roll out of the way as it slammed into the ground, then it struck again, and he had to drop flat to avoid the slashing blow as it went over his head and tore a strip of bark from the tree.

The monster snake remained fixed, its coils still around the professor, whose thin face was rapidly turning blue. Its head was raised. It gave a low, hissing scream in defiance.

Then a shot rang out, and the head dropped at once.

Silva lowered his rifle and hurried forward to pull the coils off of Illingworth. Perseus scrambled up to help, ignoring the burning stings of the insects he had fallen upon.

The snake was not quite as heavy as they had feared it might be, and fortunately it had not gone into convulsions when it died. In a few seconds they had unwound Illingworth from its body and Perseus set to work to provide artificial respiration while Silva went to see to Bill.

"It's all right!" Perseus called after a minute. "He's coming 'round."

Silva pulled Bill to his feet, red in the face and clutching his stomach. "Not a bad effort, boy," Silva said, slapping his shoulder. "You might make a hunter yet."

At that moment, Illingworth drew a sudden, deep gasp. For some minutes, he could do nothing but breathe and cough.

"There, there, Professor," said Perseus. "You'll be all right. Just relax."

Illingworth looked about him with wide eyes and saw the body of the great snake. His mouth worked as though he were trying to say something.

"Don't try to talk, old boy," said Perseus. "It's safely dead. Don't you worry."

Illingworth either didn't hear him or disregarded him, for he kept trying to speak. He drew one more deep, shuddering breath, then at last croaked the word out.

"*Magnificent!*"

"Sir?"

"Absolutely...magnificent!" he coughed, then forced himself to a sitting position. "I never dreamt...Did you see how fast it moved? How aggressive? And how it defended its prey! No snake, at least no python or boa that I've ever heard of behaves that way! And look at the size of it! More than twenty feet if it's an inch!"

He was getting his breath back, but he seemed to be getting something else as well. Rather than his usual, pedantic recitations, he was now speaking with the fervent enthusiasm of a fanatic. He turned a shining face on Bill, who was being sick in the undergrowth.

"Bill, you have my measuring tape? No? What are you about, boy? Go fetch it at once! My notebook, and the camera, of course. We must document this! No, wait, first we must move it back into that clearing..."

Bewildered and somewhat amused, Perseus, Silva, and Bill dragged the dead snake back into the more open space. Then Bill and Silva went to fetch Illingworth's equipment.

"Red-on-black markings," he observed while they were gone. "And a red underbelly. The barrel isn't as thick as *Eunectus Murinus*'s. No, this fellow wants lean, hard muscle, built for fighting. And did you see the aggression? Most big snakes will abandon their prey if seriously threatened. This one had adapted to use its length in combat, striking with head and tail while simultaneously subduing its prey. No doubt it evolved to counter jaguars and other large predators. It must require a massive amount of food to power those muscles, so it wouldn't be able to afford to let its prey go once it'd got hold of it..."

"Its prey such as yourself," Perseus pointed out.

"The greater speed and power pay for themselves, as it were, biologically speaking," Illingworth went on, ignoring him. "Its metabolism must be amazing for a reptile!"

He lifted the tail end and performed an indelicate examination. "Male," he said. "Most likely territorial, given its food requirements."

Silva and Bill returned, accompanied by Martin and Elizabeth.

"Are you all right, Professor?" Elizabeth asked at once.

"I can hardly recall being better," he cried. "Look at this creature! A new species of anaconda, and the most formidable great snake on earth! Here, Bill, the measuring tape!"

He took it and they carefully measured the snake's body, while Perseus gave the others an account of what had happened.

"Professor, are you sure you wouldn't like to go back to the boats and rest?" asked Elizabeth.

"Thirty-two feet!" Illingworth announced. "Not an inch less! If only we had a scale capable of taking the weight! Bill, are you writing this down? Well, get on it, boy! You think a chance like this comes every day? What were you saying, Lady Darrow?"

"I suggested that perhaps you might like to return to the boats and rest," she said. "Though I'm starting to think that was a silly idea."

"Rest? How can I rest when there is so much work to be done?" he answered, his eyes beaming with a wild enthusiasm. "Don't you realize that we have discovered an entirely new apex predator? That hasn't happened in...well, I don't know how long. Hundreds of years, perhaps. There isn't a moment to lose! Pity the head is so damaged..."

The next hour was taken up with a thorough study of the great snake under the rapidly failing light, complete with photographs, measurements of every conceivable kind, and detailed drawings of its markings and other characteristics. Illingworth seemed to have undergone a complete transformation. He hopped about like a schoolboy on Christmas morning, and he was so excited that he almost couldn't take notes. He nearly cried when it was pointed out that there was no room in the boats to take the specimen, nor did they have the means of preserving so large a creature.

"I shall return one day," he vowed. "And recover one of these beasts for proper study. Alive, if possible. Oh, and its habits! Its habits must be better observed. Bill, you are sure you have it well photographed? Good. Guard that film with your life!"

At last, with the black jungle night settling over them, Illingworth consented to be dragged away from the dead snake that had attempted to devour him.

"Of course," he was saying along the way back to camp. "This substantiates all those rumours of giant, man-eating monster snakes that have come down through the years. They weren't myths at all! A little exaggerated, perhaps, but not much. That fellow could take a man easily."

"Nearly did," Perseus pointed out.

"Yes," said Illingworth, sobering a little for the first time. "My goodness, that was...a terrifying experience."

"Are you *sure* you are all right?" Elizabeth asked.

"I feel wonderful," he said. "Well...quite sore, actually." He felt his ribs gingerly. "Oh, dear. I probably ought to have been sitting down." He swallowed. "But this...I never thought that there were creatures like this yet left to be discovered in the world. It...it is like being born again!"

They at last got him seated beside the fire, where he ate his dinner with trembling hands, still talking about the great snake. "I shall call it *Eunectes Imperator*," he announced at last.

"I should have thought you'd want to name it after yourself," said Perseus. "It *did* almost eat you, after all."

Illingworth gave a hollow laugh.

"Saddle a glorious animal like that with the name of a poor old stick like me?" he said. "You must be joking! I wouldn't dream of it. It needs a name that conveys the power, the vitality of the beast. *Eunectes Imperator*: the Red Anaconda. Lord of all serpents. See you get that down, Bill."

Perseus turned to Silva. "Thank you for your help," he said.

Silva waved a hand. "Least I can do," he answered. "You people saved my life. Besides, it is the way in the jungle. Help someone, they help you back." He grinned. "Maybe I am not such a snake as you think I am."

Perseus smiled back. "Maybe."

Chapter Nine
The Forbidden Valley

I am the way into the city of woe.
I am the way to a forsaken people.
I am the way into eternal sorrow.
-The Divine Comedy: Inferno, Canto III: 1-3

The atmosphere of the expedition changed noticeably after their encounter with the Red Anaconda. For most of the party, it had been a grim reminder that they were entering uncharted territory, where unknown dangers might lurk around every tree and hide in every bend of the river. There was less talk in the boats and they rode closer together, watching the solid wall of green on either side with apprehensive faces.

Illingworth himself was the exception. His brush with death seemed to have taken twenty years off his life. He had lost most of his dry, haughty manner, and indeed, had almost become the life and soul of the expedition, talking the most, eating the most, and laughing the most. He still bullied Bill a great deal, but even that was in a more jovial and less impatient fashion.

"You will note," he said one evening after they had discovered a red and orange coral snake while making camp, "the desire to warn off predators by the bright, nearly hypnotic patterns of many venomous snakes. Yet simultaneously, many other species opt for camouflage and seek to conceal themselves from sight. These two strategies must therefore be almost equally successful, or equally irrelevant, for both allow the species to survive and propagate.

"This, of course, raises questions about the whole concept of concealment and, indeed, of survival of the fittest. The fittest only means, in fact, 'he who survives.' Yet so many things, so many accidents may occur, and it seems that the dangers involved in jungle life are such that no strategy at all is truly safe. The coral snake population needn't fear the growth of its predators, for the predators themselves face a thousand threats."

He looked thoughtfully at the little snake in his hand. He had picked it up with an expert's grip behind the head, and it was now coiled quite docilely around his wrist.

"Are you saying that adaptation does not matter?" asked Perseus.

"I am wondering, that is all," said Illingworth. "Certainly pressure to survive and breed cannot be the only factor at work in a place like this. So much depends on what is called chance. I am beginning to think we have been too hasty in assuming that Professor Darwin has uncovered the secrets of the Creator's process. There is, after all, so much we do not know."

He smiled at the little snake. "You are a beautiful creature," he said. "Perhaps that should be enough for us."

Meanwhile, the Noite wound on, and they soon decided to abandon their previous back-and-forth tactic, for though paddling directly against the current was slower and more taxing, the eddy-jumping method often brought them right under the shadows of the trees. Trees from which snakes and insects hung, on which monkeys chattered, and behind which, from time to time, they saw eyes watching them. Though, as Silva cheerfully pointed out, this would serve them as little defence against any more of the great snakes, as anacondas are aquatic.

They also began to encounter rapids. And so, despite their unease, they were more than once forced to abandon the relative security of the river in order to portage their canoes. These were gruelling, tedious, and nerve-racking affairs. They first had to find or cut a path through the jungle around the rapids – often several miles – and then to return to drag the heavy dugouts along the path, laying down branches to act as rollers.

Their greatest fear was that one of the canoes would split, which would have required them to stop and spend several days making another one. Even as it was, these portages generally took at least a day, if not more, and their progress slowed to a crawl. Wasps and venomous ants tormented them, and they had to exercise great caution to avoid the many snakes that crawled along the trail. Fortunately (though to Illingworth's disappointment), they encountered no more Red Anacondas.

About the fifth day after their battle with the anaconda, Elizabeth was sitting in the boat with Perseus, watching the jungle pass by. The banks were growing higher, the stream narrower, and it seemed to her that the jungle was wilder and more tangled than ever. As she gazed mechanically at the green wall, she suddenly gave a jump as she realized what she was seeing.

"There are people," she said, pointing. "Watching us from the trees. There was one just there, but he's gone now."

Perseus nodded.

"I saw him," he said. "But don't point. Everyone keep your guns handy," he added in a raised voice to the others. "Don't start anything, though. Just try to ignore them."

From then on they caught occasional glimpses of the tribe, watching them from the trees. They never showed themselves openly, much less attempted to make contact with the expedition, but they made their presence felt. Sometimes they could hear drums beating deep in the forest. Most of the time they were merely shadowy figures glimpsed behind trees, usually toward evening.

The expedition now set two on watch each night, and Perseus insisted on either he or Martin being one of them at all times. The sentinels sat outside the tents, rifles on their laps, scanning the trees, listening to the shrieking of the insects and the innumerable, unidentifiable night sounds of the jungle. Those off duty slept uneasily, their own weapons close at hand. Every morning, when they left camp, they would leave a few beads and other small gifts for the tribe to try to show that they were friendly. No one knew whether it worked, but at least they suffered no attacks.

Elizabeth found she was often awakened by vivid nightmares of glowing-eyed figures closing in about her. The sense of being exposed and vulnerable, partly forgotten during the day, plagued her more and more by night and robbed her of sleep. This caused her to often lay awake for hours, dwelling on horrible possibilities and wishing again and again that she hadn't so insisted on coming.

In the mornings, she sometimes smiled to remember how she had herself prophesied that it would be so. But she never complained or confessed this to the others. Having so imperiously saddled them with her presence – unwanted and unhelpful as she felt it to be – she was determined not to burden them any further. After all, she thought, it only served her right for being so stubbornly determined to push herself forward in the first place.

Then, about the twelfth day after the fight with the snake, Perseus suddenly called out and pointed to the bank. There, scarce to be seen amid the trees and tangled growth of the jungle was something black and solid.

"That's it," he cried. "I'd bet my life that's the idol that Cooper was talking about."

"Perhaps," said Martin. "Let us see."

Even in his excitement, Perseus did not forget his caution. He scanned the trees for any sign of danger before pulling alongside the bank. There was no sign of the nameless tribe, nor of the anacondas.

The idol stood on a high bank that would likely be above water even in the flooded season. It was about seven feet tall and carved of black stone in the shape of a strange, reptilian figure with a wide, grinning mouth of pointed teeth. Its base was covered in queer markings, which Bill carefully copied into his notebook for further study. The expedition made a search of the ground and found several rusting supply tins and other marks of a long-gone camp.

There was no doubt about it; they had found their point of departure.

"Cooper proved right once again," said Perseus. "Now I think we must bid the river goodbye and strike out into the jungle."

They pulled the canoes up onto the bank and hid them as well as they could, leaving a good portion of their supplies stashed inside for the return journey. Gomez and Costa were to remain with the canoes, under strict orders to have one on watch at all times and not, by any account, to offend the natives.

It was fairly late in the day when they discovered the idol, and it was decided to camp that night before beginning their overland journey in the morning. So they cleared a space and pitched their tents behind the stone idol, on the very spot the ill-fated Applegate expedition had camped some eighteen years before.

Perseus felt nearly wild with excitement. The dreary, harsh routine of a jungle expedition had subdued his enthusiasm during the monotonous days of journeying, as it often did on such trips. But now that they were nearing their goal, and indeed had confirmed that such a goal existed (for despite what he said, the idea that the valley was a myth and the diary a hoax had never quite left his mind) he felt new vigour and all the hopes that had led him to embark on this expedition returned.

He thought back to Old Joe in Istanbul and his promise of great treasures to be found, and he dared to imagine that his long journeyings might at last be coming to their end. And then...well, then he would face the next challenge: that of trying to make Elizabeth feel for him what he felt for her.

At the moment, and despite her anger having long since cooled, this seemed to him a far more daunting challenge than recovering the treasure of the Forbidden Valley.

They slept uneasily. Elizabeth found that her nightmares were worse than ever. This time they were filled with a huge, unseen creature that seemed to be stalking ever closer to her while she tried desperately to hide, knowing all the while that it would find her in the end. She woke up more than once, disoriented and soaked with sweat that had nothing to do with the tropical night.

The expedition rose early the next morning, every one of them bleary-eyed and groggy from a poor night's sleep (save Illingworth, who whistled cheerfully over his breakfast). They broke out the packs they had brought for the occasion and parcelled out the goods as suitably as they could. Perseus saw to it that Elizabeth had the lightest pack and he himself had the heaviest. Illingworth, meanwhile, insisted that they all carry a number of alcohol-filled specimen bottles so as to maximize their supply.

"Though it won't be nearly enough, I'll warrant," he said happily.

"I don't see how we can make it through the jungle with all this," said Bill, shifting his own (he thought) far too-heavy burden.

"You shall think a sore back a small price to pay if we are obliged to camp for any length of time," said Martin. "A pound of sweat today saves a pint of blood tomorrow."

"Gives you an appreciation for tortoises," said Elizabeth, adopting a cheerful tone to try to counteract her own tiredness and unease. "Poor things have to carry their whole house on their backs all their lives."

"I'm sure your Ladyship knows much of such things," said Silva.

He spoke lightly, but Elizabeth felt the shot keenly and turned away in the hopes the others wouldn't see how it had hurt.

"Alright now," said Perseus. "Everyone stick close together. Jungle like this, you can lose yourself in only a few feet. Find yourself lost, fire once into the air. You all have your guns handy? Good. Our bearing, according to Cooper, is due east."

They set out, Perseus and Silva in front with machetes to clear the way. They were followed by Illingworth, then Elizabeth, then Bill. The ever-dependable Martin served as their rear-guard.

The density of the jungle waxed and waned as they went on. Some places were so thick that they were more like hedges than wild growth forest and required the whole party to stop while they cleared their way through. Others had almost no undergrowth at all, and they marched along on the damp, leaf-strewn ground amid trees like the pillars of a living cathedral.

The ground was rising slowly but steadily as they went, climbing a far-flung outpost of the ragged rim of the Amazon basin. For a while a narrow stream went tumbling over rocks and falls beside their line of march on its way to feed the Noite. Its banks were lined with beautiful flowers of a kind none of the expedition had ever seen before. They were, perhaps, some form of orchid, though with much larger flowers and thicker petals and smelling of honeysuckle. The flowers were a remarkable variety of colours; blues, reds, whites, golds, and even some that were a velvety black. The stream snaked in and out of view for most of the morning until it finally disappeared entirely.

They marched on through the steaming jungle, stopping for rest whenever Elizabeth or Illingworth seemed to be lagging behind. Illingworth also occasionally paused to make note of the snakes and lizards they passed. Once Elizabeth's boot startled what she initially took to be a rodent, until she realized it had no tail and far too many legs and was, in fact, a giant tarantula scurrying for shelter under a tree root.

"Oh, bother," she stammered, trying to pass over the scream of fright she had just given. "Now I'll *never* get to sleep again in this jungle."

"Don't worry," said Perseus. "Their venom isn't dangerous, just painful."

"That really isn't very comforting," she answered.

Despite her misgivings, they indeed made camp on the forest floor. By then Elizabeth was tired enough to fall asleep at once, spiders or no spiders, and if any nightmares plagued her, she slept too soundly to recall them.

Bill, on watch with Martin, kept finding himself nodding off and being shaken awake by his companion.

"How on earth do you do this?" he asked the third time it happened. "You walk all day in this heat with that great bloody bag on your shoulders, then you sit up half the night."

"I do it by remembering that it is my duty," Martin answered. "Our friends are depending upon us to keep them safe, and so I stay awake to do just that."

Bill flinched a little at what he took to be a reminder of the jaguar incident. "I wish I had your will power," he muttered.

"It is not a matter of will power," said Martin. "It is merely a matter of putting myself second. That, my friend, is the secret of life: if you wish to be happy, consider yourself as little as possible."

"Sounds to me more like a good way to be walked over," said Bill.

"Quite the contrary, it is wonderfully clearing. The less you worry about yourself, the more you can see things as they are. Selfishness clouds the mind."

The next day was much the same as the first. The ground continued to rise slowly, but steadily, and the trees were occasionally less thick than before, allowing them to look back and see the jungle sloping away behind them. They didn't say much as they marched along in their wet clothes, bent under their heavy packs. Silva was now the most cheerful of the party, no doubt being used to this sort of thing. He sang a bawdy song in Spanish as they marched along, chopping their way through the undergrowth.

The third day saw the ground levelling out, which made their march mildly less arduous, though the jungle was thicker than ever. It almost seemed to be crowding about them, as though the trees were curious about these little people who had wandered into their domain. The expedition went slowly all that morning, hacking and pressing their way through the undergrowth. The only consolation was that, for whatever reason, there were comparatively few biting insects in this part of the jungle

Then, all at once, they arrived.

Perseus, in front, hacked through a particularly dense tangle of vines and vegetation and suddenly found the valley open before him, as if the ground had simply dropped away under his feet. They might have passed within a few yards of the precipice and never even known it was there, yet the edge of the cliff was so close that he instinctively grabbed the nearest tree for fear he might slip over. He gazed in wonder at the sight below.

"Lady and gentlemen," he said. "We have arrived. Careful, though; it's very abrupt."

The expedition members crowded forward, taking hold of branches and vines to steady themselves as they gazed upon the Forbidden Valley.

It appeared to be almost a perfect circle, at least ten miles across, the far cliffs dim and hazy. Perseus estimated the floor to lay about a hundred and fifty feet or more below the surface of the surrounding jungle. The cliffs overhung considerably, like the edges of a vast gourd that was curling in on itself. Just as Cooper had said, nothing but a bird could ascend from the valley to the surrounding jungle. On the valley floor directly below them was a rocky slope dotted with shrubs that ran down into a dense forest. The rest of the valley seemed to be a blend of forest and shrub-lands, lined here and there with rivers radiating out both from the centre and from a large lake far off to their right.

And in the exact centre of the valley there stood a tall, narrow pyramid that gleamed bright white against the green of the jungle. Even as they looked upon it, the sun came out and it shone as though it were made of pearl.

"Beautiful!" Elizabeth gasped.

"Amazing," said Bill. "So, this is the Forbidden Valley?"

"I never would have believed it," said Illingworth, shielding his eyes to squint at the pyramid. "That must be nearly as tall as the Great Pyramid of Egypt."

"I should say at least that," said Perseus. "Seems there have been people here, once upon a time. Might be there still are. Suppose that's one of the things we'll learn."

"Well, what are we waiting for?" said Elizabeth. "Let's get down there!"

"I entirely agree with your Ladyship," said Martin. "But we must do this carefully. We don't know what—or who—might be waiting for us."

"Very true," said Perseus eagerly. "I will go first and spy out the landing place. Martin, you will follow me, so that we can have at least one man on guard while we bring the others down. The rest will follow as they like."

This was agreeable to everyone, and they set to work clearing the brush around the cliff and breaking out the ropes and climbing gear they had carried for so many miles for just this occasion. During the planning stages, Perseus had given careful thought to how they would bring everyone down into the valley once they found it. After discussing the question with Martin, they had privately provided for a practical solution before leaving Manaus. He had already explained it to the others over the course of the journey, leaving nothing left but to implement it.

A pulley system was secured to a nearby tree. One end of the rope was tossed down into the valley, the other was arranged with a kind of basket seat in which a man could sit, or a pack could be secured. Sitting thus, a strong man might lower himself by going hand-over-hand on the other line. Meanwhile, if he were to lose his grip, those on the surface could arrest his fall by throwing a locking mechanism on the pulley.

The device had been custom made, and they had not had the opportunity to test it. But Perseus felt reasonably confident of its success. Confident enough, at least, to risk being the first to try it.

He slung his rifle over his shoulders and sat in the harness. Then, taking a firm grip on the anchor line, he began to walk down the face of the cliff.

The first part, where he could brace his feet against the stone, was not at all difficult. But, about twenty feet down, the walls drew back as the cliff overhung severely, more like the roof of a cavern than anything. Here he was obliged to abandon all support save the rope in his hands.

Hand over hand, he lowered himself, swinging back and forth in the warm breeze. As he descended, he realized that the air coming up from the valley was subtly different from that of the surrounding jungle. There was an almost sickly-sweet tang to it, as though the valley were full of honeysuckle. And there was something else; a musty, dried up kind of smell, rather like you got in an old house that has not been changed or lived in for a long, long time. The two together made a somewhat nauseous combination.

He put the problem of the air out of his mind and continued to descend. Finally, his feet touched down upon the valley floor. He stepped out of the harness, unslung his rifle, and looked about him.

It was remarkably quiet, as though the whole valley were holding its breath in awe at the visitor from the world above. It was also dark; far darker than he had expected. But of course, he was under the overhang of the cliffs, and the clouds had covered the sun once more while he was descending. The sharp white tip of the pyramid stood directly in front of him, far off and just visible over the tops of the trees, and seeming to shine even under the cover of the clouds.

Behind him, the cliffs rose in a great concave arc, like an enormous wave that had been turned to stone. Nothing much grew in that shadow besides a few shrubs. Below him lay a dark, dense forest full of creepers and moss.

Something spooked and scurried away in the undergrowth, but he only caught a glimpse of it before it disappeared. From the little he saw, he judged it to be some kind of ground fowl.

Perseus took his time looking about, identifying the places where a predator or a human hunter might hide, but seeing no sign of either. At last, while the others called to him for news, he gave the word that it was all right and sent the harness back up for Martin.

The second descent was easier, for Perseus was able to help manage the anchor line from the ground. Martin soon arrived, another rifle on his shoulders, and took up his position as sentinel.

Elizabeth came next, fairly trembling with excitement. After that Perseus called up for them to send down the packs next, and they came down one by one. Then Illingworth, then Bill.

Last of all, Silva sat in the harness and gave the word. He began to descend.

But then, before had even reached the overhang of the cliff, he suddenly stopped, holding tight to the rope.

"Anything wrong, Silva?!" Perseus called.

Silva didn't answer. Instead, he reached across to his belt, and before they quite realized what he was doing, the anchor line was cut through and came down, coiling about them like a dead snake.

There was a moment of shocked, stunned realization. Perseus held the limp end of the now-useless rope in his hand. Then, as Silva furiously hauled himself back up over the cliff, Martin raised his rifle and fired. There was a burst of dust as the bullet struck the rock, missing Silva by about a foot. Martin cycled the action, but before he could fire again, Silva disappeared over the top of the cliff.

"Silva!" Perseus roared. "You bastard!"

"What are you doing!?" Elizabeth shouted. "Come back!"

Silva's hand appeared over the edge, waving.

"Adios, my friends!" he called. And just like that, he was gone. They were trapped in the Forbidden Valley.

Chapter Ten
A Lost World

"The land which we have viewed, devoureth its inhabitants: the people, that we beheld, are of a tall stature. There we saw certain monsters of the sons of Enac, of the giant kind: in comparison of whom, we seemed like locusts."
-Numbers 13:33

For a moment after Silva's departure, the expedition members simply stood and looked at one another as the full impact of their situation came upon them.

"Damn and blast me for a fool!" Perseus growled. "I should have made him come down sooner; second or third at most. Bastard!"

"Never mind that now," said Elizabeth. "We can parcel out the blame later. What do we do?"

"If I may make a suggestion, your Ladyship," said Martin. "Our first move ought to be to make camp in a defensible location. I see what appears to be the entrance to a cave that may be suitable. Once sure of our immediate safety, we can begin to consider other plans."

This, of course, was agreeable to all. Martin took Bill with him to explore the cave at once. They soon returned to report that it was dry and fairly open, apparently not going too far back. There were signs that something had been living there one upon a time, but nothing fresh.

Once everyone was inside, Perseus made a quick survey of his own. It was a strange formation, he thought; the walls were curved and bumpy, reminding him of something that had once been liquid and hardened, though the rock was certainly not volcanic. Moreover, there didn't seem any clear outlet in the cave beside the front. It was like a huge air bubble in the rock. He wondered how it had been formed.

"Looks to me like limestone," said Bill, picking up a loose bit that had fallen from the wall and weighing it in his hands.

"At any rate, it'll do for now," said Perseus. "Only one way in or out, and a fairly good view of the approach."

They made camp and sat down in the entrance to begin tackling the all-important question of what to do about their predicament.

"We are supplied well enough for the moment," said Martin. "And I am much mistaken if this valley does not provide the means for survival. We at least needn't fear starvation."

"What I can't understand is why Silva would do it?" said Elizabeth. "We never did him any harm, and you said that he'd only try to hurt us if he thought he could benefit. But how does stranding us here benefit him?"

"My guess," said Perseus, "is that he's heard rumours of the treasures of the gods being hidden in the valley and thinks he'd like to take a crack at them. Probably he made his plans almost as soon as we told him where we were going. He did all he could to help us find the place, and now that he knows where it lies, he can come back any time he likes. He'd have had a job knocking us all off at once, but now he can simply let the valley do it for him."

"He must think it's unlikely we can survive then," said Bill in a would-be casual tone.

"This valley is supposedly the abode of monsters," Perseus reminded him. "I suppose we'll find out soon enough how true that is. In any case, if he's smart – which he is – he'll haul off to the other side of the Amazon for a few months or a year. Then come back, and whether we die here or escape won't make much difference to him as long as we're out of his way. Now I suggest we forget Mr. Silva for the moment and see what we can do about making it out of here."

"I cannot believe that the entire boundary of this valley is insurmountable," said Illingworth. "Surely there must be *some* way up, some easier slope to the cliffs, or a cavern such as this one that leads to a passage?"

"That's possible," said Perseus, nodding. "We will have to look into that. A circuit of the valley, studying the cliffs is clearly indicated. But there is something I would suggest we do first. This valley has a pyramid in the centre. Pyramids don't grow up on their own, so presumably someone made it. It's just possible someone still lives about it. Therefore, I think our first move ought to be to attempt to make contact with the locals, if there are any."

"Won't that be dangerous?" said Elizabeth.

"Yes, but I don't think there are many options available to us that don't carry that adjective," Perseus answered.

"Supposing they're savages?" asked Bill.

"No doubt they are," said Perseus. "But there are savages and savages, you know. Most people, savages or not, can be reasoned with. If we are going to be here for any length of time, it'll be best to try and make friends with our neighbours. They may be able to help us. And if they aren't willing to be reasonable, then better we find out sooner rather than later."

In the end, it was agreed to. After stashing most of their gear out of sight in the back of the cave and passing out rifles and ammunition, they set out in the direction of the pyramid.

The jungle here was much like that above, though more open than one might have expected owing to its undoubted age. Nevertheless it contained places where it was so thick with tangled bushes, branches, and vines that the expedition was obliged to find a way around rather than trying to hack through.

But they had not been in the jungle long – gone no more than a quarter mile or so – when they halted. Strange sounds were echoing through the trees; low, deep, musical notes. At first Perseus took them to be horns, perhaps the natives signalling their approach. But the more he listened, the less he thought so. There was not the mechanical, tinny note of a horn.

"It's like whale song," he said aloud. "Only deeper."

"You surely aren't suggesting whales in the jungle?" said Bill.

Perseus didn't trouble to dignify that with an answer.

"It's lovely," said Elizabeth, though she looked uneasy. "What do you think it is?"

"I haven't the faintest idea," he answered. "I've never heard anything like it."

Illingworth, meanwhile, had noticed something on the ground a little to their right. Here the undergrowth was much lighter and appeared in places to have been trampled. He bent down and examined it, then jumped up as though stung.

"No..." he said. "That is impossible."

"What is impossible, Professor?" Perseus asked.

Illingworth stared at the shape in the ground. It was the impression of a round object, studded at one end and about the size of a large serving tray.

"I will not say," he said. "Not until...quick, we must confirm this!"

"Confirm what?"

"Professor, are you all right?" Bill asked.

"Don't be ridiculous," he snapped. "Now come on! We must follow this trail!"

It was all they could do to stop the old man from running off by himself. They followed the trail of broken undergrowth, Perseus forcing them to maintain a cautious pace, though he himself was bursting with curiosity. The trail bent southward, away from the direction of the pyramid, but it seemed they were obliged to follow it at present nonetheless.

The 'song' grew louder as they went. Judging by its volume, Perseus had originally guessed the source, whatever it was, to be perhaps a quarter mile away. But it was more than double that before they at last emerged from the jungle on the edge of a large clearing and beheld the most spectacular sight any of them had ever seen.

Nine enormous animals – the largest at least sixty feet long – were grazing upon the treetops, calling to each other in those deep, musical notes. They had barrel-shaped bodies rather like those of elephants, though at least three times as big. Their small heads were set on long, thick necks balanced by equally long tails ending in flexible, whip-like structures that were constantly twirling and flicking through the air behind them. The creatures were covered in pale pinkish scales like those of monitor lizards, which darkened to crimson along their spines. Five appeared to be adults, while the other four ranged from an adolescent about half the size of the largest adult to two youngsters the size of buffalo.

The animals moved slowly, but with grace and ease and something like the soft tread of an elephant. There was nothing clumsy or awkward about them. This, coupled with their musical cries and the hypnotic effects of their flashing tails, created a queer impression. It was as though they had stepped out of reality and into a dream world.

For a moment, the expedition could only gaze in awe. Even Martin's stoicism had momentarily deserted him. He stared, wide-eyed and open mouthed like the others.

No one had to say the word 'dinosaurs.' The animals before them made it as superfluous as crying 'fire!' before an erupting volcano.

"Thank you all," said Illingworth at last in a strange, choked voice. "Thank you for bringing me to this. I...I had forgotten."

"It's impossible," gasped Bill.

"I shall never say that word again," said Illingworth. "Never. Impossible indeed! Who are we, my boy, to put a limit to the Creator?"

Elizabeth found she could hardly speak, but Illingworth had said what she had thought. All her fears, all the hardships, even the danger of their current situation and the doubt of their ever returning home – all this seemed worth it for the sake of that moment. At once she felt she was back, the rambunctious red-haired girl climbing trees and pouring over the likes of *Treasure Island* and *Tales from the Odyssey*, dreaming of far-off lands and fantastic creatures. And here she was, in a valley lost to time, gazing with her own eyes upon living dinosaurs.

Perseus was no less in awe than the others. But he also was the first to return to the matter at hand. They had already stayed there longer than was wise.

"We should move on," he said. "We don't want to be out here after dark."

"A little while longer," Elizabeth pleaded. "No one's ever seen this before."

"I know," he said. "But we will enjoy the sight more if we know we'll be able to tell someone about it."

Slowly, they dragged themselves away from the sight of the herd. The animals paid them no attention, and seemed not even to have noticed them, which suited Perseus just fine. He didn't like to think what these creatures might be capable of if aroused. He had seen what elephants did to foolish humans who invaded their space; an animal like this didn't bear thinking about.

The songs of the dinosaurs followed them into the forest as they made their way northeast toward the centre of the valley.

"Brontosauruses," said Illingworth at last, unbidden. "Or something very like them. I have seen partial skeletons dug up in

America – North America, I should say – but it is…it is quite another thing to behold such creatures in the flesh!"

"Oh, if only Mr. Charles Knight could see these!" Bill exclaimed. "He would re-do his entire portfolio!"

"You bring up an interesting point, Bill," said Illingworth. "I had noticed that the animals were substantially different in their habits than we had anticipated. Note particularly that their tails were held aloft, off the ground."

"I noticed that, Professor," said Bill. "And there seems to be nothing in the way of a swamp nearby either."

"The question, of course," said Illingworth. "Is whether the contemporary animal shares these traits with its ancient ancestors. For, of course, we must not fall into the trap of thinking that we have seen brontosaurus as it existed a hundred million years ago. This must be a totally different offshoot of the species."

"Why so?"

"Use your brains, my boy!" said Illingworth, though in a jocular tone. "*Brontosaurus Darrowi* – with your permission, Lady Darrow – is a contemporary animal, no less so than the elephant or the lion. *Brontosaurus excelsus* was a creature of the Jurassic. They are not the same. These animals have had an extra hundred million years of evolution. It seems that has done little to alter their general nature, but it cannot have done *nothing.*"

"Of course, I hadn't thought of that," said Bill.

"It is an easy mistake to make," said Illingworth kindly. "I nearly made it myself just now. It is the sort of thing that comes with training."

"I don't care what you call it or what it does to scientific literature," said Elizabeth with a sigh. "I shall never, never forget that as long as I live."

"I don't think any of us shall," said Perseus.

Illingworth suddenly gave a small gasp. "What is it, Professor?" Bill asked.

"I just had a thought," he said. "A most alarming thought."

"Well?" said Perseus.

"If a species of brontosaurus has survived," he said. "It stands to reason other dinosaur species have done the same in this valley."

"Very likely," said Bill. "And I look forward to finding them!"

"Yes, but may I remind you of what some of those species were?"

Bill thought a moment, and then his face visibly paled. "Oh!" he said. "Oh, yes. I quite see, Professor."

"You mean predators," said Perseus.

Illingworth nodded. "Some of the deadliest predators the world has ever known."

The tone of the expedition changed in an instant. They looked about them, suddenly fearful of what the jungle might contain.

"Come on," said Perseus. "No sense standing about then. But keep your eyes open and those rifles at the ready."

They pressed on through the jungle, following a zig-zag path around the thicker patches of undergrowth. In this way they proceeded for several hours, while seeing nothing but several brightly coloured birds and a few small lizards and insects.

All at once, they emerged through the brush and found themselves facing a wall. A massive, grey-blue erection of masonry, at least thirty feet high, and running in a great curve to their right and left.

"Well, what have we here?" said Perseus, feeling the brick. "More marks of humanity."

"Indeed," said Martin, examining the masonry along with him. "However, I observe that this wall is exceedingly old. Note how the bricks have shifted and worn smooth in places."

"Shows that people lived here once upon a time, at least," said Elizabeth. "I wonder who built it, and why?"

"Probably to keep the wildlife out," said Perseus.

"No doubt," said Illingworth.

Putting the wall on their left, they began to follow its line. It was comforting, at least, to know that there was one direction that no danger could come. The size of the wall, though, was intriguing. Judging by its curve, Perseus guessed it must enclose an area close to a full mile in diameter; large enough for a city. But surely this wild valley could not hold such a population as that.

For a time the trees grew right up against the wall, creepers and vines climbing the very masonry itself. After some distance, however, the forest fell back and they went along more open country. There were signs of burning here, indicating the trees had been forced back deliberately, as well as stumps of trees that had been cut down. Perseus took all this to be a sure mark of present human habitation.

A short while later, emerging around the curve of the wall, they saw a line of wooden spikes driven about the base of a small hill, upon which there stood a cluster of wooden huts roofed in leaves. The huts appeared to be rude, ill built things, centred around a tall totem pole topped with some sort of idol. But they weren't nearly close enough to make it out, nor to see the whole village.

Here they came to a halt, for now they had their first sight of the natives of the Forbidden Valley. A troop of about seven men, all carrying spears, were coming down from the village to meet them. The expedition members drew closer to one another.

"Steady," said Perseus. "Keep hold of those rifles, but don't shoot unless you have to. And watch our backs! They're likely to have friends in the woods."

The natives were a totally different racial type from the peoples of the Amazon. Indeed, they were unlike any men that Perseus had ever seen. Their skin was dead black – as dark as the darkest hues of Africa – and they were very tall and very thin. The shortest man in sight Perseus would have put at six-foot-six at least, and the chief

– so he took him to be, judging by the feathered spear and the headdress of bone – was nearly seven feet. Yet they were so narrow and compacted that they reminded him of stalks of grain. It was as though they had been squeezed in from the side, so that they had a normal man's body mass, but stretched along a narrower frame.

This narrowing effect extended to their heads, which were definitely abnormal; almost bean shaped. The skull was more oblong than round, billowing out toward the top, and the jaws and cheekbones were so compact that Perseus wondered how they could eat. Their noses too were so small as to be little more than slits in the front of their face, giving them an almost reptilian appearance.

The troop of natives halted about ten yards away and looked at the visitors with expressionless black eyes, holding their spears ready, but not aggressively. It was as though they were trying to make up their mind what they thought of these people.

After a long, tense silence, Perseus decided to open communication. Though he had slim hopes, he decided to try a few words of Guarani.

"Hello," he said in that language. "We are friends."

The natives did not react in the slightest. It was clear that for all they had understood him, he might as well have just spoken English.

"We," he said, resuming his native tongue and gesturing to the expedition. "Friends." He laid a hand on his heart and extended it to the chief.

The chief blinked slowly. He seemed to get the message, but it didn't appear to interest him much.

Suddenly a tremendous roar came from somewhere on the other side of the wall, making them all jump about a foot. It was like nothing Perseus had ever heard; deep and powerful, like thunder, but ending on a high note that was almost a hiss. The sound made his hair stand on end. Elizabeth, her nerves already on edge, actually screamed aloud. It was pure luck that no one accidentally fired.

Almost at once the chief began to speak, and Perseus, still gathering his wits, could tell that the language he used was indeed nothing like that of the Amazon peoples, nor like that of the African peoples, much less like Portuguese or Spanish. Yet, it reminded him of something, though he couldn't immediately tell what.

"Etzun Cuangi," he said. "Cuangi hetz esin dou. Exkakzoon!"

He pointed straight at Elizabeth with a long, thin finger. She flinched a little and tightened her grip on her rife.

"Did you hear that?" said Martin. "Cuangi."

"You're right," said Perseus. "Cuangi?" he said aloud to the chief.

"Cuangi!" the chief replied, pointing to the wall. "Ezago!" He pointed to Elizabeth again. "Emakoma gurria Cuangi opar."

Perseus glanced back at Elizabeth, then at the chief again. Whatever the fellow had in mind, he didn't like it.

"Apparently," he said. "You have something to do with Cuangi."

"Is that so?" said Elizabeth in a shaking voice. "That's certainly news to me."

The chief, who like Perseus recognized that speaking wasn't doing much good, pointed to Elizabeth, then made a motion as if he were drawing her to himself, then pointed to the wall. He repeated the gesture while saying, "Cuangi opar."

"My own guess is," said Martin. "That he means he wants to give Lady Darrow to Cuangi."

"Human sacrifice," Elizabeth said, swallowing hard and trying to keep her voice light. "Tell him I'd rather not if it's all the same."

Perseus shook his head and made a gesture of denial, palm out. He hoped the chief would get the message.

Apparently he did, for the chief stopped speaking and resumed his stoical silence, looking hard at the visitors for a moment. Then he pointed back to the village, raised five fingers one-by-one, then pointed to the expedition. He repeated the gesture.

"If I'm not mistaken, he is trying to buy her," said Martin. "Offering five of his own women."

"Good Lord, he is keen," Perseus muttered. "Not for sale!" he said aloud, making the same gesture of denial, more vehemently this time.

Again, the chief stared at them in silence for a moment without expression. Then, without a word or gesture from him that they could see, the warriors on either side raised their spears and charged.

The suddenness of the attack was the most dangerous part, for there was no coordination or strategy; it was a pure, direct grab, the military equivalent of a toddler reaching for the jam. Had Perseus and Martin not been there, it may have worked for all that simply because it came with so little warning, but the two men reacted at once. Their rifles cracked and two of the warriors dropped.

The survivors halted halfway between the expedition members and the chief, as though they were wind-up toys that had simply stopped working. There was no expression of fear on their faces, nor of confusion, awe, or anything else that might be expected from a primitive tribe's first encounter with firearms. Only the same blank expression that they had worn throughout.

The chief didn't flinch either. He merely studied the visitors, occasionally glancing down at the two dead men. Then, again with no visible sign from him, the remaining warriors retreated and resumed their positions beside him.

Perseus checked that they were not being flanked from the trees, then pointed from the chief to Elizabeth, then from himself to his gun to the chief again. Then, to make certain he got the message, he repeated the gesture; the chief, Elizabeth, himself, gun, chief. Then he concluded by stomping on a twig lying on the ground, snapping it in two and grinding it under his heel. The chief watched these gestures with the same stoic expression, but Perseus thought he must get the point.

"The British Empire has arrived," he said aloud. "And we don't approve of giving women as gifts to anyone or anything. You play by our rules, and we all get along, savvy?"

The chief made no sign, and Perseus thought it best that the meeting should come to an end. It had not gone well.

"Let's get back to the cave," he muttered. "Before they think to try to cut us off."

"Good idea," said Elizabeth. She was keeping very close to him, and though her voice was shaking, her rifle wasn't.

Perseus raised a hand to the chief.

"We go," he said, gesturing to the expedition and pointing away. "You do not follow." He pointed to the chief and made a gesture of denial.

The expedition backed away, half turning and keeping a close eye on the natives. Neither the chief nor his men made any move to stop them, but it was impossible to tell what they thought of the encounter, or of their departure. They merely watched, like statues, as the white people retreated into the jungle.

Chapter Eleven
Encounter by Night

"I see. The plain truth is, that I am doing nothing but make life a little bitterer for you."
-Lord Peter Wimsey, *Gaudy Night*

There was no sign of pursuit as they made their way back to the cave. Though Perseus didn't expect their camp to remain hidden for long, he was at least glad they weren't facing a battle straight away.

"Not a bad first day's work," he said, eying the setting sun. "At least they know now that we mean to be friendly, but can look after ourselves. Tomorrow I suppose we'll start looking for a way out."

They built a fire outside the cave entrance and cooked dinner. Despite the exertions of the day, no one felt much like eating. There was too much be thought about: the presence of living dinosaurs, the wall and the sound that came from within it, and the strange, stoical hostility of the natives.

"Did you catch the language they used?" said Martin.

"Not at all like the local tongues, is it?" said Perseus. "Did it remind you of anything?"

"It took me some time," said Martin. "But upon reflection, it sounded very much like Basque."

"*Basque?*" said Illingworth. "You mean to say that these people are related to the Basques of Spain?"

"There is not the least physical resemblance," said Martin. "But the language seems quite similar to me, at least from the little I know."

"How on Earth can that be?" asked Bill.

"Well," said Elizabeth. "The Basque people claim that theirs is the oldest of all languages, the original one that God smote at the Tower of Babel."

"But we are surely not taking *that* as a serious hypothesis?" said Bill.

"Perhaps not," said Perseus. "But it is curious. Next time we meet, why don't you try a little of it on them and see what happens?"

"I am afraid," said Martin. "That I do not speak it. I only recall those days we spent in Bilbao."

"Oh, yes," said Perseus, thinking back on that disastrous adventure. "I suppose it's no wonder you remember that better than I do."

"What happened?" asked Elizabeth.

"I was knocked up for most of the time," he said. "We had been doing some prospecting on the French coast – looking for a ship that went down back in the days of Cardinal Richelieu – and had to make a hasty departure. I took a nasty crack on the skull and we spent a good week or so recuperating in the basement of a church."

The expedition retired for the night soon after. Perseus volunteered to take first watch alone and let the others sleep. He wanted to think.

As he sat before the fire, gazing absently in the direction of the now-invisible pyramid, he considered their situation. Perseus had been in many a tight spot before now, and many that were, at the time, more immediately dangerous. He had, at one time or another, been locked in prison awaiting execution (twice), been adrift at sea following a shipwreck, and been lost in the trackless jungle.

Yet, for sheer hopelessness, he didn't think anything could compare with their current plight. It was not the prospect of prehistoric monsters or hostile natives or even the as-yet unseen 'Cuangi' that troubled him. As far as all that went, it was only a matter of dangerous animals and dangerous people, both of which could be managed.

No, the difference between this and all his other adventures was the element of being cut off, not just from all help, but from the world at large. Here was a simple and immovable barrier between them and any hope of safety; not even the most audacious plan or the most reckless gamble could remove those towering cliffs.

Furthermore, there was, as far as he could see, no necessary weaknesses in the valley, as there would be in a prison made for men. Nor was there the possibility even of simply moving in one direction and trusting to luck that it would lead somewhere in the end, as one might when lost at sea. They were completely walled in, and the best they could do was look for some crack in that wall. He personally saw little hope of finding one.

If it had only been himself, he would have found it a daunting prospect. As it was, he felt something more: shame. He had been the one to lead them all here, in his pursuit of gold. And in so doing, he'd involved Elizabeth. That was the end to which the long pursuit of his hopeless dream had brought them; trapped like rats at the bottom of a barrel, in the deepest, darkest jungle on Earth.

A step behind him startled him and he looked around. Elizabeth was coming out of the cave, her own rifle on her back and their tea things in her hands.

"Can't you sleep?" he asked.

"No," she said. "Too much on my mind. Thought I might as well make tea."

"That certainly can't hurt," he said.

He watched her as she set to work preparing the pot on the fire. It was, he realized, the first time since they'd met as adults that he had seen her when her hair wasn't done up. It was longer than he had expected, reaching past her waist. Though of course, he reflected, it had had plenty of time to grow lately. It flashed and gleamed in the firelight.

"That was the first time I've had anyone offer to buy me," she said conversationally as she worked.

"You think I should have bargained a bit?" he asked.

She chuckled in a nervous kind of way as she poured out the tea into tin cups. "It was...really rather frightening. I was glad you were there."

"I'm glad it didn't go any further," he said, taking the cup from her hands. "But we'll have to keep an eye on you, you know. That chief is liable to steal what he can't buy."

"As if we didn't have trouble enough," she sighed. "You were certainly right. Back in Pordesol, I mean. I really shouldn't have come. I ought to have gone back then."

He sipped his tea. "Probably," he said. "Though, if we are to be honest, I would have hated to have parted from you just then."

There was no need to say that she understood.

"Tell me honestly," she said. "Did you never get my letters? During the war, I mean."

"Certainly not," he answered. "I often wished you would write to me, but I didn't expect...well, never mind that now."

"But I must have written you a dozen times," she said. "You really didn't get one of them?"

He shook his head frowning in perplexity. Then his face cleared and he slapped his forehead.

"I'm a fool!" he said. "Of course! You addressed them to Perseus Corbett, didn't you?"

"Naturally, that being your name."

"Yes, but you see, I joined the navy under the name *Peter* Corbett. The fact is, I wasn't being strictly honest about my age and I thought 'Perseus' would be too conspicuously easy to follow up on."

"Oh!" she said in pleased surprise. "That explains it! I suppose they all went into the dead letter box at the post office, then."

"Most likely," said Perseus, nodding.

"And then after the war," she said, her voice taking on an anxious tone. "You...you left right away, did you?"

"I only stayed long enough to sell whatever my father had left me," Perseus answered. "I was back at sea by Christmas."

"And you really didn't hear about my father's death?"

He shook his head sadly.

"No, I rather avoided news from England, to be honest. Kept my distance from newspapers."

Elizabeth swallowed hard, gripping her tin cup tightly.

"I wish...I wish you hadn't lied to me," she said.

"I am truly sorry," he answered. "It was pure thoughtlessness; not because I didn't trust you. I was trying to keep you safe."

But she shook her head.

"It wasn't the expedition," she said. "Or not chiefly that. It was my medal. You said you still had it, and you don't. You...you told me what you knew I wanted to hear, because you were afraid that if you didn't, I would be angry and not have given you the money. That's right, isn't it?"

Perseus flinched under the accusation. But he could not deny it.

"That is what makes it so hard," she sighed. "Because I *want* to trust you, Perseus! I want to be able to believe the things you tell me of what you knew and didn't know, and I'm not sure that I don't. Only...only now that I know you've lied to me on something so very important, it is as if there's a little voice in the back of my mind that says 'and yet, he may still be only telling you what you want to hear.' And that means that everything else is still there, no matter what you say."

"Everything else?" he asked. "What else?"

She looked at him with a pained face.

"You don't see?" she said. "No, I suppose not. I was disappointed that you never wrote back to me during the war. But then, after the war, when my father was killed I, well, I needed someone. Someone to talk to, you know. Someone to...to save me from some of pain I was feeling. I went looking for you. I wrote, I put a bloody advertisement in the paper. And you never answered. You'd left, I suppose. Of course, I understand you had to earn your living, and I daresay I was being presumptuous to think I could summon you and all. But still, I...I needed you. And you weren't there."

He was quiet for a moment, staring into the fire. In all the times he had thought of Elizabeth during his wanderings, it had never occurred to him that such a circumstance might arise.

"I've made a bloody mess of everything," he sighed. "But I swear to you, I had no idea!"

She smiled sadly and touched the side of her head.

"I'm glad to hear that," she said. "But it's still there."

"What can I do to get rid of it?"

She made a helpless gesture.

"I don't know."

They lapsed into silence. Perseus covered his feelings by fiddling with the bolt of his rifle. Overhead, the clouds cleared and the brilliant night sky shone down on the Forbidden Valley. Elizabeth gazed up at the stars.

"I'm such a horrible person," she sighed. "In spite of everything, I'm still glad I came."

"What do you mean?" Perseus answered. "Why shouldn't you be glad you came?"

"Because I'm a burden to you all," she said. "Just a passenger. A passenger on a pleasure excursion that isn't really very pleasant."

"Nonsense," he said. "You carry your weight as well as anyone. Carrying supplies, keeping watch..."

"All things you could have done just as well without me. Better, really, since you wouldn't be constantly worrying about me in the process. In fact, if you hadn't been, you may have been more on your guard with Silva and this wouldn't have happened."

"Don't think that way!" he said sharply. "It was my fault entirely."

"Regardless, you can't deny that it was really very foolish of me to force myself on you like this."

She took another drink of tea and stirred the fire.

"The truth is," she said. "That I was jealous."

"Jealous?" he answered in surprise. "Of whom?"

"You, of course," she said. "You've gone and done all the things we talked about. Meanwhile, I've spent the last ten years trying to avoid having horrible things said about me in the newspapers. I'm not brave or adventurous at all. I'd often promised myself I would go somewhere – join an expedition to Syria, or India, or somewhere like that – but then another article would come out calling me a useless drain of resources who fritters away her money while the poor starve, or something of the sort and I just couldn't face up to it. Not that it ever stopped them, of course; they'd say horrible things no matter what I did."

"Bastards," Perseus said. "Ought to mind their own business."

She smiled weakly.

"But if you knew they were going to say it anyway," he added. "Why not go and enjoy yourself?"

"Because at the very least I didn't want them to be *right*," she answered. "I thought that feeling that I was vindicating everything they said about me would have sucked all the joy out of it." She turned her face back to the stars. "I suppose I'm glad at least to find that it doesn't."

"Don't be ridiculous," he said.

"But they are right," she said. "I *am* rather useless."

"Use!" he growled. "There's too much worry about *use* these days. Damn it, you think I've been chasing around the globe for half my life looking for something *useful*? Useful is what you call a tool or a machine. No one should aspire to be useful, least of all you."

"Oh?" she said turning to him in some surprise. "And what should I aspire to be?"

"Valuable," he said. "Which you already are. I have it on good authority you're worth at least five ordinary girls."

She gave a faint chuckle.

"Truly, though," he said. "What do we value most in the world? Hammers, wrenches, cranes? Not at all. Paintings and sculptures and fine clothes and jewels. Things that are no use to anyone, but we love them because they're beautiful and meaningful and irreplaceable. Just like you."

The last words slipped out before he realized what he was saying. Elizabeth flushed a little in the firelight and took another gulp of tea. For a while, they sat and watched the stars without speaking. Then Elizabeth turned to him and opened her mouth as though to say something.

But she never got started. Her eyes darted suddenly from his face to something over his shoulder, and she screamed. Perseus whipped around, rifle at the ready, and saw something....

Something huge, dark, and fast was charging up the hill. He fired, and the thing roared, but didn't slow down. He pushed Elizabeth back into the cave, overturning the tea things as the monster came upon them.

Perseus seized the end of a log from the fire and thrust it before him. He had a glimpse of a horrible, reptilian face cast in sharp, jagged shadows before the flames, deep blue with bony red ridges over the eyes. The monster roared again, shying away from the fire. Then there was another gunshot as Martin fired over Perseus's head. He saw the bullet drive into the brute's shoulder, but with little apparent effect. It snarled again, turned away, and darted back into the jungle.

"Are you all right?" Elizabeth gasped, rushing to Perseus's side.

He nodded. "You?"

"Fine," she said, looking pale. "What in God's name was that?"

"Allosaurus," said Illingworth, his glasses askew. "Or something very like it. Those ridges over the eyes...the well-developed forelimbs...one of the most vicious creatures imaginable. Or so we guess from the fossil record."

"Your guess seems confirmed," said Perseus. "At least it's not so fond of fire."

He was disturbed by how close the monster had gotten before Elizabeth had seen it. Despite its size, it seemed capable of moving with great stealth.

"Settles your question about the predators," he said. "And the sooner we get out of this valley, the better."

Chapter Twelve
Further Excerpt from the Diary of Bill Little

Yet, I can well imagine that the day may come when we may be glad that we were kept, against our will, to see something more of the wonders of this singular place, and of the creatures who inhabit it.
-Sir Arthur Conan Doyle, *The Lost World*

September 26th

I never before understood why men would venture out into unknown, dangerous places with, it seemed to me, little other object than to see what was there. Why do men climb mountains, or try to reach the South Pole? Why did men sign up for Sir Earnest Shackleton's mad effort to cross Antarctica, or spend their lives hunting in Africa and Asia?

Yet, from the events of these past two days, so thick with both wonder and disaster, I think I do know now. On the one hand, the thought of never seeing my dear Frances again is almost too bitter to contemplate, and the hopelessness of our situation presses upon my soul like a weight. But on the other, I have never felt that my life was worth so much or my spirit so exulted as now, when I have seen and done such things.

My eyes have beheld the great monsters that once ruled the earth: the dinosaurs. Probably no white men but ourselves, and those of the unhappy Professor Applegate's party, could say the same. It is like peering back behind the curtain of God's workshop to gaze upon earlier models now long discarded. What is life for, if not to acquire such moments?

But I wander. See what this experience has done to me already? I am astonished to find such thoughts coming from my pen.

Mr. Corbett has not despaired of escaping this valley, and today we began a search – which I now believe will prove futile, for reasons I shall relate – for a way out of the valley through the many caves that pepper the cliffs.

I must say, this valley is an extremely odd geological formation. It is as though a circular segment of the jungle, perhaps ten miles across, simply sank some two hundred feet straight down. But I shall return to this point in its proper place.

Of course, this part of the jungle was on considerably higher ground from most of the Amazon basin, so that I believe we are still well above the level of the Noite itself, for all that good that does us. The cliffs overhang in most places, and as I say are honeycombed throughout with round holes or caves, though I hesitate to use the latter word as none of them extend back more than about thirty feet.

We broke camp early in the morning, about daybreak, and set out working our way southward around the valley's rim (that is, anticlockwise), with the far-off point of the pyramid on our left.

There was little in the way of jungle on the rim; too much rock and not enough sunlight, I suspect. That is not to say the going was easy, though. The ground was broken, rough, and covered in tangled thorns that gripped at your ankles and tripped you up like a snare if you weren't careful. I tripped more than once, and Professor Illingworth bashed his knee quite badly, so that I was worried for a time whether he would be able to continue. We've provided him a stout stick to ease his discomfort.

By noon we had explored at least a dozen of those honeycombs, as we have come to call them. As I say, none of them are especially large, though some have side chambers that seemed to have bloomed off of the central core. A number of them were occupied. The first such of these we encountered held a pair of small, badger-like mammals that neither I nor Professor Illingworth could identify, but which were as vicious and unrelenting as an African honey badger.

By some cruel twist of fate, the creatures fixed on me as their chief malefactor and pursued me away from the cave until I was obliged to scurry up a boulder and have them screech at me for several minutes while they tried to claw their way up the side of the rock. All this time the others, I am sorry to say, merely stood back and laughed. Why the creatures should target me simply because I was the first in the cave and leave the others alone, I can't think.

While they were so occupied, the Professor was able to observe that these creatures laid eggs and had a clutch of them in their cave, which partly explains their savagery. He has also named them *Galictis Littlei*, which I can't help feeling was in bad taste.

Needless to say, after this experience we approached each new cave with considerably more caution. We met several more of the egg badgers, though thankfully without inciting their wrath (not that it wouldn't do Corbett or Halritter or the Old Man some good to have one of those monsters at his heels to see how funny he thought it).

Most interesting of all were the honeycombs which contained what I can only describe as mated pairs of dinosaurs. They were of a light, birdlike species, perhaps six or seven feet long, bipedal, and with strong grasping forelimbs. The Professor identified them, hesitantly, as a species of Ornitholestes. They had built a nest in the cave – I suppose all creatures in this valley use the caves for such purposes if they can, which means it was jolly good luck that the first one we found was uninhabited – and were brooding over a clutch of eggs.

Or rather, one, which I shall take the liberty of identifying as the female, was brooding. The male stood by, and when he saw us he made a fearsome display of displeasure, baring his pointed teeth, flexing his claws, and making little darts at us. It seemed quite as fearless as the egg badgers, and just as willing to give its life in defence of its mate and young.

This struck me forcibly, for I had never anticipated such behaviour in reptiles. Though, of course, crocodilian mothers *do* protect their young in the first years of life – and savagely too – but they do not form mated pairs. It seems that dinosaurs – or at least some species of them – do. Whether they did so a hundred million years ago is, of course, another question, one to which we are unlikely to ever know the answer.

We did, however, find several empty caves, and these we explored thoroughly without success. At no point did we discover anything that might even possibly be a way to the surface.

I had high hopes for one particular cave, from which a stream was flowing (we've now come across several of these, this being the first). I thought for sure that erosion from the stream must create a passageway of some kind. But we found instead a vertical chute down which a faint trickle of water dripped to feed a large pool, which overflowed into the stream. Mr. Corbett attempted to ascend some way up this passage, but found that it soon became nothing more than a few cracks in the rock. It seems that water soaks down through the soil overhead, passes through chinks in the limestone, and finally comes to swell the pool in the cave.

This led to yet another discovery, which I must note with care. Where the water ran down over the back wall of the honeycomb, it had worn away the limestone, and instead trickled over smooth, dead white stone. It was more like tile than anything. We did not especially note this at the time, but it later proved highly significant.

We concentrated our efforts on these caves from which streams flowed, thinking that if water were coming in from above, that must surely create some kind of passage sooner or later. But we had no such luck; every one of them was much the same, and had the same pale stone revealed against the flow.

About noon we had our daily downpour, and so we paused in one of those unoccupied honeycombs to rest, take a meal, and watch the rain falling outside. And I must pause to say how refreshing it was to watch the rain fall from a sheltered place once again. I had almost forgotten that a good rain can be pleasant, if one has a dry place in which to watch its fall. The smell of the damp ground and leaves was really quite lovely, even mixed with the queer sickly-sweet smell of the valley air. The low songs of the brontosaurs rolling across the valley blended with various hoots and cries from we-knew-not-what-animal made for an eerie counterpoint to the rolling thunder.

This particular cave appeared to have held its own watercourse until recently, for there was a low, stagnant pond at one end, and once more the pale stone was exposed.

"Professor," said Corbett while we ate. "Do you know what kind of stone that is?"

"I am no geologist," the Old Man answered. "I really would not know where to begin classifying it."

"Curious, isn't it, that we've found it in every cave so far? At least, every one where the stone has been stripped away."

"Yes, I suppose it is," the Professor said without much interest. Halritter, however, looked up.

"You have some idea, then?" he asked.

"No, not an idea," said Corbett. "Only a sense that it is strange. It doesn't seem to me to fit somehow. As a matter of fact, this whole valley doesn't fit."

"What do you mean by that?" I asked.

"I can't quite say for sure. Just something about it strikes me as odd."

"You mean apart from the dinosaurs, the deformed natives, and the mysterious pyramid guarded by a wall and an unseen mythical beast?" Lady Darrow asked dryly.

"Well, yes," he said with a faint laugh. "Something even apart from those. I don't mean anything *in* the valley; I mean the valley itself. It struck me the moment I set eyes on it. It is...well, it doesn't fit."

"I felt the same," said Halritter. "It is not part of the scheme, as it were."

"Do you know," said Lady Darrow. "I think I know what you mean. It didn't strike me before, really, but now that you mention it, there *is* something off about this place. Like you say, it doesn't...*fit*. Not, um, not quite natural."

"That's it!" Corbett exclaimed. "You've hit it. The valley doesn't appear to me to be a natural formation."

"Nonsense," I said. "What else could it be?"

"That is exactly the question," said Lady Darrow. She looked excited, her lovely hazel-green eyes sparkling with delight. "What else *could* it be?"

"I believe we may be going too fast," said Halritter.

"Quite," said the Old Man. "I am still in the dark as to what you think is wrong with the valley."

"To begin with, it is too symmetrical," said Corbett. "Almost a perfect circle."

"One does get such coincidences in nature," said the Old Man.

"True. But that raises the question of how it formed in the first place. It wasn't cut by a river, surely. It appears as though it simply dropped out of the land around it."

"The crater of an extinct volcano, perhaps. Or of a meteor impact."

"Quite true, quite true," said Lady Darrow. "Those are possibilities."

"Yes..." said Corbett. "They may account for it. Must have happened a deuced long time ago, though, with the dinosaurs. So why it hasn't filled in or fallen in over the years?"

"You have me there," said the Old Man. "Though if it were somehow artificial, as you seem to suggest, that question would still remain."

"So it would," said Corbett. He tapped his lip with the end of his fork, thinking. His eyes rested on the pale stone.

"But this stone bothers me as well," he said. "We keep finding it, and nowhere have I seen a single crack in it. Now that is not natural, is it?"

"N-no," said the Old Man slowly. "No, one would expect at least some fracturing, even in the hardest stone. But then again, we have not seen much of it, have we?"

"All the more reason to wonder that we keep finding it," said Corbett. "And always at the back, a little below the surface..."

Then, as though struck by an idea, he set his plate aside, seized a pick from his bag, and went to the limestone wall of the cave at the other end from the pond. He struck it hard, making a deep crack, and chipped away until, only about eight inches into the wall, the pale stone was revealed again.

"There you have it," he said. "I suspect we shall find it in the back of *every* cave in the valley wall. In fact, this *is* the valley wall."

He drew the pick back and struck the pale stone as hard as he could. The pick rebounded in his hand, but there was not even a chip in the stone. He struck twice more, but then had to stop as the pick head was beginning to bend. Not so much as a crack or scratch in the stone was to be seen.

"My God," said the Old Man, running his hand over the exposed stone. "I've never heard of rock *that* hard before. It's like diamond."

"Then I suppose that's the end of finding a passage up," said Lady Darrow. "If it really does run all the way around the valley, I mean."

"Not quite, your ladyship," said Halritter. "Assuming that this substance is the valley wall, there is still a chance – slight though I confess it to be – of finding a vertical water passage."

"True," said Corbett. "In any case, there seems no reason to stop looking. After all, it isn't as though we have an engagement elsewhere."

"I should say," said the Old Man, still following his own train of thoughts. "That this would lend credence to the meteor theory. An object formed, perhaps, of some element unknown on this planet strikes the Earth, liquifies on impact, then solidifies around the rim of the crater. Explains why the boundaries haven't fallen in at least."

"Seems a mite smooth and even for that, Professor," said Corbett. "But I suppose it's possible."

"Could it also explain the cliffs and the honeycombs?" I asked, struck by a sudden idea.

"How do you mean?" asked the Professor.

"It would be like stalactites in a cave," I said. "The pale stone solidifies in place, and water drips down the surface. Over millions of years, limestone collects on it, building outward rather like mould. But the water courses naturally alter as they follow the changing surface – hence honeycombs. That is, the caves were not carved *out* of the rock, the rock formed *around* them."

The Old Man, I was pleased to find, did not dismiss this theory at once. He looked about the cave thoughtfully, then said, "From what I understand of the subject, I suppose that is possible. We must make careful documentation and consult with a trained geologist to say for certain. But that is a most interesting theory, Bill, and I commend you on it."

It was the most complimentary thing he had ever said to me. Oh, dearest Frances, I really think he might be warming!

I am writing this while we wait for the rain to stop. At least, I hope we will not resume our journey until then. It is uncomfortable enough without walking in a downpour.

Chapter Thirteen
Continued From the Diary of Bill Little

"We are accustomed to look upon the shackled form of a conquered monster. But there you could look upon a thing monstrous and free."
-Marlowe, *Heart of Darkness*

It has been quite a day since I wrote the above.

We did not, in fact, have to wait long before the rain stopped and we were able to resume our journey around the rim of the valley.

The point of that pyramid keeps winking in and out of sight over the trees. I don't know why, but I don't like it. It feels almost as if something were watching us from that pale, distant peak...but I must not grow morbid. Lord knows there's enough danger already without imagining things.

We had not gone far before we passed by a field of tall ferns. I hardly paid it any mind, until Halritter suddenly tapped me on the shoulder.

"Look," he said.

I paused to look, and so did the others. But I couldn't tell what we were supposed to see; the field appeared deserted of animal life.

Then there was a low, quick whistle and something moved in the corner of my vision. But when I looked, there was nothing there.

"My goodness!" the Old Man exclaimed. "Do you see them?"

"No," I said, but Lady Darrow said "Yes!" at the same time.

"What are they?" asked Corbett. "Look like some kind of bird to me."

Then I underwent an abrupt reversal of perception. What I had taken to be a tall stalk of some green plant suddenly blinked and ducked down below the surface of the ferns.

"I saw it!" I exclaimed.

"Keep your voice down!" the Old Man hissed. "You'll spook them."

Another head popped up with a quick whistle, not unlike that of a songbird, and I was able to get a better look at it. It was very well camouflaged, with dark, mottle green scales and black markings rather like a leopard's that broke up its outline. All that was presently visible was a beaked head with enormous black eyes perched on a long, flexible neck. It turned this way and that, evidently scanning for predators. It whistled twice and I could see the throat jumping as it made the sound. A moment later, another head popped up and the one I had been watching ducked back down amid the ferns.

"Much like a herd of giraffe," said Corbett. "One keeps watch while the others eat."

Bit by bit, I was able to make out more of the animals. Their backs rose a little above the ferns, though as they had the same leopard-pattern on their backs as their heads, and the green of their scales was the exact colour of the ferns, it was difficult to fixate on them. They seemed to be bipedal, with long, flexible tails sticking out behind them for balance. At one point, one of them moved into a position where I could observe that it had well-developed forelimbs, which it used to gather ferns to its mouth.

"Species of Ornithomimus, I should say," muttered the Old Man. "Wonderfully well camouflaged! And note the herding instincts..."

At that moment, the sentinel suddenly gave a particularly loud, sharp whistle, almost exactly like that of a policeman. Seven or eight heads rose at once, turning this way and that in the way a flock of birds will when startled, as each tries to get its bearings. Then there was another whistle, and all at once the whole herd took off into the jungle, bounding and leaping over obstacles to vanish into the trees.

But they had not gone before I observed something that I would never have believed. I doubt I should even have recorded it had not the others confirmed that they saw the same thing. As the creatures ran, their markings changed. It was as if their spots were flowing off them like water, or like passing shadows. The whole herd seemed almost to shimmer out of sight as they moved, so that the eye had a devil of a time following them.

"By Jove, no wonder their camouflage is so good!" exclaimed the Old Man. "They're like chameleons...no, better than chameleons. Like cuttlefish. Not only can they change their colour, they can do so continually and while in motion."

"Yes, unlike leopards, they *can* change their spots," said Corbett. "Devilishly useful."

"What I wouldn't give to get those skin samples under a microscope!" the Professor sighed.

"What concerns me," said Halritter, "is what scared them?"

That brought a chill upon us all. We eyed the trees at the edge of the fern grove with deepest suspicion, but whatever it was didn't show itself.

"Probably caught a scent," said Corbett. "Might even have noticed us. They must have marvellous eyesight."

He kept a good grip on his rifle all the same.

"Come on," he said. "Best not stay around here."

We kept a careful watch at our back as we went, but no predators appeared to be following us. My own thoughts were full of the monster we glimpsed last night – the allosaurus. If one of those should take a mind to hunt us out here in the open....

"Mr. Halritter," I asked as we walked, trying to keep my voice casual. "Just how powerful are these rifles?"

"This is a .30-06 Mauser Sporter," he said. "Sufficient, I should say, to take down most large game."

"So, a tiger, say, or a bear?"

"Yes," he said, though in a hesitating kind of way. "Mr. Corbett and I have hunted tigers in India and have also had encounters with the grizzly bear of Wyoming. I have seen firsthand what this weapon can do to such creatures."

"It stops it, then?"

"Yes. Eventually."

"What do you mean eventually?"

"You must understand how a rifle works," he said. "It sends a projectile into the animal, causing tissue damage and loss of blood."

"Yes, I understand that."

"Then you must understand that, unless it hits *vital* tissue, such as the heart or brain, the bullet will not kill immediately. It may not kill at all. It all depends on what it hits and how much blood is lost."

"So, a creature like what we saw last night..."

"I should say it was entirely possible to kill such an animal with this weapon," said Halritter. "Large as it is and strong as it is, it could not live without the heart or brain. Though I should not attempt a brain shot, as I am sure the skull would deflect the bullet, unless it were fired through the eye or the open mouth."

"Then, a shot to the heart would kill it?"

"Very likely, provided it did not deflect off the ribs and provided the scales and muscle mass did not stop the bullet before it penetrated deep enough."

I thought about this. The odds of actually stopping such an animal with the weapons we had seemed to be vanishing rapidly.

"So," I said lowering my voice even further. "What will we do if one of them attacks us?"

"We shall do what we are able," he answered. "And trust to God for the rest."

His confidence, or rather his calmness, astonished me. He had all but admitted that these weapons would probably do us no good against those monsters, and yet he still seemed perfectly tranquil and resolved. How he managed it, I can't imagine.

Not long after, Corbett suddenly signalled for us to stop. He raised his rifle and scanned the trees. My mind still full of allosaurs, I didn't immediately see what had alarmed him.

"Clear off!" he shouted suddenly, making me jump and nearly causing me to fire. "I told your chief what would happen if he didn't drop the idea. Now go on! Shoo!"

I lowered my gaze and saw them. Two of the tall, grotesquely thin natives were crouched behind the trees, watching us. They were gripping bows, but seemed unwilling to try to shoot at us. For a moment it was as if they hadn't heard or understood him. But then, without a word or change of expression, they turned and melted back into the forest.

"Seems they haven't given up," said Lady Darrow with, I think, really admirable pluck. "I call that a compliment."

She was gripping her rifle rather tightly and staying close to Corbett all the same.

"At least they've learned to be afraid of these rifles," he said. "I suppose as long as they know we know they're out there, they'll think twice about actually *trying* anything."

We moved on. The cliffs became slightly less overhung as we rounded the southern tip of the valley, and I think I had some hopes that perhaps an ascent might become possible. However, this also meant that the trees came up right to the edge of the cliff, obliging us to leave the relatively open, rocky ground we had been following to pass through the tangled, twisted jungle. Trees grew right up against the rock face, and sometimes even out of it. Vines and creeping plants snaked up the sides. The green growing things of the forest appeared to my mind to be clawing at the cliff, as though they too were seeking an escape from this terrible valley.

The closeness of our surroundings worked horribly on my nerves, aided by the reminder of the native threat on top of that of predators. I wondered how the others could stand the suspense. So, in an effort to keep myself calm, I began to whistle a cheery tune. I don't see how any man could have done otherwise, and I think it really shows good sense and courage on my part to do anything so calm and contrary in such surroundings. Certainly no one objected at first.

I was, as I saw, near the back of the party, alongside Mr. Halritter. And so, we were the first to notice anything. It was not much; just a soft crunching kind of sound from behind and to the left. I stopped whistling, and Halritter and I turned about to see if we could determine what it was.

But we saw nothing. I certainly didn't. Who could in such a jungle? So, we moved on, and I resumed my tune with rather more jauntiness to try to counteract the unease I felt. But we hadn't gone far when we heard it again, and this time something else; like a single, heavy breath.

Again we turned around, and again I saw nothing...at least, not at first. But Halritter did.

"Run for it!" he shouted. "Get to shelter!"

That is when I saw the red crests amid the shadows, and the blue-black bulk of the allosaurus, hardly to be discerned in the gloom under the trees. The dinosaur charged a second later. We ran for it, making for the cliff wall. By the grace of God, there was a honeycomb nearby, with a small entrance. Lady Darrow, Corbett, and the Old Man disappeared like rabbits down a burrow, and I was just behind them. It's a mercy none of our packs became caught!

We ran straight up against the far wall, then turned to see the huge, hideous head and foreparts thrusting in after us, filling the whole entrance. It glared with its evil, elliptical eyes and snarled, showing teeth the size of steak knives; great, yellow, curved teeth. Its hot breath, smelling of rotten meat blew against us. I could see the nostrils dilate as it sniffed.

Lady Darrow raised her rifle, but Corbett put a hand on it. I couldn't at the moment understand why, but then, my mind was not working properly. Of course, the brute couldn't possibly squeeze its entire bulk into the cave after us, and it would be senseless to waste ammunition.

Indeed, the allosaur only glared in at us for a few moments, then withdrew. With a roar of frustration, it returned to the forest.

There was a rather long silence as we all tried to catch our breath.

"Bill," said Corbett. "Kindly refrain from whistling in the future."

I was confused at the connection and said so, though I don't recall my exact words. I was too frantic with the recent fright.

"Those other dinosaurs, the ornithomimi, they were whistling as well. I suspect that the allosaurs associate the sound with prey."

There is little to tell of the next few hours. The allosaurus had gone, and we saw nothing but a few birds, snakes, and more of the egg-badgers. The Old Man insisted on cataloguing every one of them. I expected that he would have forgotten about such small, commonplace animals in the light of all that had happened, but not so. The snakes were all new species as far as we could tell; a brightly coloured viper with extra-long and thick fangs (no doubt for puncturing dinosaur scales), and a rather jolly little striped colubrid (and as I've already written extensive descriptions of them for the Old Man, I am not going to repeat those here).

About five o'clock or so we came to the shore of the lake, which lies across one curve of the valley's perimeter, covering perhaps two square miles, perhaps a little more in a roughly half-moon shape. Some two hundred yards from where we stood on the shore a great waterfall plunged over the rim of the cliffs to feed it. It had cut a deep gash in the valley wall, and even from this distance we could see that it flowed down a sheer face of pale stone rising all the way to just below the line of cliffs. This lent further credence to our suspicion of the strange substance making up the whole wall of this accursed valley.

The lake, of course, meant that we will now be obliged to leave the relatively open and uninhabited perimeter of the valley and strike through the jungle itself. It was unanimously decided to put this off until the morning.

And so we have made our camp in a small honeycomb overlooking the shore. This one, I am thankful to say, contained neither any ornitholestes nor egg-badgers.

We are able, from our position, to observe the animals of the valley as they come down to drink; yet another experience that I confess to have been worth many, many pains, and my sketchbook has had nearly half of its remaining pages filled. There was a small herd of the ornithomimi, if not the very same one we saw this afternoon, which allowed us to observe their build and their remarkable colour-changing abilities better than we had been able to before. When obliged to go into the open, which they evidently didn't like, they adopted a muted grey colouring bedecked with continually shifting spots and stripes. Their motions were quick and bird-like; not at all like coldblooded animals. I suspect their metabolism is much closer to an ostrich than to a chameleon. This accounts for the restless shifts in colour, as no doubt the relevant muscles and blood vessels are working constantly.

Even more interesting was a small herd of iguanodon. Or so the Professor identified them after some considerable thought, as their stance and build was quite different from any reconstruction I had seen. It was not until he used a set of field glasses to confirm the presence of the distinctive thumb-spike that he was sure. The herd consisted of four adults and two youngsters. They walked on all fours, with their tails sticking back up into the air, but every now and again one would rise onto its hind legs and look about it, suggesting they were partly bipedal.

They were rather like huge, reptilian cows to my mind, with much the same air of stupid placidity. Their scales were brick-red, with white stripes along their backs and pale undersides, while their beak-like mouths were lined with white bands. As Corbett said, this made them look as though they had just had a good drink of milk and hadn't wiped the resulting moustache off.

A fat, saw-backed stegosaurus came down soon after; no mistaking *that* creature. It reminded me of a hippopotamus in its movements, both the heavy tread and the contrasting impression of being much nimbler than its bulk would have suggested. It was a dull, bluish-grey in colour, dotted with white spots, while its plates were a riot of warm colours; reds and yellows and violets. It was as if the animal were carrying a set of kaleidoscopes on its back. No doubt, as the professor said, that was meant to warn off predators. The animal's long tail, ending in four massive spikes, was gently sweeping the air behind it, almost as if it had a mind of its own.

The stegosaurus at once bent its beaked snout down to the water, seemingly unconcerned of its surroundings. But the iguanodons were sitting up on their hind legs, eyeing the massive herbivore with unease. They soon retreated back into the jungle. It seems that even other herbivores know to give that animal a wide berth.

The most exciting part of the evening, however, happened just as the sun was going in. Two great allosaurs came down to drink together. This gave us our best look so far at these animals, and fearsome as they were, they were also quite magnificent. They were a rich, royal blue, fading to black underneath, with red crests over their eyes. The larger, which the Professor took to be the male, was crowned with large crests flecked with gold, while the female's were smaller and of a dull crimson. They remained close together, one drinking while the other stood on watch.

"A mated pair, perhaps," said the Old Man. "This seems to be the pattern with dinosaurs, or at least the predatory species."

Then, once they had drunk, they did something I would never have expected. The female nuzzled the male under the chin, and then proceeded to do the same all along his flank. At the same time, he performed a similar exercise along hers. It was, unmistakably, an affectionate, nay, a *romantic* action.

"What on earth are they doing?" asked Lady Darrow.

"I should say they're grooming each other," said the Professor excitedly. "Cleaning off parasites or other irritants. Look, you can see their jaws working, filtering along the scales. Amazing! I never would have thought it in such animals!"

Nor had I. The tenderness which these monsters showed toward one another made for a startling image. I thought of you, Frances, while I was sketching the scene, and I can only hope I have captured some of the magic for your sake.

Once they had finished grooming each other, the allosaurs wadded out a little ways into the lake and plunged their heads into the water, apparently to clear off any remaining parasites. Then they emerged and shook themselves all over. Just before they returned to the forest, the male leaned over and nipped affectionately at the female, exactly as if he were giving her a swift kiss.

I don't know why, but somehow in that moment everything became clear to me. These animals, these great beasts, they did not dither about what they desired or wonder about how they were to acquire it. These monsters knew exactly what they were, and that knowledge made them free. Not for them the doubts, the second-guessing, the uncertainty of what one is to do with one's life; they saw what was needed and threw all their awesome strength at it.

And here was I, in the most absurd way, hopping about the jungle because I hadn't had the sense to do the same.

My dear, darling Frances, how right you were! What a bloody, silly little coward I have been, not to stand up for myself sooner. I might have been married to you already if I had. Though I suppose then I may never have gone on this expedition, and so would have missed such wonders as we have seen. How curious! This has been the worst few weeks of my life, this very day I was pursued by a prehistoric monster, and even now I am not sure whether I shall ever see my beloved again. Yet, I actually question whether I would have preferred to miss the experience! My uncle the vicar used to tell me that God permitted evil in order to bring good out of it. I used to think that was nonsense, but now I wonder whether there might not be something to be said for it.

What a strange world it is!

There is but one other thing to say. I would not ordinarily mention it, but damn it, I shall! I shall speak my mind. Why shouldn't I?

While we were watching the above scene of those two tremendous animals tenderly attending to each other, I happened to glance over at Corbett. I saw that he was looking, not only at the animals, but also at Lady Darrow. There was such an expression on his face as I can only call desire. It was as though the romantic scene before us had brought *her* to his mind, as it brought you, Frances, to mine.

Thinking back, I have noticed this more than once in our journey, though I did not then credit my own observations. I have come to think rather highly of Mr. Corbett, despite his past duplicity, and I suppose in our current predicament one may be tempted to lose sight of propriety, but this really astonishes me. He must understand that, though we are in the jungle, she is yet a baroness of a very ancient family and he is no gentleman. To entertain such thoughts merely because Lady Darrow is, at present, in a position of distress I would call most unmanly.

These suspicions are painful to me, as I have the greatest respect for Lady Darrow and I like Mr. Corbett very much. I know his character is not the best, but I would be very sorry to think so ill of him. But I must not judge too harshly. I may be mistaken. Anyway it may be nothing but a hopeless inclination on his part, which he shall keep within its proper bounds. Certainly it would be understandable, given her manifest charms.

But that is neither here nor there. I close, as always, thinking of you, dear Frances, and praying that tomorrow may reveal a means by which I may return to you.

Chapter Fourteen
By Swamp and Lake

"Wherefore Christian was left to tumble in the Slough of Despond alone; but still he endeavoured to struggle to that side of the slough that was still further from his own house and next to the wicket-gate."
-John Bunyan, *The Pilgrim's Progress*

Bill was really a very good sort of boy, and had a genuine, disinterested care for all his companions, particularly Lady Darrow. He had always thought that she ought never to have come, and consequently had a chivalrous desire to see that she suffered as little from her poor decision as possible. He thought all that night about how he might best head off the danger he suspected, and in the morning decided that he could do no better than to confide his fears to Martin. He had come to have a very high opinion of the Austrian's judgment and it had long since seemed natural to apply to him for advice.

And so, when they set out the next morning, he hung back a little and shared what he had observed and suspected with him as soon as he was tolerably sure they wouldn't be overheard

Martin, however, seemed uninterested in the matter. "Do you really think that is any of your concern?" he asked.

"Not exactly," Bill admitted. "But I do have a strong regard for Lady Darrow, as well as for Mr. Corbett. I just want to make sure he doesn't, well, do anything foolish."

"Supposing that Mr. Corbett were drawn to her, and even in love with her. Why would that be foolish?"

"Good God, man! I know he is your friend, but surely you can see that a...well, a fellow like that and a fine noblewoman like her, it...it would not be practical. And I'm sure it would be most painful to her."

Martin considered this.

"I shall tell you," he said. "I have as high a regard for propriety as you can, my boy. As I have told you before, I passed my childhood and youth in service to a gentleman of most unquestioned nobility. And I will tell you this now: having now spent several years with him, and I believe that Mr. Corbett is as much a gentleman in truth as she is a lady."

Bill stared at him.

"You will please not mention this to either of them, but it is so," he said. "He lacks title and money, of course, but so do all noble families to begin with. She is the flower of an oak; he is a sapling. I believe they would do quite well together."

If Martin retained any caveats or doubts on that assertion, they were not to be read on his face.

Meanwhile, the expedition skirted the edge of the lake, keeping in sight of it as much as possible, while a ridge of rising ground some distance to their left blocked the pyramid from view. In most places the trees grew thick right to the shoreline, and it was often a challenge to find a dry route through. The heavy air was alive with the sounds of insects, birds, and the periodic lowing and growling of dinosaurs from far off. Mosquitoes the size of humming birds buzzed in clouds about them, obliging them to wear netting which the insects attempted to push right through. They caught sight of several of the ornitholestes perched in the trees, watching them pass with a kind of contemptuous curiosity, as though they were bemused by the idea of these obviously unprepared strangers penetrating their domain.

Before long they were mud-stained, tired, and driven nearly mad by the insects. Even Illingworth had stopped noticing the snakes, frogs, and lizards scooting about in the undergrowth. The ground was growing more swamp-like by the minute, and in places they were more wading than walking. It was miserable work, and Perseus was beginning to wonder whether they ought not to turn back and seek a dryer route when something quite terrible happened.

Martin, as usual, was acting as their rear-guard. As such he was able to see the difficulties the others ran into and more or less avoid them. So, when Bill stepped onto what appeared dry ground but turned out to be particularly deep mud with a layer of moss on top, Martin stepped nimbly aside onto a solid patch of earth to avoid the same trap.

As he did so, he became suddenly aware of a low, eerie keening in the air; like the sound of some woodwind instrument. He turned in the direction of the sound and saw, not ten feet away, a huge, squat plant, about the size of an automobile, with three big pods growing out of the central mass. Over these grew stalks of what looked like long flowers or tubes of a spotted, venomous-looking purple. These were moving slightly, and it was no doubt from them that the odd music was coming.

The others heard it too and paused to stare.

"A musical plant!" exclaimed Elizabeth. "That would make a fine addition to any garden."

"Deuced ugly though," said Perseus. "All bloated like one of those opera singers."

"Still, like a dog on its hind legs or a lady's preaching, one is impressed that a plant sings at all," she answered, moving closer to get a better look.

Suddenly, Martin became aware of movement about his feet. As he looked down, four of five thick, thorny vines suddenly wound themselves around his legs in a convulsive movement. It gripped him so tight that it felt as though they had fused to his flesh right through his trousers. He cried out in pain even as he was jerked off his feet and the vines began to drag him toward the plant.

Bill and Elizabeth both screamed. Illingworth shouted in alarm. Perseus darted forward to help his friend, drawing his machete. He hacked down at the vines with all his might. The blade cut through one, but stuck against the second. He jerked it free, but before he could strike again he saw more of the tendrils crawling toward his own feet like brown snakes. He jumped back, seizing Martin by the hand. The power of the contracting vines surprised him and nearly yanked him off his feet in turn, but he braced his foot against a mossy hillock of earth and held on like grim death.

Elizabeth and Illingworth rushed in to help as more vines crawled toward Martin, creeping further up his body. He cried out in pain as they constricted him, pulling him, threatening to rip him in two. Elizabeth took Perseus's machete and tried to start cutting them back, but by now there were so many that it seemed hopeless. Each one was half an inch thick and sticky, like spider webs.

Meanwhile one of the great pods opened, revealing a deep red interior lined with sharp thorns. There was no doubt what it was – a predatory plant designed to take large prey. A man could fit inside there easily.

"Are you planning to help at all?!" Perseus snapped at Bill.

For a moment when the attack began, Bill had stood rigid, in shock at the sudden violence. Then an idea had suddenly flashed upon his mind. He didn't pause to wonder whether it would work; he simply whipped off his pack and began fishing around inside it. By the time Perseus shouted at him, he had found what he was looking for.

"I-I have an idea!" he stammered, fumbling with the jars of preserving alcohol that he always carried on hand. "Just hold on for a second!"

"Make it fast, for God's sake!"

Bill unscrewed one of the lids, drew out his handkerchief, and soaked it in the solution, then screwed the top back on so that the handkerchief was trapped under the lid, the better part of it dangling out the side. He fumbled for his lighter, found it, and set the alcohol-soaked cloth alight. For a moment, he held the burning glass in his hand. Then with the arm of a lifelong cricket player, hurled it as hard as he could into heart of the plant.

The jar shattered, spilling its contents all over the bulbous mass. The flames caught and in an instant the thorn-lined pod was a bowl of fire. The plant shuddered and contracted. Bill threw a second jar, not bothering to light this one, and the flames leapt higher.

The vines abruptly released Martin from their grasp, so abruptly that the whole party toppled backwards with the sudden release. They dragged Martin through the mud, away from the burning plant as it twitched and shuddered under the flames.

For a moment, the whole expedition stood ankle-deep in filthy water, watching the flames and trying to catch their breath. Then Martin reached over and patted Bill on the shoulder.

"Thank you, my friend," he gasped. "That was well thought of."

"It certainly was!" said Perseus, smacking him on the back. "Three cheers for Mr. Little here!"

"Well done, my lad. Well done indeed!" said Illingworth, gripping him by the arm.

"It...it just came to me," Bill stammered, a little overwhelmed both by the praise and by his own audacity. "How do you hurt a plant? Burn it. And I remember warning you about the fire hazard of all those ethanol jars back home, so...."

"So you saved the day," said Elizabeth, beaming a radiant smile on him. "The hero of the hour!"

Bill looked rather embarrassed.

***

They retreated from the swamp after this adventure. It was agreed on all sides that the man-eating plants—Elizabeth dubbed them Purple Sirens, and the name stuck—were too dangerous to risk continuing the passage. And so the rest of the morning was spent going back over the same unpleasant ground they had already been over, only now soaked and covered in mud and most of them having lost their mosquito netting.

All in all, it was a miserable morning, and they were almost glad to find themselves back on the relatively open shores of the lake, where they could wash themselves off in the clean water and discuss what to do next. The iguanodon herd – or another like it – was basking in the shallows about a hundred yards off, watching them with tranquil curiosity.

No one liked the prospect of trekking across the valley through the jungle. Perseus, for his part, had no doubt that the natives, though afraid of their rifles, were on the lookout for opportunities to surround and ambush the expedition in the hopes of capturing Elizabeth.

"Though I will say," he added quickly, seeing how the idea affected her. "That I believe we would have as good a chance as not of fighting them off. Our greatest advantage, as I see it, is that they can have very little experience fighting other human beings. They've been the only people here for God-knows how long. I saw that when they tried to rush us the other day."

"I'm glad to hear that there is some good news at least," she said, eying the trees uneasily.

"If I might make a suggestion," said Martin, who had rolled up his trousers to bathe the angry red welts now running up his legs. "I submit we should avoid the jungle and skirt the swamp on the other side. It would not take too long, I judge, to build a raft. Then we might pass the swamp by the lake."

"I say, there's an idea!" said Perseus.

"Are you sure that would be safe?" asked Bill. "What if there are...creatures in the lake?"

"No doubt there are," said Martin. "And I do not say at all that it will be safe. I do not think safety is to be expected in this Forbidden Valley. I say it may be *safer*. Or at the very least, unexpected."

"I agree," said Perseus. "Come along, Bill. We'll have some of these branches. The rest of you keep a steady eye with those rifles."

They set up on a small promontory sticking out into the lake, from which they had their backs to the water and a clear view of the shore. Elizabeth and Illingworth stood guard while the other three set their machetes and hatchets to work on the trees by the shoreline. It was hard work, and Perseus half-expected a spear in his back at every moment. But in about four hours they had a crude-yet-functional raft that would hold all five of them, and the natives had not appeared.

"I dub this ship the *Dauntless II*," said Perseus, rolling the raft out onto the smooth surface of the lake. "Good fortune follow all who sail on her."

He stepped gingerly onto the raft while Martin held it in place with a long branch.

"That would certainly be a welcome change," said Elizabeth as Perseus helped her aboard.

"Things could be worse," Perseus answered. "But I won't say how for fear of giving Dame Fortuna ideas."

The lake was very still and they kept close to the shore. Perseus pushed them along using the branch as a pole, like a Venetian gondolier. The mist that came with the hot, damp air cleared a little as the playful sun once again poked his head out from the clouds, drenching the valley in light. The expedition members kept their hands steady on their rifles, eyes peeled for any sign of danger.

"Look!" Bill shouted suddenly.

Three long, flexible necks, like those of swans, rose above the waters of the lake perhaps twenty yards off. Except these necks were covered with scales rather than feathers, were a murky brown with black stripes, and ended in pointed heads like pliers, with huge round eyes. Perseus estimated the necks to be at least five feet long. Every so often one would dive and disappear for a time before popping back up a minute later.

"Plesiosaurs," said Illingworth in a low voice.

The animals, noticing the passing of the *Dauntless II*, turned their heads to watch them for a moment, as a man out fishing might watch someone walking on the shore. But they soon lost interest and returned to their feeding.

"I shouldn't think they'd bother us, unless we annoy them," said Illingworth. "They're after the fish. Look!"

As he was speaking, one of the plesiosaurs rose from its dive with a large fish caught between its needle-like teeth. Then it tilted its head back and swallowed its still-wriggling catch in much the manner of a heron.

"Fascinating," said Illingworth with a sigh. "This valley is a treasure trove of wonders!"

"I don't disagree," said Perseus. "Though I should much prefer it with a way out. And without the neighbours."

They were floating along the edge of the swamp now, where the lake flowed over the lowlands in an ambiguous mass of land and water. They could see more of the Purple Sirens, like plump, ugly purses left carelessly by giant women. From what they saw from the raft, Perseus thought it unlikely they could have made it through the swamp at all; the mix of land and water soon became completely flooded, and the only way through was by the trees.

Several ornitholestes, in fact, were passing through in that very manner. They hopped from branch to branch like scaly monkeys, using their strong front arms and flexible tails to keep themselves aloft, or else perching like featherless birds, squawking to one another.

As the expedition passed on, they observed one of these creatures moving on its own, apart from the group, and in a very different fashion. It was hugging the side of a tree after the manner of an enormous lizard, its eyes focused upwards. As they watched, it very carefully gathered its hind limbs under it, then suddenly sprang straight up and backwards, twisting in the air, and seized a large bird that had just that moment perched unwittingly on a branch in the tree opposite. Clutching its squawking prey, the ornitholestes fell through the air for about ten feet before landing nimbly on a lower branch. It silenced the bird in mid-fall with a snap of its jaws.

It was as they were reaching the end of the swamp that Elizabeth noticed an island out against the cliffs. The lake was reaching the end of its expanse, and so the island – really an outcrop of the valley wall – was not far from the shore; say about a quarter mile. After a little discussion, they decided to attempt to reach it.

The island was perhaps thirty yards across and mostly bare, sitting as it did under the overhang of the cliffs. A few tough bushes and shrubs were the totality of its plant life and no animals were visible, except for a snake which darted out of sight as soon as they arrived.

At the back of the island was another honeycomb cave. It was with little hope that they entered it.

But this one, they soon found, was different. It ran no further back than any of the others, but it opened up below, running deep into the earth along the line of the cliffs.

"Worth taking a look at the foundations," said Perseus, lighting his lantern and leading the way down the narrow passage. It was damp and smelt of mould. Several huge roaches and other insects scurried away before their light. Every step, Perseus expected it to narrow beyond their ability to continue. But it kept going, running along the line of the cliff in a smooth descending slope.

Eventually, the cave opened up a little. They found themselves in a low-roofed cavern, so low that everyone except Elizabeth had to duck their heads. The floor of the cave was covered with perhaps six inches of water, with more running in along the walls.

"Pale stone all the way down," Perseus said, feeling the cold surface of the wall. "I think we have to consider it confirmed that this stuff indeed makes up the whole wall of the valley – and its foundation, I shouldn't wonder. This place isn't the treasure house of the gods; it's their washbasin."

"Then that means there's no way out, is there?" said Elizabeth.

"It's still just possible we'll find a vertical ascent," said Perseus. "But I should lay very long odds against it. It was always a long shot, to be honest."

"Then what do we do?" she asked.

There was a long pause.

"Let's go back to the surface," he said. "We may as well make camp right here on this island; it's about as safe as could be expected. Neither the allosaurs nor the locals are likely to swim out here after us."

Chapter Fifteen
Cuangi

"Anyway neither beast nor man. Something monstrous; all powerful. Still living. Still holding that island in a grip of deadly fear.... Well, every legend has a basis of truth. I tell you, there's something on that island that no white man has ever seen!"
-Carl Denham, *King Kong*

Perseus had had an idea that they might make a permanent camp on the island, but one night proved that was not to be. The allosaurs might not be able to swim across, but another kind of predator was found to swarm on the damp ground of the island: a new kind of leech the size of a mouse and equipped with stubby little legs. The whole cave was alive with the little beasts, and they spent a sleepless night fighting them off.

As soon as it was light, they abandoned their island retreat. After making certain that nothing predatory was waiting for them, they paddled along the line of cliffs to the shore, where they hauled the *Dauntless II* up onto land and hid her as well as they could.

The land on the northern shore of the lake was rocky and fairly open beyond the swamp, and soon began to rise steeply. This was enough to raise hope that perhaps the cliffs on the northern curve of the valley were not as inaccessible as those on the southern end, but those hopes did not last long. The ground rose to little more than fifty feet or so above the surrounding valley floor and the overhanging cliffs, though a little less towering, were no less inaccessible.

Perseus, however, felt his heart lifting in spite of himself. It was good, at least, to have a clear view of the land around them. The pyramid was more clearly visible than ever, flashing in the sun like a spike of pearl, and one had to exercise some effort to keep it from constantly drawing the eye. There was a cave entrance near the top of the ridge, and the expedition, more by habit than anything, dutifully explored it.

This proved, by far, the most interesting honeycomb they had found yet. It was one of the larger ones, though like all the others it ended abruptly against the sheer white stone only a short way in. On the right hand side was a second, smaller chamber set a little lower than the main one, with a small pool of water fed by cracks in the roof. A third chamber, with a much narrower entrance, opened on the opposite side near the back.

They had not been in the cave long and had not even begun to explore the dark third chamber when Bill gave an exclamation of discovery and held aloft a discarded tin. An eager search of the ground by the whole party disclosed several spent cartridges, a broken pocket knife, and the ancient remains of a fire.

"No doubt about it," said Perseus. "The Applegate Expedition made their camp here. I wonder if they left anything else…"

Meanwhile, Elizabeth had gone to the entrance of the yet-unexplored chamber at the back of the cave. She held her cigarette lighter aloft and peered inside. The small, flickering light fell on a pile of rocks built against the far wall of the chamber. Drawing closer for a better look, she saw that there were words carved into the limestone above the pile.

"Perseus!"

He came hurrying inside, followed closely by the others. "What is it?"

Elizabeth held her lighter up to the wall and read aloud.

"'Here lie the mortal remains of Professor Charles Applegate, scientist, born 1855, died 1911.'"

She moved the lighter to another section of the wall, where more letters were carved. "'In this valley also died Captain John Miller, born 1882, died 1911, Simplicio, birth unknown, and Angelo, birth unknown. May God grant them peace.'"

After she had finished reading, silence fell. The expedition members gazed down at the little pile of stones that covered the body of the ill-fated Professor. It looked strangely small to hold the body of a man. The men doffed their hats and Martin silently crossed himself.

"He was a good man," said Illingworth. "I remember him well. The most harmless, good-natured plodder you could imagine. Totally bound up in his subject. His wife often had to remind him to eat. Poor fellow...."

"At least you'll be able to tell her he received a proper burial," said Elizabeth.

"She died herself some years ago, I am afraid," he answered. "Killed, in fact. Burglary gone wrong or some such thing. Never mind. Let's get out of here."

They returned to the main chamber in a thoughtful silence.

"I wonder how they got out," said Bill after a moment.

"They didn't have a treacherous snake with them," said Illingworth. "Probably had a rope handy the whole time."

Perseus sat down and drew out the battered old book from his pack, unwrapping it and once more flipping through the mouldy pages, frowning over the now-familiar passages.

"But they were scared," he said after a minute. "It's plain from every word that Cooper writes. Something about this valley scared them badly. So much so that they didn't want the world to know about it."

"Easy enough," said Bill. "The valley's a death trap."

Perseus shook his head.

"Large predators and hostile natives wouldn't scare a man in that way," he said. "Not enough to create this kind of...well, of spiritual dread one could say. And yet they stayed long enough for four of the party to die."

"That isn't so surprising to me," said Illingworth. "Applegate was not the least superstitious. I can well imagine his insisting on remaining in the face of just about anything. Then he dies and the others leave."

"That is true, yes," said Perseus.

"Also, maybe they didn't find whatever frightened them until later," Elizabeth suggested. "Like you say, they wouldn't be disturbed by the dinosaurs themselves. Perhaps it had something to do with that pyramid."

Perseus shut the book and nodded vigorously.

"I think you have it exactly. That pyramid is the biggest mystery of this whole valley. Who built it? Why? What does it contain? Might be that Applegate and his people got in somehow and discovered...well, something that shook them badly."

"It is possible," said Illingworth noncommittally.

Perseus's eyes glinted. Even amidst their dangers and the conundrum of escape, the idea of the pyramid and its secrets had never been far from his thoughts ever since he first set eyes on it. The mysterious structure had been a constant presence on their journey, drifting in and out of sight, but never quite forgotten. What, indeed, might they find there?

"It is interesting," said Martin. "But, if I may, I think it is hardly our most pressing concern at the moment."

With an effort, Perseus withdrew from the visions of gold and gems and unfathomable secrets that passed before his eyes.

"Quite right," he said. "The great thing at the moment is to find a way out and to ensure we don't end up like Professor Applegate and his party."

"What would you suggest?" asked Elizabeth.

Perseus thought a moment, looking around the cave.

"I submit to you all that we may have to face the possibility of remaining in this valley for some time. I do not for a minute despair of making our escape, but it would be wise to make provisions for the present. Therefore, I say that we make this cave our fortress and base of operations. We have fresh water, the cave is reasonably defensible, and we'll be able to see anyone or anything coming from decent way off. Once we are secure here we can consider other means of escape. Frankly, I don't think finding a passage to the surface is at all likely at this point, but we can complete our search once we have made our camp."

"How long do you think we can survive here?" asked Bill.

"As long as we need to," said Martin. "A man can always do what he must."

"What about the natives?" asked Illingworth.

"As far as they're concerned, we are now about as far from them as we can possibly be in this valley," said Perseus. "Since we know they haven't forgotten about us..." he looked at Elizabeth, "that is all the more reason for us to prepare a defence."

"Well, I'm not going to argue," said Elizabeth. "The accommodations really are quite adequate, all things considered. Where do we start?"

From there they had some discussion as to the best way to secure Castle Darrow (as they began to call it). Elizabeth wanted to focus on defending against the natives, while Illingworth considered the allosaurs the greater threat, as the cave entrance was large enough that a dinosaur could get in, though it would be very cramped. In the end, Perseus and Martin sided with Illingworth on the grounds that, of the two dangers, the natives would be much the easier to fight off if they came.

Their defence was formed in the following manner. Perseus, Martin, and Bill went out and felled two young trees, then dragged them back to the cave. The trees were then mounted over the entrance and bound together in an 'X' shape, such that a person could enter by ducking his head under the cross section, but an allosaur would never fit between them. They were lashed in place and secured with stones. Then, to ensure the dinosaurs didn't simply use their powerful heads to smash through the barrier (Illingworth declined to guess at their potential strength), several of the stripped-off branches were sharpened into points and secured in place on the logs.

The work consumed the rest of that day and a good deal of the following one. No dangers threatened that night, though they had a bad scare in the afternoon, while mounting the logs, when an allosaur went ambling by about a hundred yards off. It paused a moment, looked at their activity and seemed to consider them, but ultimately continued on its own business.

"I suggest," said Illingworth. "That like most carnivores they prefer to take prey unaware, while it's at rest. Activity and showing that we know he's there discourages him."

"That's something," said Perseus. "Good to know these ancient brutes follow the same rules as any other animal."

That evening, Martin took Bill out hunting, and they returned with an ornithomimus slung over Bill's shoulders. It tasted rather like turkey.

"At least we won't starve here," said Perseus.

"Not so long as we have ammunition, at least," said Martin.

"You're perfectly right; we ought to reserve that as much as possible. Tomorrow we'll set to work making bows. Save the firearms for the neighbours."

Elizabeth nodded, looking uneasily in the direction of the pyramid. "Funny they haven't made any trouble yet," she said.

"Maybe they've given up," Bill suggested. "Maybe they think we're some kind of gods or powerful spirits they don't want to anger."

"I doubt that," said Illingworth. "More likely they're just patient brutes and are waiting for us to let our guards down."

"Suspect you're right," sighed Perseus. "All the more reason to keep the guns in reserve."

The low, musical calls of the brontosaurs drifted up from the forest at the bottom of the hill, together with cracking and tearing sounds that said the beasts were gorging themselves. Elizabeth, despite the danger, found she couldn't resist the urge to go and watch. Perseus and Illingworth went with her. A large, flat stone near the top of the ridge gave a good view of the animals busily stripping the leaves.

"This is a different group than the one we saw the other day," said Illingworth. "He wasn't there. You see? That big red one. And the make-up of the group is quite different."

He was frowning, as though perplexed.

"Look," said Elizabeth, pointing. "There are little ones. Little dinosaurs."

So there were. Scampering about the feet of the brontosaurs and catching the scraps that fell from their mouths were a gaggle of miniature, two-legged dinosaurs about the size of chickens. They darted about on two spindly legs, nimbly avoiding the massive feet of their giant benefactors while pouncing on the showers of greenery.

"Interesting," said Perseus. "And symbolic. The little ones of the earth feed on the scraps that fall from the tables of the great. At least brontosaurs needn't fear going to hell for want of charity."

Elizabeth flushed and looked away uncomfortably, but Perseus, intent on the dinosaurs, didn't notice.

"That is precisely what troubles me," said Illingworth, who was following a train of thought of his own. "This valley now; it supports at least two populations of these giants, not to mention the stegosaurs, the igaunodons, the ornithomimi, those little creatures, and who knows what else. Now, for these species to have survived all this time, the valley must maintain an amazingly stable environment. Yet these creatures gorge themselves every day, and still the forest appears thick and healthy, not over grazed at all. I would think that even a small increase in population would destroy the ecosystem entirely in short order."

"That is curious," said Elizabeth. "Perhaps...oh, I don't know."

They watched the herd for close to an hour, until thunder growled overhead and they were obliged to retreat into the cave to avoid a dousing.

"There is something else I wonder about," Elizabeth said, leaning on the crossbars to watch the downpour from the cave entrance. "Let's assume, as we now believe, that this pale stone runs all around and even under the valley. Well, then where does the water go?"

"The water?" asked Bill.

"Yes, *this* water," she said, indicating the downpour. "We're in one of the wettest places on Earth, as we've had ample opportunity to observe on this trip. So there must be an outlet somewhere, otherwise this would be the Forbidden Lake."

"My God, you're right!" said Perseus. "I can't believe we hadn't thought of that. There must be a tunnel under the lake somewhere..."

"Not just that," she said. "Didn't you notice that most of the water flows to the centre, toward the pyramid? The lake's an exception because of this ridge here, but all the other streams we've passed were flowing to the middle."

Perseus felt a great leap of excitement.

"That's it!" he said. "There must be an outlet! A...a kind of natural drainage system. Or unnatural. I don't care which at this point."

"Do you mean a way out?" said Bill.

"Well, if the water can escape, then it might be that we can as well."

"But even if there is such an outlet," said Illingworth. "Is that likely to help us? Surely it would be no larger than needs be to carry the water. Not enough for us to survive a passage."

Perseus thought about it.

"No," he said. "No, I don't think so. You yourself, Professor, said that this valley would have to maintain an extremely stable environment. That means it can't be flooded out all the time, so the drain would need to be large enough to carry any amount of water even during the wettest months of the wettest years. This is still the dry season. It's at least an even bet that any such passage would have room to spare."

A new air of restrained excitement settled over the expedition. Here, at last, was a clue; a crack in the wall that had closed in around them.

"There is one other problem," said Martin. "If the outlet is somewhere in the centre of the valley, under the pyramid, then to reach it we would have to go over the wall."

"True, but that should be no difficulty," said Perseus

"No, but what of this Cuangi?"

A chill seemed to blow in at the mention of that name. Elizabeth in particular felt an unpleasant lurch in her stomach.

"That is a question," said Perseus sobering at once. "But the problem is we don't even know what he is, much less whether we can get past him."

"Then you suggest a scouting expedition?" said Martin.

"Yes, that seems called for," he answered. "In any case we ought to find out just what the fuss is regarding him. With luck, it might even be we can put an end to all this sacrifice nonsense."

***

So it was that, early the next morning, Perseus and Martin set out to test the theory. It was, they knew, an extremely risky operation; the natives would be on the watch, and eager to make use of an opportunity to attack the party while they were separated. Besides that, and the other known dangers, there was always the possibility that the valley held yet more nasty surprises like the Purple Sirens.

But the two adventurers had been through many similar perils before. They knew how to move quietly in the jungle and to stay alert for the presence of either man or beast, and consequently they reached the north face of the wall without encountering anything more dangerous than a stegosaurus grazing on a bush, which they gave a wide berth to. They soon found a tree growing close enough beside the massive expanse of masonry to overhang the wall slightly. They climbed it easily and looked over.

The jungle on the other side appeared much the same as on theirs, unless it was perhaps a shade thicker and darker. No sign of any living thing was visible. Meanwhile, the tall, white pyramid rose closer than they had yet seen it, towering out of the jungle to its sharp point and seeming to shine even under the cloudy morning sky. Perseus wondered whether it might be made of the same pale stone as the cliffs.

They secured a rope to the tree and let it fall inside the wall. The plan was for Martin to remain as lookout while Perseus descended to explore. The Austrian took his position and gripped his rifle, his keen blue eyes scanning the jungle. But all was quiet as Perseus descended.

His feet touched the soft, leaf-strewn ground, and he immediately unslung his own rifle, looking about him. Still all was quiet. He walked forward a little ways, eyeing the trees and the twisted undergrowth. The trees, he saw, were almost all scarred by deep gashes, long grown over, as though something with huge claws had slashed at them.

"Do you want me to come down?" Martin asked.

"Not yet," Perseus said, waving him off. "I'm going to have a look 'round first..."

He moved on into the jungle. It was, he thought, unnaturally quiet. There were insects buzzing about him, of course, but other than that all was still. Not a bird, not a rodent, not a snake to be seen. He walked on for a few paces more.

Then he heard it.

Thump.

Perseus froze. Then the sound came again, like a great bass drum.

Thump. Thump.

Faster and faster, accompanied by crashing, cracking sounds as if something were moving through the trees

Thump! Thump! Thump!

Footsteps. Giant footsteps.

Perseus ran back to the wall. The crashing and thumping were getting closer. Then the whole jungle was shaken by a deep, earsplitting roar, the same roar they had heard their first day in the valley.

Perseus reached the wall, took hold of the rope, and then looked back.

Cuangi was coming.

He was, broadly speaking, an allosaurus. That much was clear from the powerful forelimbs, the bony red crests over his eyes, and his midnight-blue colouring fading to a black belly. But he was a very different creature from the ones they had observed thus far. In the first place, those had walked with their tails held parallel to the ground and their heads thrust forward, like birds. Cuangi walked straight upright, like a kangaroo or even like a man, his long, powerful tail dragging along the ground behind him. Perhaps it was the effect of this stance, which held his head more than fifteen feet off the ground, but he also seemed much, much bigger than any of the other allosaurs they had seen.

More than that, Cuangi had a wasted, thin, evil look about him. His body was covered with scars and his bones stood out sharply under his flesh. His blood-shot eyes were sunken deep into his skull, yet they blazed with the mad frenzy of a rabid dog.

This, Perseus realized at once, was no ordinary animal.

He took in the sight in an instant, then began to climb faster he had ever climbed in his life. Cuangi came roaring after, head thrust forward, running in great, bounding leaps. He was faster than Perseus had expected. *Much* faster.

There was the crack of a rifle. From his perch on the tree, Martin had fired. His bullet—a solid .30-6 round meant for taking down large game—struck Cuangi dead in the chest. The monster checked his stride, snarled a moment, then leapt forward once more. Martin cycled and fired again. This time, Cuangi didn't even pause, but merely flinched as the powerful bullet hit him in the chest.

Perseus reached the top, just as Cuangi slammed into the wall below them, causing the bricks to tremble. He looked up, teeth bared, his reptilian eyes ablaze with vicious hunger.

Martin and Perseus both aimed straight down. Cuangi roared at them, and the two guns roared back, sending two .30-6 rounds into his open mouth, directly into his brain.

The monster staggered backwards, as though surprised by the blow. He stumbled, his knees buckled, and he fell with a crash to the ground.

"Whew!" said Perseus. "A close one that, but at least now..."

He didn't finish. For at that moment, Cuangi suddenly rolled over and stood back up, shaking his head and snarling.

"That...that is impossible."

Cuangi turned back to the two men, teeth bared, then took a sudden, flying leap and snapped at them. Perseus and Martin dropped out of the tree and back over the wall just as the great jaws closed over the branch they had been sitting on seconds before, escaping death by inches.

They struck the ground hard. Perseus felt the wind knocked out of him, and Martin cried out in sudden pain. The tree before them bent as Cuangi pulled on the branch. Then with a crack like gunfire, the branch tore off and disappeared. A roar of thwarted fury echoed over the wall after them.

"Are you all right?" Perseus gasped as soon as he had breath.

"Ankle..." Martin grunted, clutching his foot.

Perseus examined it.

"Broken," he said. "Damn! Well, come on. We've got a long and unpleasant walk back."

Leaning on his friend and using his rifle as a crutch, Martin gritted his teeth and began to limp back through the jungle. Perseus kept a careful eye out. If they were attacked now, in this position...Well, he couldn't help that.

Meanwhile, his mind was racing, trying to make sense of what he had just seen. Cuangi had taken two high-powered bullets to the brain and stood right back up, apparently unhurt a moment later. That, as far as he knew, was not possible.

Yet it had happened. He had seen it.

Somehow, they managed to make it back to the cave without incident. Martin, now green in the face, gratefully sat down and let Illingworth look at his foot. Meanwhile Perseus told what had happened, first warning them that they would not believe his story.

They were very quiet when he had done.

"You mean this creature...it really *is* something supernatural?" Elizabeth asked in a soft voice.

"I don't know," Perseus admitted. "At this point I don't know what is and isn't real about this valley. All I know is that no animal, whatever the size, could have possibly survived that. And he simply got back up like it was nothing."

He didn't want to admit it, but the experience had left him badly shaken. Up until now, he had always thought that cleverness and courage could get him through any obstacle. But here was an obstacle that seemed to simply ignore the normal rules. It disturbed him on a profound level.

"No wonder Cooper thought no one would believe him," said Elizabeth. "I mean, if he met Cuangi, and tried to shoot him...well, I wouldn't have believed it."

"Nor I," said Illingworth. "I still cannot help thinking that you must have missed, or that some kind of fluke..."

"We did not miss, Professor," said Martin with unusual sharpness. "One could hardly miss a target that size which is ten feet directly below one. And while I may posit one bullet being deflected by a bone or some such thing, two at once being equally neutralized by chance is a little much."

"So we can't kill Cuangi it seems," said Elizabeth. She was staring blankly into space, her face pale, her fingers working uneasily at her shirt.

"Yes, but he can't get us either," said Perseus. "So don't you worry about it."

"In the meantime, the water passage is out," sighed Illingworth.

"Not necessarily," said Perseus. "We may be able to...oh, I don't know. Slip past him or something. Remember that legend Newgate told us. Not, of course," he added hastily as Elizabeth shot a sharp glance at him, "that we are going to offer our beautiful maiden as bait. But a more suitable animal—say one of these ornithomimi—might be just as effective."

"That sounds...risky," said Bill.

"Cuangi is quite fast," Martin reminded him, indicating his bandaged and splinted ankle.

"Yes, I know," said Perseus, frowning. "We would, of course, have to take that into account."

"And what if we find that there is no way out after all?" said Elizabeth. "We'd risk being trapped there, just like the warrior in the story."

"We may be able to bring more than one bait," suggested Illingworth. "Though it still seems extremely uncertain to me."

"Very well," said Perseus. "We'll set that idea aside for now."

The rest of the night was spent discussing possible alternatives. But they were forced, in the end, to let the matter drop.

Perseus went to bed still thinking of the pyramid. He wondered whether, if they became desperate, they might be obliged to divide their forces. Mightn't he, on his own, make a dash to the pyramid and so find if that escape route existed? And then, what else might he find there?

For even now, he had not despaired of entering that enigmatic structure and bringing off the treasures of the gods that supposedly rested inside. How could he, with Elizabeth sleeping not ten feet away?

Chapter Sixteen
Escape from the Forbidden Valley

"Fortune good-night: smile once more; turn thy wheel!"
-King Lear: Act II, scene II

Bill took the first watch that night. He had grown somewhat accustomed to the tedious, yet unnerving task over the course of the journey. Enough, at least, to be trusted with it, though certainly not enough to make it anything less than terrifying for him.

Yet, though he felt fear that night, he found it didn't trouble him as much as it once had. The dangers they had passed through, his own close calls, and the responsibility he'd been given seemed to form a kind of protective padding over his heart. He sat with his rifle upon his lap, looking out into the night and listening to the sounds of the jungle.

Frogs and insects played their incessant high notes, while the lowing of dinosaurs gave a periodic bass counterpoint. The fire burned beside him, and occasionally a set of yellow or green or red eyes would look in from the shadows outside, but nothing showed itself, and no vast shadows heralded the arrival of an allosaurus.

So he passed three quiet hours before the fire, listening to the night sounds and gazing up at the riot of stars overhead while he thought of Frances. He wondered what she was doing at the moment, a world away from him.

Perhaps it was that, near the end of this watch, his thoughts indeed became a doze. Or perhaps what happened would have

202

happened anyway. Be that as it may, he was caught completely off guard when an arrow suddenly struck him in his chest.

The impact knocked him backwards, and he was conscious of a searing pain in his right breast. He could feel the rough tip of the arrowhead scraping against his ribs. He tried to cry out, but the impact had knocked the wind out of him.

In a daze, he looked down past his feet. Dark, slender forms, swift and silent – like the figures in a nightmare – were closing in on the cave with its sleeping expedition members.

Bill thought for sure that he was dead. He had been shot, and in his mind being shot equaled death. But he also knew that he was on watch. He was responsible for keeping his friends safe.

"We do what we can and trust to God for the rest."

His trembling hand went to his rifle, bracing the stock against the ground. He worked the action one handed as the nearest native passed the barrier, a long knife of bone in his hand, his eyes fixed on Bill. He meant to make sure of him. To silence him before attending to the others. Bill's hand shifted from the action to the trigger.

The man bent over Bill just as he raised the rifle and fired.

The bullet tore through the native's chest, the impact knocking him back off his feet. The other figures paused at the roar, and the rest of the expedition were awake in an instant.

Perseus was up with his own rifle in hand before his conscious brain had shaken free of sleep. He saw the slender, dream-like figures in the flickering firelight and fired. A second native dropped, then a third as Martin added his own rifle. The others turned and fled into the night.

"Bill!" Illingworth cried aloud.

The young man lay on his back, one hand still gripping his rifle, the other clutching the arrow that stuck up out of his chest.

"Watch the entrance," Perseus ordered Martin as he dropped beside him. Elizabeth knelt at Bill's head, cradling him in her lap while Illingworth stood staring down at his young assistant in blank shock.

"That was well done, lad," Perseus said as he examined the wound. "You saved us all with that shot."

Elizabeth, stroking Bill's hair, watched Perseus anxiously as he worked. His face was grave, but it soon lightened.

"And you, my friend, are also one of the luckiest young men I've ever met," he exclaimed "That bloody arrow hit your sketchbook! Only penetrated about an inch."

He spoke cheerfully, but inside he was not nearly so sanguine. A wound that deep was more than enough to kill a man if it became infected. Or worse, if the arrow was tipped with poison. But it could have been so much worse. At least the arrow had not punctured his lung.

With a warning that it would hurt, he pulled the arrow free and quickly staunched the bleeding with a bandage, then ordered Bill to sit up to elevate the wound. Once he was safely propped against the wall with Elizabeth and Illingworth watching over him, Perseus joined Martin at the entrance.

"Well?"

"No sign of them," said Martin, leaning against the cave wall to take the weight off his splinted ankle. "As you say, they don't know much about strategy, but they are learning. No doubt studying us."

"That's two of us injured," Perseus grumbled. "How are we on ammunition?"

"Could be worse," came the answer. "I should say we are at about forty rounds per rifle, and about the same for the handguns."

"As you say, it could be worse. Though right now I'd also trade quite a bit for a cigarette."

The two men stood guard for the remainder of the long night. Bill, who had rapidly recovered his spirits upon realizing that his wound was not mortal, fell asleep after an hour or so.

With the dawn came relief, or at least the relief of seeing no living natives in sight and no longer having to fear a sudden arrow from the darkness. As soon as it was light, Perseus stripped the dead of their tools and weapons. Under Martin's guard, he then dragged the bodies off into the forest to ensure that the allosaurs didn't associate their camp with free meat.

It was when they were back in camp after this grim errand, standing around the fire and examining the crude weapons, that Perseus had his inspiration. It came so sudden and so complete that it hit him like a physical blow.

"My God!" he exclaimed, making them all jump. "I have been an idiot! Here we are marching all around the valley, fighting natives and unnatural monsters, and the whole time the answer was so bloody simple!"

"Indeed?" said Martin, raising a quizzical eyebrow.

"*This* is our way out," Perseus said triumphantly, brandishing one of the native bows.

The others frowned at him. Then Elizabeth's face broke in a look of wonder.

"Oh, my...do you think that would work?"

"If this one doesn't, we'll make one that will!" He felt so giddy with relief that he actually threw his arms around her and spun her about before he quite knew what he was doing.

"Pardon me," said Illingworth. "But I seem to have missed the idea."

Perseus let go of Elizabeth, both rather red and embarrassed.

"Don't you see?" he said. "We simply shoot a line over the cliffs! Fire an arrow with a hook into the trees overhead, and we have a lifeline!"

Illingworth's eyes widened as he took in the idea. Bill sat up a little straighter, wincing as he did so.

"Can that be done?" the professor asked.

"We'll test it at once," said Perseus.

And seizing the small quiver of arrows, he rushed straight out of the cave. He looked up at the cliffs, weighing the bow in his hand, then bent it and released. The bow, as he had suspected, was a crude, rather weak weapon; probably meant for shooting the ornithomimi. The arrow didn't rise more than half the height of the cliff before falling back to earth.

"No matter," he said. "Shouldn't take too long to make a better one."

Perseus went out at once to try to find some suitable branches. He and Martin spent all the rest of that day carving and tempering the wood, only to have it split when they attempted to string it, forcing them to begin all over again. Yet no one felt particularly discouraged by this, for the idea of escape was now fixed in their minds as almost a certainty. As Elizabeth pointed out, it now appeared no longer a question of *if*, but only of *when*.

This second bow held together, and late in the afternoon of the following day (their eighth in the valley), they all came out to see the test. Perseus took the arrow, aimed straight overhead, and let it loose. It soared to a hundred feet over the top of the cliff before turning and dropping back to bury its head in the soil beside them.

"Now for it," said Perseus. "And I suggest you all make ready to depart."

Martin bound an iron hook to the next arrow, with their rope looped through the eye. It would certainly affect the arrow's flight, but accuracy was hardly important; all they needed was for it to catch onto something. Perseus took it, aimed straight up, and let it fly. The heavy hook flew into the air and disappeared over the line of the cliffs. The rope went slack. Perseus pulled slowly, dragging it back, and the hook caught and held. He tried his weight on it and jerked it back and forth a few times. It seemed well secured. Everyone let out a long, slow breath.

"Right," he said. "Now for the interesting part."

He looked around at his companions and grimaced. As he did so, his eyes fell on the pyramid, and it was as though an iron hand closed on his stomach. The strange attraction that the structure held seemed to pull on him stronger than ever. Here was his last great chance, about to be abandoned like all the others. And there was Elizabeth standing right beside him, as unattainable as ever. Could he have the heart to bid her good-bye again after all this? To go back to his fruitless chase?

"I say," he said, letting go of the rope. "Perhaps, now that we're assured of our way out, maybe we shouldn't be quite so hasty."

"What are you talking about?" Illingworth asked.

"There's that pyramid still," said Perseus. "You can't tell me you aren't interested in seeing what it contains?"

Elizabeth looked back at it.

"No," she said slowly. "I can't."

"We are surely not going to stop now, on the verge of escape, to worry about *that*?" said Illingworth.

"No, of course not," said Elizabeth, as though rousing herself. "Besides, we can't get to it, remember?"

"We could distract Cuangi, as I suggested the other day," Perseus answered. "Be a risk, I admit, but..."

"But nothing!" said Illingworth. "This is sheer insanity. It is a curiosity, yes, and I would say that a proper expedition to thoroughly explore it would be called for, but we are in no position to do that!"

"He's right, Perseus," said Elizabeth. "It's a beastly shame, but you'll have to leave that for someone else."

He looked at her and gritted his teeth. For someone else...that was the story. That was always the story. That wonderful way of life he had tasted so long ago, the comfort of wealth, Elizabeth herself...all for someone else. Not for him.

For a single mad instant, he wondered what might happen if he simply refused to leave until he had been to the pyramid. They couldn't leave without him; none of them could climb the rope. He was really on the point of declaring his intention to do exactly that when he caught sight of Martin's face. He read the disapproval, the disappointment behind his friend's stoic demeanour; the same expression that he had worn when Perseus made his plan to lie about the diary.

The madness passed, leaving only a faint horror of what he had nearly done. He cleared his throat.

"Of course," he said. "Please excuse me. Don't know what I was thinking."

He took hold of the rope, gave one more glance at Elizabeth, and began to ascend. It was a long and difficult climb; the rope didn't feel nearly as secure as he would have liked. More than that, though, his heart was heavy within him. He felt as though he were leaving all he had ever wanted behind, climbing out of the pit of his delusions. There would, he was sure, be no more adventures after this. Back home, he would have to part from Elizabeth once more and forever. These days in the valley, like his days at Sangral House, had been a dream; nothing more. Soon it would be time to wake up.

With such gloomy thoughts as these, he ascended hand over hand, trying to channel his frustration into the climb. The Forbidden Valley receded further and further beneath him, spreading out below like a map. The pyramid glittered in the sun.

At last, his hand reached over the rim of the valley and touched the world he knew. The very Amazon jungle itself seemed almost familiar, commonplace, even comfortable after the Forbidden Valley. He scrambled over the edge, then turned back and waved to let them know he was safe. Cheers rose up from below.

Perseus unhooked the rope from where it had caught securely on a tree branch and bound it tight around the trunk. Below him,

Martin tied the end of the rope into a secure loop. They had, of course, lost their harnesses when Silva betrayed them, but this would serve something of the same purpose.

"All right!" Perseus shouted down to them as soon as Martin signalled that all was ready. "Martin, you first!"

Martin climbed into the loop and Perseus hauled him up, foot by foot, using a stout sapling as a pulley and winding the slack rope around a heavy log as he pulled so as to provide an anchor. It was brutally hard work, and his arms were growing weary, which was one reason he wanted Martin to ascend first. He'd need the Austrian's wiry muscles if he were to bring the others up.

In a few minutes, Martin appeared over the edge of the cliff, and Perseus gave him a hand over. Next came some of the packs, pulled as quick as they could.

"You next, Bill!" Martin shouted.

"You wanted to remain?" Martin said in a low voice as they hauled on the ropes, sweat standing out on their foreheads.

"It's why we came here, isn't it?" Perseus growled. "It's what we've been looking for all these years. I admit it was a foolish idea, but I felt I had to...to make at least one final effort."

"Why?"

"Why?" Perseus repeated. "You know perfectly well the reason why: she's waiting below as we speak..."

As he said it, a sudden doubt came into his mind. Had they been wise not to bring Elizabeth up sooner?

"And I say again, what do you need treasure for?"

"Do I really need to explain? She is a lady. I am not a gentleman."

"I beg leave to differ."

"What do you mean?"

"Permit me, *Sir*, but you are as much a gentleman as any I have ever known. And she thinks the same."

Perseus was so surprised by this that he nearly dropped the rope. "What are you talking about?"

"With all due respect," said Martin. "You must be the greatest fool in the world not to see that she is as much in love with you as you are with her."

Perseus stared at him, but at that moment Bill appeared at the edge of the cliff and he and Martin went to help him over and assist him to a place where he could sit down. It was just as well; Perseus couldn't think at the moment. His brain was echoing Martin's words, wondering if they could be true...

But then, Martin didn't know everything, did he? He didn't know of the little voice of mistrust that he, Perseus, had planted in her mind.

**

Elizabeth and Illingworth watched Bill's ascent with anxious excitement. So far all was well. They were almost free. Elizabeth, for her part, could hardly believe it. Her whole body fairly trembled to think that the ordeal was nearly over. The fear that had formed a constant weight on her heart the whole time they spent in the valley was about to be lifted forever.

Bill disappeared over the edge.

"You go next, Lady Darrow," said Illingworth.

Eager as she was to be gone, Elizabeth felt a little uncomfortable about that. Of course, this was a flaw in the plan that, in their eagerness to escape, no one had really considered; the fact that someone would have to go last. Someone would have to spend a degree of time completely alone in the Forbidden Valley.

"I insist," he told her, giving her a very serious look. She understood by it that he was thinking much the same as she was and trying to convey that this way was only sensible. Elizabeth was directly targeted by the natives; Illingworth wasn't.

She nodded reluctantly as the rope descended. "Very well."

"Oh, I don't think so."

The shock of hearing that voice momentarily stunned her. She whipped around just in time to see the butt of a rifle slam into Illingworth's face. The old man dropped to the ground with a small gasp, and Silva turned a grin of uneven teeth on her.

Elizabeth wanted to scream. But the surprise, the impossibility of what she was seeing momentarily took her power to do so. It was as though a nightmare had suddenly intruded upon reality, causing her to doubt whether what she was seeing could be real.

Perseus's warning about him flashed through her. She was now alone with him; alone in the Forbidden Valley, her only possible protector unconscious or dead at his feet. It could not be real...It was too horrible to be true....

The fit lasted only an instant, but it was long enough for a strong hand to close over her mouth and another to grab her arm and twist it behind her back. Gomez held her while Costa grabbed the rifle out of her hand and took the knife and revolver from her belt.

"Quick, now," Silva snapped. "Before they start coming back."

Elizabeth's screams came at last, but they were muffled by Gomez's hand as she was dragged away, down the slope and into the forest. There, to complete her terror, stood the native chief and four of his warriors waiting for them.

"There you are," said Silva, gesturing to Elizabeth. "A donation, as promised!"

Two of the warriors stepped forward and took hold of her, each gripping an arm, while one held her mouth shut to muffle her screams. They were terribly strong, and their skin felt cold against hers.

"You two stay here," Silva said to the *comaradas*. "Watch if anyone comes after her. If so, try to take them alive if you can, just in case we need a spare."

In the midst of her terror for herself, Elizabeth thought of Perseus and felt something very like despair. If he came after her, he would walk into a trap. But if he didn't....

Silva and the natives carried her off through the trees. But she wasn't about to give in that easily. With an effort born of desperation, she forced her mouth open and bit the man's hand with all her might. He grunted and his hand flinched away.

"It's a trap!" she screamed as loud as she could. "Don't come, it's a trap!"

Silva struck her hard in the stomach, knocking all the wind out of her. Elizabeth doubled over, gasping.

"Enough of that, ladyship," he snarled. "We can make this a lot harder for you than it needs to be."

She glared at him, trying to convey all her hatred in a single look. But she couldn't scream and could barely speak as they carried her on through the forest, far out of earshot of the cliffs.

Chapter Seventeen
Human Sacrifice

Andromeda was there, doom'd to atone
By her own ruin follies not her own:
And if injustice in a God can be,
Such was the Libyan God's unjust decree.
-Ovid, The Metamorphosis: Book IV

"All right, Elizabeth!" Perseus called once Bill was safe and the rope was being lowered once more. "You next!"

He leaned over the edge, feeling slightly giddy. He wanted badly to see her, to try to discover whether he could discern in her face any of what Martin had described. For if so, then perhaps in time....

But the scene that met his eyes far below banished all happy thoughts from his mind.

Illingworth was on the ground. Elizabeth was being dragged off toward the trees by three men. It was too far to make them out, but they certainly weren't natives.

Immediately, he thought of Silva.

He gave an inarticulate shout of horror and anger, which brought Martin limping to the edge just in time to behold the scene.

"Lady Darrow!" he cried.

"What's going on?" Bill called.

Perseus didn't hesitate a moment. He slung his pack and rifle over his back and took hold of the rope.

"Stay here," he ordered Martin. "Watch Bill!"

His climb down was the fastest such climb he had ever made; far faster than was at all safe, but he was reckless in his fear. Elizabeth...in the hands of Silva. Probably in the hands of the natives by now. All other thoughts gave way to that.

About halfway down, he heard a scream from the forest. He thought there were words in it, but he couldn't tell for sure. He gritted his teeth and climbed faster.

He dropped the last ten feet and bent over Illingworth's prostrate form. The old man was groaning feebly.

"Professor! Can you hear me?"

Illingworth only moaned and felt his head.

Perseus had no time to give him proper care. He dragged him to the rope and tied it around his waist, entwining it around his arms and wrists to make sure he couldn't slip out.

"Martin!" he shouted. "Can you hear me?"

"Yes, I can hear you!" came the answer.

"I'm going after her. Illingworth's hurt. Bring him up and do what you can for him. Then take them both and make for the river! We'll catch up with you."

There was a pause.

"Very good, my lord! God go with you."

Perseus was momentarily caught by the unexpected title. But there was no time to discuss or declaim it. He waved a hand to Martin then turned and ran for the forest after Elizabeth. He was near wild with fear, covering the distance while hardly seeing where he was going.

He had not penetrated the trees more than a dozen yards when a voice spoke out.

"Drop the rifle, Corbett."

Perseus halted as though turned to stone. Gomez and Costa had appeared from behind a tree, covering him with their own guns. His anger at the delay was nearly enough to overcome his good sense, but he checked himself in time. Elizabeth needed him alive; he would do her no good by getting himself killed. He cursed himself for the recklessness that had led him to rush in headlong like that.

Slowly, he let the gun drop and raised his hands in surrender. Gomez covered him, while Costa retrieved the rifle and took his knife and pistol.

"Go," Gomez snapped, jerking his gun. "And no tricks."

Perseus drew a deep breath. Fear would not help him. He needed to be calm, focused. Clever.

They started through the jungle, Perseus going in front, the two *comaradas* behind. His sharp senses took in the sounds and smells around him; the hooting of the birds, the distant lowing of the brontosaurs, the hum of the insects. At the same time, he was considering his position. He would not allow them to take him all the way to the village; that would be to place himself in a far worse situation. He must escape before then, preferably with a weapon. He knew these men were good shots, however, and entirely willing to kill him if he tried. They were armed and he wasn't.

The only advantage, as he could see it, lay in the fact that he almost certainly knew more about the Forbidden Valley and its inhabitants than they did.

Walking through the jungle, Perseus began to whistle.

It's a long way to Tipperary...

"Calm, are you?" said Gomez with a sneer.

"I don't think a cheering song is uncalled for at the moment," he answered. And he resumed his whistling

To the sweetest girl I know...

He heard the men behind him muttering something in Portuguese and laughing. They evidently didn't think much of his whistling.

It's a long, long way to Tipperary...

Thunder rolled overhead, and a downpour began. Perseus cursed it to himself, thinking the rain might muffle the sound. Then, as though in answer, he heard drums beginning far ahead in the jungle.

But my heart's right there.

Another roll of thunder...no, not quite that. Perseus, still whistling to himself, glanced back over his shoulder.

"Look out!" he shouted to his captors.

Gomez and Costa instinctively looked back. As they did so, the two allosaurs charged. They were still a good way back, and evidently had hoped to creep closer before pouncing. But now that they were made, they ventured a direct charge, roaring as they came. The two men screamed and whipped around, bringing their rifles to bear. But as they turned their backs on him, Perseus sprang. He hit Costa hard on the back of the neck, then turned on Gomez, who was so fixated on the oncoming monsters that he hadn't even noticed. He got one shot off at the oncoming allosaurs before Perseus seized the rifle, twisted it from his grip, and jabbed him in the stomach with the butt before turning and running as fast as his legs would take him. There was a confused jumble of shouting, then two screams cut short as the allosaurs descended on the men.

Perseus glanced back and saw the pair bending over the ground, apparently well satisfied with their prey and paying him no more heed. The idea just flashed through his mind that this might be the very same mated pair they had seen at the lake.

He really felt almost fond of them now.

The storm intensified around him, and he forced himself to slow down and proceed with caution. Meanwhile, the pounding of the drums ahead of him grew faster and louder.

***

Elizabeth moved in a nightmare; a dream of rain and thunder, of misshapen black faces, of hands that gripped like steel, bruising her to the bone

The natives took her through the jungle, which was alive in the storm. They marched her at a pace beyond what she thought she could endure, dragging her whenever she stumbled and bruising her shins against stones and logs. Ahead of her, she heard drums rolling wildly.

All at once, she was in the village and the drums were all around her. She saw the natives standing in line, heedless of the storm, men and women both. Dimly, it occurred to her that she hadn't seen any of the native women before.

They were as tall and gauntly misshapen as the men, and seemed somehow even more withered, whether young or old. Their hair was short, and they had almost no visible breasts. Men and women watched her without expression, save that they were pumping their forearms up and down and chanting.

"Cuangi. Cuangi. Cuangi."

At a sign from Silva, the natives released her, and the drums and the chanting stopped. All seemed silent but for the rain. Elizabeth stood in midst of the natives, rubbing her bruised arms, breathing hard, and looking about her in despair. For a second, she thought of making a run for it. But she was surrounded by a solid wall of black figures; she wouldn't make it a yard.

Such was her numb terror that Elizabeth didn't immediately realize that Silva was talking to someone. Someone who definitely did not belong in that village. Then she saw him, but thought she must be delirious.

"Colonel Newgate?" she gasped.

It was him. Broad-faced, cleanly dressed in white, but no longer smiling. He looked at her and shook his head.

"I tried to warn you, Elizabeth," he sighed. "I told you to go home. I didn't want you involved in this."

Elizabeth kept staring at him, as though she thought that she might break through the trick her senses were playing on her. This was impossible...unthinkable. She glanced at Silva, who was grinning at her from Newgate's side.

"What...what are you doing here? And how?"

"I followed you, of course. About three days behind. As soon as I was convinced you really had discovered the way to the valley, I sent my friend Mr. Silva here ahead so that he would be able to accompany you and so guide me to what you found."

He drew a deep breath and looked around.

"I have been searching for this place for so long," he sighed. "Almost since the end of the war."

"Why didn't you just come with us then?"

He shook his head.

"Because you wouldn't have understood," he said. "Those others you were with, they would have tried to prevent me when it came to the point."

"What point? What are you talking about?"

"This valley, Elizabeth, this pyramid, has the means within it to change everything; to clear away the old, stupid, violent world and make a new one in its place. That is something that so few people can understand. They see all the waste and horror, but they still won't give up what they have to pursue something better. I've tried to convince people before now. Your father chief among them. I laid the whole thing out before him, but he hadn't the ears to hear. Damn fool."

The thunder rolled overhead. The natives were watching the exchange with inscrutable eyes. The rain seemed to increase, casting a veil over Newgate's face.

"He didn't believe you, then?" she said.

"That's the worst of it," he groaned. "He *did* believe us. I showed him Cooper's manuscript."

"The...you mean you had it?"

He nodded. "When we attempted to acquire it, there was a struggle and the book was torn. Joseph – Cooper's valet – escaped with the front half, while we were left with the back, the one that told what to expect in the valley. Combining it with certain information we had from other sources, we knew what the account meant. I showed Lord Darrow all these proofs, so that he would know that the thing was true.

"But he was like so many others – he'd rather cling to his own sad little bit of the world that is than give it up so that everyone might have something better. He was willing even to betray me, his best friend, to the police rather than let go of his precious privilege. We had no choice but to arrange that accident."

Those words took a moment to sink in. When they did, Elizabeth's fear was suddenly swallowed in fury.

"You...you...!" She stammered, and forgetting everything else she leaped at him. Instantly, two strong natives seized her and held her back.

"You see what I mean!" Newgate said. "You don't understand! Here we are on the brink of a new world, a paradise on earth, and all you can think of is that you're upset your father died!"

"Don't talk to me about your new world!" she spat back. "You're nothing but a common murderer!"

She strained to break free, not to escape, but to attack. But the cold hands that gripped her were like iron.

"Words," he said. "Simplistic words. But it doesn't matter now. I wanted you to try to understand, to see how important this is, but you won't. I don't think you can. You never were anything but a silly, spoiled rich girl who can't see an inch beyond her own wants.

Otherwise you might realize that this is the most useful thing you have ever done or likely ever could do in your life!"

"And just what am I about to do?" she demanded. She had stopped struggling, not because her anger had abated, but because it hurt too much to strive against those immovable hands.

"Don't you see?" he answered. "All that I need is in that pyramid. And as you may recall from my story, the only way past Cuangi is to offer him a sacrifice. Distract him."

Icy cold fingers gripped her heart. She understood fully.

"I see," she said, straining to keep her voice as steady as she could. "Then I can only hope you meet the same fate as the bastard in you bloody story."

And she spat in his face.

He looked rather shocked, as though she had done something totally unreasonable, but merely shook his head in irritation and waved to the natives. The drums rolled again and they took up their chant once more. The men holding Elizabeth dragged her with irresistible force past Newgate and Silva to the back of the village.

She saw now that it was built right up against the wall, and indeed laid out before a huge gate of solid wood. In front of this was a crude kind of staircase made of branches that had been lashed together with vines that led up to a wooden platform standing level with the middle of the gate.

Time seemed to be moving oddly to Elizabeth, in sudden jumps. She was seeing the wooden structure for the first time. She was at its feet, perhaps a chance to break free if she struggled hard enough. She was at the top, being bound between two posts. Her skin seemed more sensitive than usual, and the rough cords scraped painfully against her wrists. And surely it was much too tight, unnecessarily so? Why would they stretch her arms out so cruelly?

But of course; it was meant for the native girls, who were far taller and had longer limbs than her. They had to stretch her to make it work. This struck her as funny for some reason, and she thought she laughed a little in the midst of her agony.

Then she was alone, abandoned, her arms spread out at their furthest extent and bound painfully tight. Twisting to look over her shoulder, she saw that the natives were gathered in a crowd well back from the altar – for altar it was – watching her, still chanting. The only exception was the chief himself, who stood on another raised platform beside the gate, looking out at the tribe. Silva and Newgate were nowhere to be seen.

All at once, Elizabeth felt the full weight of her position crash in upon her. Dimly, her mind realized the impenetrable fact that there was no hope; no hope at all. No one was coming to help her, and they wouldn't be able to do anything if they did.

There was no escaping it. She was about to die.

For sheer hopelessness, Elizabeth threw back her head and screamed aloud, a scream that ended in a sob. All the tomorrows she had anticipated, all that she would do and feel and enjoy 'someday', all that was now about to be destroyed forever. She screamed again, and then found herself praying. There was nothing else to be done.

The chief was saying something. She kept stammering out prayers and occasionally relieving the agony of her spirits with another cry of despair.

Then a gong sounded, and the chief pulled upon a great rope, causing a section of the gate right in front of Elizabeth to slide back. It was like a slat on a normal door through which someone might check to see who was knocking, only it was about six feet high. Elizabeth stopped both her prayers and her screams when she saw it starting to open. This was it. Her death lay on the other side of that door.

Thump. Thump. Thump!

Heavy, rapid footfalls. Her final breaths were coming quick and shallow, as though her body wished to get as many of them in as possible in the time it had left. Then a huge, dark shape appeared through the rain on the other side of the gate. Her eyes widened in unbearable terror as the great, hideous head of the monster bent down to peer through the opening at her. Its lips pulled back from its long, yellow teeth, and it roared.

Elizabeth shut her eyes and screamed for what she was sure would be the last time. Strangely, her mind went to Perseus; to that one and only kiss they had shared so long ago.....

But as Cuangi thrust his head through the gate to snatch his victim, something flew through the air and smashed against his face. Instantly the monster's whole head was aflame.

With a shriek that might have split stones, he jerked back, cracking his head against the gate and splinting the boards in his haste to withdraw. Elizabeth's eyes snapped open at the sudden change, and the natives all stared in silent disbelief.

But Perseus didn't wait for them to realize what had happened. He scaled the side of the altar with the speed of a monkey. A second later his machete was in his hand and hacking at the ropes binding Elizabeth in place.

***

Perseus had entered the village from the side, while everyone was gathered in the centre to watch the ceremony. He saw the altar, where Elizabeth, her long red hair flowing down over her pack, stood bound in cruciform fashion. He had crept as close as he could, taking his position against one of the huts a little behind the altar. There he paused to try to think of a plan. He had only a machete and a single rifle with six rounds and was facing what looked to be over a hundred natives. If he could only get Elizabeth away, it might just be possible to escape in the jungle, where at least they would have a fighting chance, but he would be swarmed the moment he tried to approach her.

Elizabeth's despairing screams had been almost more than he could bear. But he had to control himself...he had to *think*....

Then an idea flashed across his mind. Possibly the only option he had. He unslung his pack and hastily rummaged through until he found what he wanted; three empty specimen bottles (thanking Heaven that Illingworth had insisted that they all carry a supply). Tearing strips of the cloth they had been wrapped in, he unscrewed one of the bottles, soaked the cloth, and screwed the lid back on, trapping it in place. He only prayed that the alcohol would still burn in the rain.

He had finished the work as the gate was opening. He managed to light the first improvised weapon just as Cuangi appeared. Out of time, he seized what seemed the only chance he had. He threw the bottle at Cuangi himself and ran for the altar before it even hit. Even if the fire didn't kill him, he thought, it would at least keep him busy for long enough to cut Elizabeth free.

But Cuangi wasn't the only threat.

With startling agility, the chief sprang from his perch beside the wall, thrusting his spear at Perseus. Perseus only had time to cut one of the ropes holding Elizabeth in place before he had to step back to avoid the blow. He stumbled partway down the steps, and the chief closed in after him. Meanwhile, the rest of the village was rushing toward them, just as he had suspected. None of them shouted or indeed made a sound as they came.

The chief thrust at him again, and Perseus parried the blow with his machete from his knees, then seized the haft of the spear and pulled, rising to his feet as he yanked the chief off balance. He swung his machete and had the satisfaction of feeling it hit bone, but he didn't wait to see how much damage he had caused. He pushed past the chief to Elizabeth's side, where she was frantically trying to untie herself with the numb fingers of her free hand.

But even that brief amount of time had been enough for Cuangi to recover. As Perseus reached her, they both saw his murderous red eyes fix on them. With an enraged bellow, he thrust his now burned and charred head through the opening, while at the same time slamming his whole bulk against the gate with terrific force.

Perseus saw the attack coming and did what seemed the only thing possible. He seized Elizabeth about the waist and leapt off the side of the altar with her, hacking at the remaining rope even as they fell. It was enough; the frayed end caught, but their combined weight snapped it an instant later, and they landed hard in the dust.

At the same time, the chief had been charging back up the stairs at the head of his people, bleeding from his side, and he thrust his spear at the interloper just as he and the girl vanished over the side. The spear missed, and it is likely the chief didn't even have time to realize his mistake before Cuangi's great jaws snapped shut on him.

The other natives screamed – harsh, grating cries as if from throats long parched from disuse – and turned to flee, but Cuangi's assault on the gate had carried him further into the opening than he ever had been before. His multi-ton body, smashing against it, had partly splintered the boards outwards. Now, as he attempted to withdraw, he found he was stuck.

This, of course, only enraged him further. He hardly seemed to even notice the bloody victim in his jaws, for he bellowed, spewing pieces of the chief across the village as he clawed at the gate, pushing harder against it, lacerating his own flesh in his mad effort to escape. The wood split and buckled, and a moment later the monster tore free of the gate and stepped forth into the village, crushing the altar before him like matchwood.

The natives fled. Cuangi, howling as if to split the sky, charged after them, flattening their huts and pursuing them this way and that in a frenzy of hunger and rage.

Perseus and Elizabeth, in his very shadow, passed unnoticed. But Perseus saw at once the insanity of trying to escape into the jungle under that monster's watch. Pulling Elizabeth after him, he ducked past Cuangi's madly swinging tail and fled through the gate.

Whatever else it contained, the pyramid was their best shelter now.

Chapter Eighteen
Treasure House of the Gods

There are two ways of getting home; and one of them is to stay there.
The other is to walk round the whole world till we come back to the
same place.
-G.K. Chesterton, *The Everlasting Man*

They didn't stop running until they had reached the pyramid's nearest side, which was steep, perfectly smooth, and (as Perseus had suspected) appeared to be made of the pale stone. Seeing no entrance on this side, they hurried around to the next: the east face. There they saw a high, open archway into which a river was flowing. Following it inside, they found themselves in a vast open space below a vaulted ceiling. The floor was partly covered in dirt and growing plants, beneath which many coloured flagstones were visible. A flight of stairs—with very wide, yet tall steps—ran up on either side of the entrance, and they hastily took one of these up to a wide landing that stood some thirty feet or more over the courtyard.

Here at last they stopped to catch their breath. Perseus did not, however, let go of Elizabeth's hand. He could feel her trembling violently.

"Are you all right?" he asked.

Slowly, she nodded.

"Not quite a sea monster," she said at last in a shaky voice. "But close enough."

He laughed. Somehow, it seemed the funniest thing he'd ever heard. Without thinking what he was doing, he pulled her into a tight embrace. He ran his hands up and down her back and sides, rejoicing to feel her solid and alive beneath his fingers.

After a minute, he released her. Remembering the tight knots still constraining her wrists, he set to work untying them. As he worked, she stammered out the story of Newgate's treachery. When she had finished, she looked at him with something like confusion.

"You came back," she said at last after he had undone the ropes and was vigorously rubbing her arms to restore circulation.

"Of course," he said. "You didn't think I'd just leave you, did you?"

"I didn't want to," she answered. "But you did once."

He stopped and stared at her. It took him a moment to realize what she was referring to. "This was a *slightly* different set of circumstances."

"I know," she said hastily. "I shouldn't even mention it now. It's only that...I needed you then too."

"If I'd known..." he began.

"You would have come," she said. Her hand suddenly tightened on his and a faint smile crossed her face. "It's good to know that."

They smiled at each other.

"Why did you stay away?" she asked suddenly. "All those years, I mean."

"I was after treasure," he admitted. "Trying to make my fortune."

"Yes, I know, but there are lots of fortunes to be made in England. I would have been happy to give you a job if you needed one, and...and you might have at least written or come for a visit."

Perseus had long since considered the possibility of this question arising, and had prepared an answer. He had been rather surprised that, in all their conversations during the journey, she had never yet asked it. But that answer wouldn't do now. Neither would the truth. So he said nothing and merely dropped his eyes, ashamed to look at her.

"I think I know why," she said softly.

"You do?"

"Yes, you...you never really liked me very much then, did you?"

He stared at her in amazement. She was pale and trembling. All her defences were down at last.

"I was so bossy and selfish and all that that it wouldn't surprise me at all," she went on. "But I hope...well, I've been trying to be better."

"Trying to be better?" he repeated in amazement.

"Yes," she said. "Less haughty and sure of myself and so on. Am I?"

"You...you really think *that* was why I stayed away all that time?"

"Well, yes," she said in some surprise. "I'm not offended, you know...."

"You idiot!" he exclaimed. "The only reason I left at all was so that I could earn enough money to become a gentleman!"

"To become..."

"Because," he pressed on in reckless abandon. "That was the only way I could imagine that you might marry me."

There was a heavy silence. Dimly, he was amazed at himself for saying that aloud. Elizabeth was staring at him as though she wasn't sure she'd heard him right.

"It was stupid, I know," he said. "But it seemed at least possible at the time."

She swallowed hard.

"It *was* stupid," she replied in a constrained voice. "Because if you hadn't left, I certainly would have."

Her words hit him like a bullet. All at once he saw his life for what it was; he had travelled the world, enduring war, famine, disease, and every danger known to man, and finally had trekked into the deepest, darkest jungle on earth...all chasing something that had been waiting for him at home all along.

He blinked at her in wonder for quite half a minute. Then, once again, he roared with laughter.

"God!" he gasped. "What an ass I am! What a stupid, silly ass!"

Elizabeth laughed too. The worry, the anxious pains that had gnawed at her heart for so many years had been revealed in a moment to be nonsense – an illusion of her own. She had tormented herself, punished herself over mere phantoms. What she had taken for abandonment and rejection had been pursuit; the most serious and absurdly devoted pursuit she had ever heard of. He had not forgotten her or despised her; he had gone to the ends of the earth in the hopes of winning her.

They at last gasped themselves back into seriousness. Perseus looked at her, thinking she was even more radiantly beautiful than he had ever realized.

"And what about now?" he asked.

She grinned at him. "Ask me again after we get out of here."

"Right!" he said, jumping to his feet. "I wonder what old Cuangi's up to now?"

He looked around him, taking in more of their surroundings than he'd yet had the attention for. It was very dimly lit, but he could get an impression of intricate patterns of geometric shapes covering the vaulted ceiling. The only light came from the two great archways, one facing east, the other west. Through each of these flowed a river, which poured down a big, circular pit in the exact centre of the floor.

"There's our drain," said Perseus. "You were right. Do you suppose we can get out that way?"

"Perhaps," she said. "Though personally, I think I'd rather go back to camp and use the rope again, if it's still there."

"It is," he said. "And in that case, I suppose we had better go sooner rather than later. Before Cuangi comes back."

"Y-yes," said Elizabeth slowly.

He turned to her. She was looking around the chamber and biting her lip thoughtfully. He knew that expression; it was the one she had worn when they were children, and she had come up with some scheme that she was sure would get them into terrible trouble. He couldn't help grinning at the sight.

"You know," she said. "I think we might as well take a look around first. After all, we may be the first civilized people to set foot in this place."

His heart leapt. It was what he would have wanted himself. But he still hesitated, thinking of Martin.

"It probably would be safer to leave now."

"I'm certain it would be," she said, with a small, trembling laugh. "But do you know it occurs to me that, if I had been eaten just now, I would have spent most of my life avoiding the things I really wanted. And now, so long as I am *not* dead, I think I am going to do what I like, and to hell with the risk!"

He laughed. "As your Ladyship wills," he said.

They ascended the stairs together, trembling with the kind of excitement that comes of doing something you desperately want to do, but are not quite sure you ought. The climb was difficult and unnerving; there was neither curb nor rail, and each step was a good fifteen inches high and set wide apart. The idea occurred to Perseus that they weren't built for normal humans. Even the eerily tall natives would, he judged, have had trouble with them.

The steps ran alongside the slanting wall of the pyramid, tending inward along with it, and with almost nothing in the way of support underneath. Only the breadth of the stairs – each step was at least nine feet across – afforded them any comfort. Upon reaching the ceiling the stairs continued through a passage and it was quite a relief to have walls on either side.

At the same time, though, Perseus became aware of a change in the air. It was hard to say what it consisted of, but there was a kind of heaviness and oppression upon his eardrums and a tang like smoke at the back of his throat. This, he realized, had been present ever since they entered the pyramid, but it had been faint enough to escape his notice. Now it was growing stronger as they ascended into the interior.

Elizabeth felt it as well. She kept a firm grip on Perseus's hand.

Reaching the top of the stairs, they emerged into the true interior of the pyramid. As they did so, they reeled as though hit by a blinding light. It was not brightness that dazzled them, but the sheer complexity and confusion of the space they entered. Perception, shape, colour – everything we use to categorize and understand the images that meet our eyes were all jumbled into incomprehension by the strangeness and intricacy of what lay before them.

The colours were only the ones they knew; white and grey, pale variants of green and pink, all very muted. The light – which was dull, steady, and rather red – seemed to emit from the very walls themselves and banished every hint of a shadow. This added to the confusion, as this made it difficult to discern shapes and distances, which were delineated only by colour and shade.

Bit by bit, they were able to make sense of their surroundings. They were in a great space that seemed to take up the majority of the interior of the pyramid, the walls rising to a point far overhead. Before them was a pale pink aisle or road running between lines of structures made of green and grey stone and topped with domes. There were no visible entrances to these structures, and Perseus was put in mind of tombs. To their right and left a line of the same pinkish stone ran along the outer edge of the space, no doubt providing access to other, similar roads. They could make out taller structures on other 'streets,' these with pointed domes rather like those on Russian churches, only far narrower.

Directly in front of them, in the centre of the space, was a second pyramid, exactly proportional to the first on a smaller scale.

And covering the walls of the chamber was a pattern of geometric shapes and colours of such intricacy, and yet precision as overwhelmed them. It was not chaos. No, it didn't give the smallest impression of chaos. It was that, when they looked at it, they found that its very rationality and precision invited their brains to try to understand it, but its complexity swiftly overwhelmed them. It was too much for their minds to grasp or to hold, and yet they could hardly help but try.

It was this more than anything that staggered them and made them lean on one another.

It was some time before they were able to keep their attention off of the pattern and so to get their bearings. When they did, they found that the air was thicker here than ever. There was something more as well, something hard to define. It was almost a sense of unbalance, like one felt upon first stepping onboard a ship. Yet Perseus, who was well used to ships, thought it was less a matter of the ground moving than of something in the air buffeting them, though Elizabeth's long hair hung about her untouched by any breath of wind.

"Come on, then," he said after they had recovered sufficiently. He was speaking low, though he didn't know why. "Let's have a look at that."

They walked down the street between the doorless tombs. The closer they got to the smaller pyramid, the more the impression of strangeness increased. Perhaps it was a trick of the odd light, but Perseus kept imagining that the angles and shapes of the structures around them were changing. A tile on the floor might appear hexagonal at a distance, but prove square when they got closer. A dome would appear now circular, now oblong. And he was never quite sure whether the path they were walking on was level with the floor the tombs were built upon or somewhat elevated or sunken.

More than that, the sense of being buffeted about increased. Their steps felt now heavier than expected, now lighter, sometimes causing them to stumble. Yet there still was nothing that could be called a wind. It was more like the ground was shifting up and down beneath them, or that they were continually gaining and losing weight as they walked.

The inner pyramid was completely solid, but where the street met the base there was a double flight of steps leading down into the foundation. They descended a short passage and a moment later found themselves inside the treasure house of the gods.

It was laid out as a kind of inverted pyramid, with six levels leading down to the centre. Below the top level, which ran uninterrupted around the walls, each of the four sides had three paths leading down the steps. Between them were low walls topped with stone chutes running down to meet in the middle. These chutes were all filled with rivers of gems, each chute a different colour. They were gems ranging from the size of a hen's egg to the size of an orange, all precisely cut, all gleaming in the dull, reddish light that seemed to come from the very walls. It was as though they were in a frozen fountain of many colours, or a rainbow made of stones.

For a moment, they stood and gazed with wonder on the scene. Perseus had never seen so many jewels in one place; he doubted whether anyone had. It was difficult, owing to the strange light, to judge the size of the chamber. It was at least thirty or forty feet across, and each of the twelve chutes was overflowing with hundreds of precious stones.

He began to descend the steps, passing amid the streams of jewels and gazing at them. He picked up a handful of red gems – rubies, perhaps – and felt them. They were cold to the touch, and when he held one up to his eye he found it to have perfect clarity without an imperfection to be seen.

Wonder gradually gave way to excitement. Here, if ever, was what he had sought. Here was all the wealth he would ever need; a mere handful would make him rich. He began to pile the gems into his pack.

Elizabeth, meanwhile, had noticed something else. Around the top level were recesses set in the wall, and in each of these there was set some weapon or artefact. They were all of exquisite and intricate workmanship, wrought in what appeared to be silver and polished steel, inlaid with gems and carvings. The latter reminded Elizabeth of Celtic knots, only of a much denser complexity.

Yet the workmanship was the only thing she could discern about them; of their purpose or meaning, she could say almost nothing. They seemed to be *almost* like things she recognized, but not quite. There was a large circlet of silver that could have been a crown, except that the interior was decorated with waving lines of metal that would seem to preclude anyone's wearing it. Likewise there was something that she assumed was a tall, narrow goblet, but upon examination it proved to have a hole in the base, making it impossible to have been a drinking vessel.

This confusion, however, could not dampen her excitement at seeing and handling objects from God knew what lost civilization. She took off her pack (which she was a little surprised to find she had been wearing this whole time) and carefully placed the 'crown' and the 'cup' inside of it, along with a silvery rod she thought might be a sceptre, or perhaps a weapon of some kind. She would have them examined back in England.

While Elizabeth was examining the artefacts, Perseus reached the bottom of the chamber. Here gems of every colour were laid in a circular trench or pool surrounding a shallow bowl, not of stone but of what appeared to be silver and which was almost completely empty, except for a single small jewel. He thought it must have fallen in from the overflowing piles at some point over the millennia. It was about the size and shape of a sparrow's egg and perfectly white, except for the top of the narrow end, which was a swirl of many colours.

It was a pretty little thing; not as striking as the larger jewels, but its presence here all alone amidst the greater treasures lent it a kind of glamour of its own.

He glanced up at where Elizabeth was examining more of the artefacts, and an idea occurred to him. With a smile, he slipped the little gem into his pocket.

This done, he became curious to know what she was looking at and joined her on the upper level, his pack heavy with jewels. Elizabeth had set her own heavy bag down for a moment and was examining something.

"Look at this," she said, holding up the object in her hand. It was, or at least appeared to be, a huge gem, royal blue in colour and about the size of a football. Only, where the others were of a perfect uniformity and clarity, this one was lumpy and opaque. Elizabeth thought it looked like a pudding that hadn't cooked properly.

"Not quite ripe, I should say," he answered. She laughed, but hastily stifled it. There was something about the heavy, dense atmosphere that made her laughter sound odd and out of place.

"I've never seen anything like it," he said more soberly.

"Nor I," she said, tucking it into her pack. They were both speaking in whispers, though they didn't know why. She looked around at the chamber and shivered a little. "What kind of people do you suppose built this place?"

"Very strange people, I should say," he answered. His excitement, sated by the wealth weighing on his shoulders, had ebbed a little and questions were beginning to arise. "Do you notice there's no art? No statues, no pictures, nothing but these abstract shapes."

"Yes," she said. "And where does this light come from?"

She put her free hand to the wall, which was warm and seemed to be vibrating slightly. Withdrawing it, her palm glowed faintly with luminous dust.

"Fascinating," he said, taking her hand and feeling it. "We'll have to bring some of this back for the Professor to see..."

His eyes and his mind drifted from the luminous dust on her hand to her lovely face. She smiled slightly as his hand closed over hers.

The moment was shattered by a gunshot. Elizabeth screamed as the bullet tore dust from the wall behind her. Perseus yanked her back behind cover, pressing her against the wall.

"Are you all right?" he demanded, unslinging his rifle.

She felt her side with trembling hands. Her nerves were on fire, but a brief examination showed no wound. The bullet had just missed her.

Perseus leaned out from behind cover. His ears were singing with his anger. They had tried to shoot her.

"Hold your fire!" called Newgate. He and Silva had taken shelter beside the stairs they had just come down. "There's no need for any further bloodshed!"

"Really?" Perseus answered. "Then that was a friendly shot, was it?"

"Mr. Silva is, as you know, a little impulsive," said Newgate. "It won't happen again."

"Forgive me if I don't take your word for it, you murdering swine!"

"Be reasonable, Corbett!"

"Come on out and I'll show you just how reasonable I can be," Perseus answered. "Nothing more reasonable than shooting a rabid dog, is there?"

His mind was racing. He very much wanted to kill Silva and Newgate, but not nearly as much as he wanted to get Elizabeth to safety. They had known that exploring the pyramid was a reckless gamble, and now it looked as though they were paying for it. How could they have been so stupid as to forget that Newgate would be on his way here as well?

"Don't you have the slightest curiosity to know the reason for it all?" said Newgate.

"Not particularly," Perseus answered.

There was a flight of steps right next to the recess that they were sheltering in. If they made a dash for it, they could be up onto the streets in a moment, and then they just might be able to make it out of the pyramid before the others could hit them. It was risky, but it seemed to him the best play. He had only a few shots – and nothing prevented Newgate and Silva from dividing their forces and flanking them.

He looked at Elizabeth, who was trembling violently after her close call. In a whisper, he explained the plan.

"I'm game if you are," she said in a shaky voice. She slung her bag over her shoulders and pulled the straps tight in preparation for the move.

"Stay close," he told her.

He fired a shot at Newgate, who ducked back behind cover as the bullet struck the luminous dust from the wall. At the same time, Perseus and Elizabeth darted out from cover and dashed to the stairs, racing up as fast as the awkward size of the steps would permit.

They reached the top before the others could retaliate. But one glance told them that they were not outside, on the odd streets amid the doorless tombs.

Instead, they were inside the inner pyramid.

Chapter Nineteen
The Seed of a New World

Time present and time past
Are both present in time future,
And time future contained in time past.
-T.S. Eliot, *The Four Quartets: Burnt Norton*

The chamber they had just entered was very tall and the walls sloped in all the way to the sharp point at the top. Like the outer chamber, the whole inside was lit by a constant, reddish light, only this was more intense and of a deeper colour than the one outside. The walls were lined with what seemed to be furrows in the stone, crossing and re-crossing one another in an infinitude of shapes and angles. Yet they had that same sense, not of chaos, but of overwhelming order.

In the centre of the chamber was a circular pit. And rising out of the pit all the way to the apex of the pyramid, completely dominating the scene was...well, it was hard to say what it was. It was like a fountain, if the water were flowing infinitely back upon itself. It was like a dynamo, if it were made of quicksilver. It was like lightning or St. Elmo's fire contained and made fluid. It was like a column of light, except denser, with the more the appearance of metal.

The best way they could describe it was as a continual stream of brilliant, glowing liquid silver, reaching all the way to the summit of the pyramid before flowing back down upon itself, and continually revolving upon its point like an impossibly narrow fountain. The whole apparatus was of a size that was difficult to ascertain. Judging by the amount of space in the chamber it could not have been more than ten feet across, yet it seemed to loom over them like a moving hill.

It was so strange and so hypnotic that in spite of everything they paused to gaze at it. At the same time the heaviness and smoky tang of the air became so intense that they had trouble breathing. The odd buffeting sensation nearly knocked them off balance.

Only with a great effort did Perseus force himself to recall the danger. Catching hold of Elizabeth, he began to lead her around the terrible device. He had no plan; only an instinct to keep moving.

But by then it was too late.

"Stop!" Newgate ordered, appearing at the top of the stairs behind him. "Drop that rifle!"

Perseus turned on him, hoping vaguely that the great engine would distract Newgate as it had him. But Newgate seemed to be better prepared for it and was pointing his pistol straight at him. Silva, on the other hand, was gazing at the thing, his rifle slack in his hand.

"I said drop it," Newgate repeated.

There was nothing for it. Perseus let the gun fall. Newgate gestured for him to back off and then kicked the gun aside.

"Hold him, Silva," he ordered.

Silva didn't move.

"Silva!"

The poacher shook himself and affected his old sneer.

"Why not kill them now?" he said.

"A moment," said Newgate impatiently. "Don't you see where we are?"

His eyes fell on Elizabeth, who was glaring at him with a hatred that left no room for fear.

"I killed my best friend for this," he said. "I want his daughter to understand why, if she can."

Newgate went to Elizabeth and took her by the arm. Perseus started forward, but Silva stopped him with a gesture of his own gun. He could only stand and watch as Newgate led Elizabeth before the terrible machine, covering her with his pistol.

"You see it?" said Newgate. He still held Elizabeth, but his eyes were fixed on the engine. "Do you realize what it is?" he said. "It is power. Power beyond anything mankind has ever known. The power to remake the whole world."

"So you say," she replied, shaking but defiant.

"Listen," said Newgate in an eager voice. "Why do you suppose Cuangi cannot be killed? He dwells in this pyramid, sleeping beneath this very engine. It gives him life, endless life. Why do you think the valley remains green and never experiences famine, despite those giants gorging themselves day after day? The very soil of this place is made endlessly fertile by this device. A tree stripped of its leaves in the morning grows back in full by the afternoon. And here, even now, can you not feel the very force of the Earth's gravitational pull being bent by its power? And it does all that when it is merely idle. Can you even conceive what it might be capable of if harnessed and directed to a purpose?"

"And what do you intend to do with it?" asked Elizabeth. "What was worth murdering my father and me over?"

"We will remake the world," he repeated. "No one could resist us with the power this machine can bring. We will strip away the old, broken system and then create a new one. One where no one is ever hungry, or poor, or ill. Where there is no war, no petty squabbles over nations or religions. No reason to go on killing each other."

He looked at Elizabeth. In his reverie, his gun had dropped to his side. Though he was still holding her arm, it was in a loose, almost gentle way.

"Don't you think that's a worthy cause?" he said. "So many men died for nothing in the Great War. Isn't it worth a few men dying to make a world where nothing like that can happen again?"

Elizabeth looked into his eager, open face, then jerked her arm free and stepped away from him.

"A world founded in betrayal and murder doesn't sound much better to me."

Newgate's face went cold. He shook his head.

"I'm sorry," he sighed. "More sorry than I can say to find you so selfish." And he raised his pistol.

All the while that Newgate had been speaking, Perseus had been slowly, almost unconsciously sliding his pack – heavy with gems – off his shoulders and down his arm. He had no plan, was conscious of no decision; he had simply been instinctively preparing the closest thing to a weapon he had. Now, even as Newgate took aim at Elizabeth, he acted.

"Newgate!"

The colonel turned, no doubt expecting some plea for mercy or bargaining. Instead, Perseus slung his pack as hard as he could right into Newgate's chest. Caught completely by surprise, Newgate instinctively caught it, and the impact of the bag with its weight of treasure caused him to stumble backwards. His foot slipped over the edge of the pit, and he fell into the very heart of the machine. A single cry, a dazzling flash of light, and he was gone.

Perseus hardly waited to see him fall before he turned on the stunned Silva, jerked his rifle aside, and knocked him to the ground with a blow. Elizabeth was at his side an instant later, and he seized her hand and ran down the steps as the machine flashed with many colours and a terrible wind shot through the air, nearly knocking them off their feet. Another flash, and a grumbling, growling hum as of electricity.

Apparently, Newgate hadn't agreed with the machine. Perseus dimly wondered what the outcome would be. In any case, it was clear they needed to be gone.

Hand in hand, they ran for it down the steps, around the edge of the treasure chamber, then up out onto the weird street, between the tombs. The air seemed to be trembling with energy, and the whole pyramid was beginning to shake.

Not daring to look back, they fairly flew down the stairs, risking death with every step as the pyramid groaned and trembled about them. When they at last reached the ground, Elizabeth felt a leap of relief. They were only a quick dash from the drain...

Then, as they turned to make their final race, something sprang from the stairs behind them. It landed on Perseus before he could turn, the sudden weight bearing him to the floor. His knees struck the hard tile. Elizabeth screamed. Perseus tried to recover his bearings, but before he could a booted foot kicked him hard in the side, knocking him over.

"You killed the colonel!" Silva shrieked, sitting astride him and striking at him with the savagery of a jungle cat. "My payment! You ruined it all! I'll kill you!"

Perseus, dazed from the sudden assault, instinctively raised his arms to guard his face as Silva rained blows upon him. The poacher seized his left arm, pinning the other with his elbow, then drew his machete in a flash before Perseus could pull free of the grip and raised it over his head for a killing blow.

But he had forgotten or neglected Elizabeth. She came on him from behind now, grabbing his wrist with one hand and his face with the other, clawing like a jungle cat. As she did so, her finger hooked into Silva's left eye. He screamed and twisted away from her. Keeping hold of the machete, he hit her in the stomach with his other hand as he rolled off of Perseus. She doubled over, gasping in pain and Silva wrenched himself free of her grip, backing away from her.

Probably he would have killed her right there, had he not been disoriented and blinded with the pain of his ruined eye. He stood back a moment, his pale face flush and covered in blood, gripping his machete with one hand, his eye with the other. He shot her a murderous look, but his chance was gone, for Perseus had staggered to his feet and now stepped protectively in front of Elizabeth, drawing his own machete and facing the poacher with grim resolve.

Then, suddenly, he looked past Silva at the archway. At once he seized Elizabeth by the hand and they turned and ran for the drain.

Silva, mad with rage and pain, gave immediate chase, his machete raised. He was the faster now, and in a second, he would...

His mad delight ended when he heard an earthshaking roar. Forgetting all else, he turned back.

Cuangi, his burned face healed and smeared with blood, had just ducked through the archway. Above him, the pyramid was rumbling as though in an earthquake. But his eyes were fully fixed on the three small figures before him.

With a roar, he bounded forward. Silva screamed, but the momentary hesitation as he turned back was all that Cuangi had needed. The great jaws snapped shut and Silva's scream was cut short.

But Cuangi did not pause long to savour his meal. He had scarcely gulped down the poacher's bloody remains before he leapt after the other two. Perseus and Elizabeth, not daring to look back, called on all their remaining strength for the final dash as the pyramid rocked around them. Without pausing or waiting to see what lay below, they leapt out into the drain. Cuangi's jaws snapped in the air just behind them as the waterfall took hold of them and bore them down, down until the warm, black water closed about their heads.

As they hit the water, there erupted a confusion of heat, sound, and pressure far above that told them the pyramid had met its end. But they only had a fleeting impression of the explosion, for an instant later they were swept away into utter darkness, leaving the sounds of destruction further and further behind them.

What followed was a long, confused, and frightening journey. They were in absolute blackness, unable to see anything. The echoes distorted all sound, and the water rushed them along so fast that it was all they could do to keep their heads above the surface. Every minute Perseus expected to run into a stalactite or be ground against a rock, or to have the roof suddenly sink and plunge them under the surface.

But the tunnel seemed remarkably smooth and even. As far as he could tell in the dark, it ran on almost perfectly straight for mile after mile. He couldn't feel the bottom and he had no idea how high the roof was. Only the walls – smooth and hard – could be felt if they cared to swim off to the right or left. Otherwise he and Elizabeth might have been floating on an infinite, timeless river, on out of all knowledge. All they could do was hold on to each other and tread water as they were swept along.

After some period of time that might, for all he knew, have been several hours or a whole day and a night, Perseus suddenly bumped up against a rock, grunting as he hit it. Elizabeth yelped as she did the same. Soon there were rocks all through the tunnel, and they had to try to swim back against the current to feel their way around them.

Then it happened. The ceiling dropped suddenly, and before they knew where they were they had been swept underwater. For a moment, they were in a blind, suffocating world of hard stones and rushing water, the only other thing in the world being their clasped hands. Then, like the dawning of a new creation, they were hurled out into into a small stream under the blazing tropical sun, amid innumerable flowers of bright, vivid colours, smelling of honeysuckle.

Gasping and sore all over, Perseus struggled to shore, helping Elizabeth out after him. They looked around, and he realized that this was the very stream they had passed by on their way up from the river, what felt like years ago. He laughed.

"How about that?" he said. "We went right by the waters of the valley and didn't even realize it!"

Elizabeth laughed too. They were out. They were free.

Wet, sore, and tired as they were, the journey back down to the river seemed as easy and as quick as a stroll across the lawn at Sangral. They found the idol – shorn of its terror now that they had seen the original – and soon uncovered their canoes, which had (almost miraculously) been left untouched. They also found a third canoe drawn up on the bank, no doubt the one Newgate had come in. These would have to be prepared and staged for the return journey, but all that could wait. For now, they sat down on the bank, looking out over the Noite.

"Now all we have to do is wait for the others," said Perseus.

"They'll be all right, won't they?" she asked.

"Of course they will!" he answered. "Martin's looking after them, and he's got more sense than the rest of us put together."

"He is a marvel! Wherever did you find him?"

"The Caribbean. He was working for a hotel, if you can believe it."

"Scandalous!"

They laughed. Elizabeth drew a long, deep breath, smelling the damp, fragrant air of the jungle. It felt wonderful to be alive. She was acutely aware of every nerve, every vein, every muscle of her body. Her very soreness seemed a joy just for the fact that it testified to her continued existence.

Perseus, meanwhile, reached into his pocket to see whether any of his matches had survived the trip through the underground river. As he did so, he felt something hard and smooth. He had quite forgotten the little jewel he'd pocketed. He took it out and held it in the palm of his hand, smiling down at it.

"Fourteen years," he said. "Fourteen years hunting for treasure all across the globe. Of war, intrigue, adventure, and God knows what else from Russia to Singapore. And this is all I have to show for it."

He tossed it into the air and caught it. Then he turned to Elizabeth.

"It isn't a ring," he said. "But it's the closest I've got, or am ever likely to get."

He rose and knelt beside the river, holding out the little stone.

"Elizabeth Alban, Baroness Darrow, will you marry me, after all?"

She took the gem, and then, without a word, she kissed him for the second time.

Chapter Twenty
Of The Return to Sangral House

"Through darkness you have come to your hope, and have now all your desire. Use well the days!"
-Galadriel, *The Lord of the Rings*

Bill did not write in his diary again until they were well on their way home, and most of what he wrote then has already been told. But his account of the events after leaving the valley bears some mention:

"I wanted to wait, but Halritter said that Corbett had given strict orders, and that in any case there was nothing we could do to help. I can tell you that I ground my teeth and cursed my wound that made it impossible for me to climb down and join in the rescue. We left the rope where it was in case they should need it and began our journey back to the Noite, all three of us limping and injured.

"Circling around to the eastern edge of the valley to pick up our return trail, we found two *comaradas*, strangers, waiting beside a rope-ladder hung over the cliff. They drew on us, but Halritter shot them dead before they quite knew what was happening. This shocked me immensely, but he explained that these men were obviously part of the party that had kidnapped Lady Darrow, and he did not mean to let us be captured as well. Such is the harshness of life in the jungle, I suppose, and after all, they did draw first.

"We found the trail, freshly cut by the enemy party and started back along our route, making good time despite our injuries owing to the brush being cleared. Then, around toward evening, the Earth suddenly shook beneath us and there was a roar like the worst wind you ever heard. We looked back and saw a beam shooting out of the valley into the sky. It was of a colour...well, I can't say what the colour was; I'd never seen a shade anything like it. It fired straight up for about ten seconds and seemed to pull the clouds up after it, as though it had made hole in the atmosphere. Then there was a kind of screaming sound, almost like tearing metal, the ground shook, and that was that. We couldn't imagine what had happened. Martin said it must be the pyramid, though he had no idea how. One thing we were sure of, though; our friends were done for.

"It was a long, melancholy journey back to the river. We made camp that night and the next, saying little. I cannot tell how wretched I felt. Though Martin insisted that we would still wait for them by the river – wait a whole week if we had to.

"The next day was much the same as the first, and I tried very hard to find reasons for hope. We made the same good progress as before, aided by our going downhill, and we reached the river near evening.

"What do you think we found, but Lady Darrow and Corbett sitting beside the river upon one of the canoes with a pleasant fire before them. After two long days of worry and dread, there they were, as if on a holiday! If that wasn't the most absurd capstone to this absurd journey....

"They rose at once and greeted us heartily. But before we could stammer out the hundred questions we had, Lady Darrow said, 'I am so glad you are all here! You should all know that Perseus and I have recently become engaged.'

"Exactly as if we were at a dinner party!

"It need not be said that I was shocked, but I could not feel the slightest disapproval. Nor can I do so now. It was not only a matter of relief at finding them alive, nor of Martin's opinion of his master's gentility. Much more than that, it was that I had not known that anyone could look so radiantly, so unrestrainedly happy as Lady Darrow did at that moment."

***

The Illingworth Expedition returned to London with no news of a lost world of dinosaurs and ancient pyramids. On their return journey, Perseus and Elizabeth had told the others of all they had discovered and of Newgate's treachery and fanatical ideas, and all five of them had agreed. The valley, it seemed, held terrible secrets, some of which had perhaps survived the destruction of the pyramid. Like Cooper before them, they judged that those secrets were better off hidden from the world.

Nevertheless, the expedition was accounted a great success, being the first completed zoological survey of the Rio Noite. Professor Illingworth's description of the Red Anaconda, coupled with photographs and drawings of the great snake, made a sensation. More serious scientists also took interest in the less spectacular specimens of wildlife that he reported and brought back. It was generally judged that Professor Illingworth had made a truly distinguished contribution to the science of zoology, and at a time of life when most men would be thinking of retiring.

That it was soon followed by the marriage of his only daughter to his young assistant (whom he declared to one and all as a most promising and worthy young man with a brilliant future ahead of him) only served to confirm it as the crown jewel of his illustrious career. This was only slightly tempered by his subsequently producing a popular book titled *On the Blindness of Darwin*, which shocked and offended many in the scientific establishment with its critique of Natural Selection as a framework for understanding nature.

Of course, the scientific sensation was nothing to the reaction of the society papers when it was announced that Lady Elizabeth

Alban, Baroness Darrow was going to marry her jungle guide. Tongues wagged, of course; talk of 'primeval passions' aroused in the Amazon and so on. Many a novelist took inspiration, and many a psychologist wrote learned articles on the event, while the gossip columnists and editorialists had an absolute field day.

But, strange to say, the lady at the centre of the excitement paid very little mind. When asked about the subject, she would say that the whole thing had in fact been arranged years ago. At least, that is what she would say when she didn't invite the questioning journalist to go boil her impudent head.

Though the story remained fixed in the public mind for many years to come, her own friends soon lost interest. Perseus Corbett, it turned out, was not at all the rough, barbarous man of the wild they had expected (and half-hoped) to find, but rather a perfectly amiable, well-mannered, and rather witty young gentleman. Soon most people were denying the story altogether and saying that he must be the son of some impoverished genteel family, a rumour that neither Lady Darrow nor her husband bothered to correct. When, some years later, he was in fact made a baronet, it was generally agreed to be only fitting.

No newspaper, and only a few of her friends commented on the quietly beautiful necklace – set with a most unusual gem – that Lady Darrow had brought back from her journey, though she was never again seen without it. Just as Perseus was never seen without the Charles I medallion that he had promptly redeemed from the pawn shop upon his return to London.

The happy couple themselves settled in Sangral House amid the hills, the dogs, and the horses, the suits of armour, the paintings, and the books, and all the other things they had loved together as children.

Old Tredwell the butler said nothing on the occasion of the wedding, except that he was very glad her Ladyship was settled at last, and that in his advancing years he was grateful for the assistance of Mr. Corbett's private valet: an implacable and extremely efficient Austrian who was a positive terror to journalists, though much beloved by the local children.

Professor Illingworth (or Sir Julius as he now was) became a frequent visitor, together with his daughter and son-in-law. They often had long conferences in the library, discussing the valley and its secrets (for Frances, of course, had been included in the circle). Then Elizabeth and Perseus would take out the few treasures that she had managed to bring away with them – the jewel, the cup, the crown, and the sceptre they called them – and they would wonder who made them and for what purpose. But though Sir Perseus and Lady Darrow went on to became famous for their archeological and zoological journeys, making real contributions in both areas, and though they subsequently brought several highly learned archeologist friends into their confidence and had them examine the artefacts, they never did find any clues to these questions.

Sir Perseus, for his part, wasn't particularly bothered. The mystery was intriguing, but it did not prey on his mind. Any time it threatened to do so, he only had to look at his dear Elizabeth, and it all seemed quite unimportant, as did the prospect of a new world waiting to be made out of those secrets.

His world already had everything he wanted.

Epilogue

"Then Feanor swore a terrible oath. His seven sons leapt straightway to his side and took the selfsame vow together, and red as blood shone their drawn swords in the glare of the torches...vowing to pursue with vengeance and hatred to the ends of the World Vala, Demon, Elf or Man as yet unborn, or any creature, great or small, good or evil, that time should bring forth unto the end of days, whoso should hold or take or keep a Silmaril from their possession."
-The Silmarillion

Rain lashed the windows outside the little room. Thunder rolled. Inside, the fire crackled in the grate and the old grandfather clock struck out its even measure of time.

A man sat in the big armchair before the fire, turning the leaves of a great book, and waiting. He was about forty years of age, and of massive girth, filling the chair so thoroughly that he seemed almost to be a part of it.

It had been several weeks since the return of the Illingworth Expedition. A newspaper on the table told of the wedding of Lady Darrow and Perseus Corbett that had taken place that very day. But despite all the speculation of what had happened in that jungle there had been not one word or hint of the Forbidden Valley.

The fat man did not know what to think of that. So he thought nothing until he learned more.

The door opened suddenly and the man called Byron stepped in, stomping the mud off his boots and shaking out his umbrella.

"It's confirmed," he said. "Newgate is gone."

252

Silas Prosser silently closed his book. Byron threw himself into a chair, poured himself a drink, and tossed it off at a draught.

"Then," said Prosser. "He is dead?"

"Seems that way. We would have heard from him by now otherwise."

The other shook his head sadly. "I am sorry. He was a good man."

Byron waved this aside. "Never mind that now; what are supposed we do about it? This is the worst possible outcome we could have had. He sits there for years waiting for someone to show up with the other half of that damn book, then as soon as he thinks he has something he runs off without telling us and disappears! Idiot."

"We must begin again," sighed Prosser. "From the beginning."

"Yes, the very beginning. Not even a trail to follow. And this guy," the American said, tapping the paper. "Doesn't even breathe a word about it. Nothing at all about whether they found it or not."

"I strongly suspect they did," said the older man. "Only, for reasons of their own, they have decided to keep it a secret. Perhaps Newgate let slip what the valley truly is."

"We may be able to find it through them..." Byron suggested. But Prosser shook his head.

"That would attract far too much attention," he said. "Lady Darrow is too prominent a figure, and this Corbett is no longer a mere vagabond wandering the earth. And if Newgate *did* tell them the truth, then they will be on their guard. Interrogating and disposing of my brother was risky enough. Even then we never learned where the valley lay. No, I am afraid that line of research must be entirely set aside until our own strength grows."

"Then we're stuck," Byron growled. "All that work for nothing!"

He threw his glass into the fire, causing the flames to leap up as though in sudden rage. Prosser merely regarded the younger man with the detached interest that he might have shown to a specimen of beetle.

"Do you wish to give up then?"

Byron seized a new glass and poured himself another drink. For a moment he stared darkly into the fire.

"The Hell I do!" he said suddenly. "There's too damn much at stake. We'll keep going. Keep going to the end of the world, as long as we can still draw breath!"

"I would expect nothing less," said Prosser, raising his own glass. "Then let us begin anew."

About the Author

David Breitenbeck considers the art and philosophy of storytelling to be one of the great passions of his life. He delights in stories of all kind, whether old or new, high or low, frothy as foam or deep as the abyss. His greatest ambition is to spend his life creating his own.

He is the author of several books including *The Wisdom of Walt Disney*, *The Ten Commandments of Murder*, and *The Walk Home and Other Tales of Suspense*, and his short fiction has appeared in anthologies such as *Fantastic Schools vol. 2*, and *Adventure Stories for Young Readers*. He has also written for several sites including *The Federalist*, *The Everyman*, and *Catholic Match*.

Mr. Breitenbeck's other interests include art and philosophy as such, history, religion, and martial arts. He is currently laying the foundations for a writing career and lives in southeast Michigan.

More of his work can be found at *www.NobleCobra.com*.